I0577390

"Daniel Holub cultivates a special blend of history, nonstop action, and political revelations as this fast-paced, tense thriller evolves. It's unusual to find a page-turner that incorporates equally powerful elements of psychological, social, and political discovery, but here you have it—all tied together by heart-stopping action that makes *Article 9* a standout."
—Diane Donovan, Senior Reviewer, *Midwest Book Review*

"An action-packed read from beginning to end! Very riveting storyline with a hint of scandalous side drama. It may be fiction, but not too far-fetched from reality. I couldn't stop reading *Article 9!*"
—Joel Maldonado, retired U.S. Border Patrol Agent and author *of The Binding Oath: A Border Patrol Journey and The Mayorkas Effect*

"*Article 9* is a fast-paced story of survival, reckoning, and redemption. Holub delivers an everyman protagonist whose particular set of skills drive the recovery of an ordinary life from extraordinary threats."
—Dana King, Intelligence Analyst

"An extraordinary tale of the new west in which mortal peril is met with fearless resolve. The book's opening paragraph grabs your attention and doesn't relinquish it until the end. It is an intense and gripping hybrid of physical courage and political intrigue."
—RH Stewart, DVM, PhD, Clinical Professor, Texas A&M University

"*Article 9* is written by a man who has an intimate understanding and knowledge of the modern Southwest and the border problems that Texans face every day. Holub can also construct a cast of strong characters. The reality that cartels are more than willing to move with international terrorists fits the story like a glove. As Texas cowboys would say, '*Article 9* is like leaving cow camp on a frosty morning. Get ready for a wild ride!'"
—Cotton Elliot, former Sheriff of King County, Texas and current Justice of the Peace of Briscoe County, Texas

"If you love action, political fiction, and a badass main character, then *Article 9* is written for you. The protagonist's ability to dig deep and repeatedly escape danger made me reluctant to put it down. If you are a fan of adventures set in today's troubled world, *Article 9* should be at the top of your must-read list."

—WR Harlin, DVM

"Holub's debut novel grabs you from the beginning, shakes you in the middle, and doesn't let go, promising more in the future. This political thriller is a fast-paced, character-driven saga you'll want to finish in one sitting. Hold on and buckle your seat belt for a supersonic ride that will not disappoint."

—Julia Brewer Daily, award-winning author of *No Names to Be Given* and *The Fifth Daughter of Thorn Ranch*

"Dr. Holub has been known as a great storyteller for a long time, but now he's done it in print in his debut novel. *Article 9* comes at you like a charging bull and doesn't back off. This is an amazing tale full of intrigue and plot twists that keeps the reader on the edge of the seat. The adrenalin rush sets you up for a single-sitting read. I hope the sequel is in the works."

—Mack J Boyd, DVM

ARTICLE 9

A GRIPPING WESTERN POLITICAL THRILLER

ARTICLE 9

DANIEL HOLUB

Dos Palomas Press

To contact the author about speaking or ordering books in bulk, visit www.danielholub.com

Edited by David Aretha
Cover art by Tigerlily Collins
Book design by Christy Day, Constellation Book Services
Digital logo art by Wilson King
Author photo credit: Bob Collier

ISBN (paperback): 979-8-9929630-0-7
ISBN (ebook): 979-8-9929630-1-4

Library of Congress Control Number: 2025906836

Printed in the United States of America

This work is dedicated to all the people who blink and find themselves in the final third of their lives. I suggest you put on your trifocals and search out that avocation you have put on the back burner for far too long. That avocation may well lead your frontal lobe back to the middle third of your life.

You need eagles wings to get over things
that make no sense in this world.
–Tom Petty

And alone and without his nest shall the Eagle fly across the sun.
–Khalil Gibran

CHAPTER ONE
Death to the Infidels

November 22, Thanksgiving Day, San Diego, California

Ryan McDill, the CEO of General Atomic Aeronautical Systems, had just begun carving the holiday turkey for family and friends when three armed men burst into the room. They wore black ski masks and carried MP5 submachine guns.

"If you move, everyone will die," screamed the apparent leader of the team. The startled dinner guests did as they were told.

Two of the men rushed to the CEO, pulled him away from the table, and knocked the carving knife to the floor. They handcuffed his hands behind his back and placed a hood over his head.

The leader produced a bag and shouted, "Cell phones in the bag, now!" The victims gave up their phones without a word.

As the other two terrorists ushered the CEO out of the room, the leader warned, "A guard is stationed outside to kill anyone who leaves the room."

As he backed toward the entrance of the room the leader paused and shouted, "Allah Akbar!" The whole operation was completed in less than two minutes.

It took one brave dinner guest fifteen minutes to garner the courage to get up and see if the kidnappers were gone. Those fifteen minutes were all that was needed for the terrorists and their victim to disappear into the holiday traffic of San Diego.

Because of the terrorists' Islamic invocation and the fact that the kidnap victim was the CEO of the company that made the US military's Predator Drones, and it occurred on US soil, the news became national by that evening. The FBI and the NSA also opened special monitoring groups to begin to ratchet up attention.

November 29, National Security Agency, Fort Meade, Maryland

A low-level analyst sat in front of a multi-screened computer workstation sipping coffee from a Yeti insulated mug. He was part of a large team tasked with monitoring terrorist websites. The analyst's workstation was tied to the NSA's Cray supercomputers that were programmed to look for key phrases or images that might be of value in the battle against radicalized Islamists.

The upper right sub-screen began to show an alert icon indicating the interception of a site that met the criteria for possible significant incoming data. A secondary icon indicated that the image was a live feed. The analyst continued sipping his coffee while his eyes went to the screen. The screen showed the image of three hooded men who stood behind a kneeling man with his hands secured behind his back. On the wall behind the men was the black flag of ISIS.

The analyst slowly lowered the Yeti to his desktop and touched a function key that centered and enlarged the sub-screen image. When he saw the large knife in the hand of the center terrorist, he whispered out loud, "Holy shit!"

With a shaking hand, he keyed an alarm function that sent the image to other workstations and to the head of his department. As other analysts listened to the standard anti-American rhetoric, they all began to experience the sickening certainty that they were about to see the kneeling man die.

The head of the department touched the screen of his computer, causing a small box to form around the face of the doomed man. He opened his fingertips, causing the image of the face to enlarge. When he was sure, he picked up his phone and pressed a set of numbers. "Get the assistant director down here ASAP. We've found Ryan McDill."

As he hung up, the center terrorist finished his speech and the accomplices to his left and right restrained McDill's shoulders. The leader grabbed his victim's hair and jerked his head back. Without a pause, he slit McDill's throat with one bold stroke that severed both his left and right jugular veins and common carotid arteries. The gory display lasted less than twenty seconds. The leader held up McDill's head by the hair and spoke one last time to the camera.

"Be prepared, you minions of the Great Satan. Your punishment begins." With that, the website went dark.

The NSA analysts sat in stunned silence until one female team member retched and vomited on the floor. The assistant director looked at the head of the department and said, "Oh, I've got a very bad feeling about this."

Within hours, the NSA analysts concluded that the grisly event was uploaded on very high-quality, high-definition equipment. There was nothing about the images of the room or the hooded killers that would be helpful in the investigation. Voice print analysis of the man who made the anti-American speech was compared to a large collection of known terrorists, but no match was found. The surprising oddity was that the voice did not belong to a person with English as a second language. Instead, the language analysts all agreed that the man had a vocal pattern consistent with someone raised in the upper Midwest, possibly Chicago.

On December 7, the president of Fox News was taken from his Manhattan penthouse. Five days later he was beheaded by a different set of terrorists using the same video equipment. His purported crime against Islam was biased reporting on the evening news.

The graphic murders of two such prominent Americans brought President William A. Martinez, the recently elected first Hispanic president, promptly in front of the cameras for a prime-time statement to the nation from the Oval Office. The president assured the nation that the full weight of federal and state police assets was being brought to bear against these heinous criminals. He also reminded the nation that these perpetrators were in no way representative of true believers of Islam. He even quoted a couple of passages from the Koran to prove his point and to send a subliminal message to other radical Islamists to please stop causing such problems while he was getting used to his new office. Neither the Islamists nor his political adversaries were amused.

With Christmas around the corner, the nation held its collective breath that the terrorists would use the holiday as a way of making yet another statement. When the 25th and 26th came and went with no kidnappings, the nation collectively exhaled. ISIS waited until the 27th to kidnap retired Army General Louis Reed from his home in Phoenix. The terrorists were getting payback for Operation Cobra, which had been designed and executed by Reed during his last tour in Afghanistan. On January 7 during the college football championship game, his beheading hit the net.

With the score of terrorists three and Americans nil, the US intelligence community was getting heat from every direction. During a daily status brief at the CIA, a young analyst asked the work group a question for which he got no answer.

"Where are the bodies? These guys usually broadcast the beheadings and then dump the head and body somewhere convenient for discovery. We've got three very dead guys, but no bodies. What's that all about?"

With a direct attack on a high-ranking American military man, the scrutiny of all things Arabic was ratcheted up. No other kidnappings occurred in January. With no other ISIS attacks by February 15, false security began to build.

CHAPTER TWO
Brooks Davis—A Truly American Guy

Monday, February 15, 1:45 p.m.

Tina Landry slowly wound a tuft of her boss's chest hair around her index finger. She studied his rugged good looks for the thousandth time. She loved the way he fell so peacefully asleep after they made love. Her long, mahogany hair was in casual disarray that tumbled around sculpted shoulders. Her skin color spoke to the generations of Corsican women from her maternal side. To say that Tina tanned perfectly was the understatement of the century. Her impossibly long right leg was strategically draped over Brooks' leg. Her great toe slowly stroked his ankle. She chuckled softly, wondering if old Molly put as much athleticism into their lovemaking as she and Brooks did.

She had been Brooks' primary construction superintendent since he hired her out of college four years earlier. Now, at twenty-seven, she was reaching her prime both professionally and…well…personally. She was more than ready to be co-owner of a top-tier custom home construction company. There was just one minor problem…Brooks' wife and their three sons.

Tina nudged him awake. He caressed her face and then her breast. With a sleepy smile he said, "We've got to get back to the site. They are supposed to be delivering eighty yards of fill for the backyard, and I've got to make sure that they put it in the right place."

"When are you going to talk to Molly?" Brooks was startled by the question.

"I don't know," he said irritably.

"You can't put it off forever." Brooks hated it when she ruined a perfectly great afternoon by starting in on huge problems.

"Well, Tina, it's going to be put off today." He got up and found his pants. Tina wasn't about to let him punctuate the conversation.

"She's going to find out one way or the other."

Brooks cast her a sideways glance. After a pregnant pause, he asked, "And what exactly does that mean?"

"That means if you don't tell her yourself, and somewhere down the line something bad happens to you like you have a heart attack or something, I'm going to tell her what a lovely relationship we had."

Brooks assessed her chocolate eyes for a long moment and noted that she never blinked. As he turned to find his shirt he mumbled under his breath, "Shit."

CHAPTER THREE

When It Rains on Brooks Davis—It Pours

Molly and Brooks Davis produced three fine, smarter-than-average sons. James, the eldest, at nineteen was the mirror image of his father. James came from a lengthy line of men, who, when they were adolescents, were dangerously rebellious. When his great-grandfather was twenty, he shot two men over a dispute about a fence line. In turn, he was shot by a sheriff, in a minor way, and spent some time in jail. Young James always thought of his great-grandfather in Herculean terms. James was at that dangerous time in his life and really didn't care what anybody thought about it. He had caused his parents a fair amount of grief of late, but because he graduated as the salutatorian from high school and picked up a four-year engineering scholarship at the University of Texas at San Antonio, how much could Molly and Brooks say about their son being an adolescent dumbass? They were just glad he decided on a local university so they could keep an eye on him while his brain finished developing.

Andrew, the middle child, at fourteen, looked and acted like Molly and the calmer, more civil side of the family. He was a first-year student at the same Catholic high school where his older brother had left a lasting impression. He frequently pulled his older brother's chain by telling him that his goal was to graduate as the valedictorian. He would then ask James if he knew what that was.

Zane, the youngest, at nine, went to the same Catholic elementary school that both of his older brothers attended. He was happy to tell them that his teachers liked him better than the both of them.

Monday, February 15, 7:00 p.m.

One of the things that Molly and Brooks insisted on was that the evening meal was a family affair...no exceptions. When all four, Y-chromosome-bearing individuals that she lived with sat down at her table with their smartphones open and ignored her beautifully presented dinner, Molly shouted, "PHONES!"

A flurry of button pressing and phones being pocketed followed.

"James, grace," ordered Molly.

"Zane, grace," the eldest brother transferred the order.

While Zane dutifully launched off into the blessing, Molly and Brooks looked at each other and shook their heads. Molly nodded at Brooks, indicating that the floor was his. It was his fatherly duty to lead the dinner discussion.

"Well, James, you said that you had your first two major exams of the semester today. How did it go?"

"Calculus, stupid easy. Poly sci...prof is an ignorant Marxist...she needs to get back on the boat and go back to wherever she came from."

"James! What the hell!" sputtered Molly.

"What's a Marxist?" asked Zane.

"A dumbass commie!" replied the eldest brother.

Seeking to regain a bit of control before complete deterioration, Brooks asked, "Anything at all good about your day today?"

James stared thoughtfully for a moment at the chandelier over the table. "Oh yeah! I met a girl at the student union...spectacular... no, check that... breathtaking. Blond, green eyes, no bra...mercy!"

"Not at the table, James!" demanded Brooks.

"How do you know she didn't have a bra?" inquired the youngest.

"Ask Andy," advised the eldest, causing the middle child to crack up.

Molly put her forehead in her hand and mumbled, "I live with animals."

Her comment triggered Zane to jump back into the conversation. "Did you know that Dweezel dug up all your iris bulbs over by the pool?" A wild-eyed Molly looked in Brooks' direction.

Brooks held up one hand in surrender. "I'll take care of it."

Molly looked at Andrew, her middle child, the good child. He rarely caused any trouble. Maybe he could save the dinner conversation.

"Andy, do you have anything good to add to this conversation? How was school today?"

Andy put down his fork and took a sip of iced tea. "Well, I probably shouldn't say much about the big topic around school today. Your less intelligent sons have already messed up dinner. Incredible pot roast, by the way. I don't know how you do it."

"Brown-noser!" opined James.

"What *is* a brown-noser?" asked Zane.

Molly and Brooks were now very interested in what the big topic was around a Catholic high school.

"Well, the big topic was this ISIS thing and the beheadings. Some people downloaded the stuff off the dark web and were showing it around school. By noon, probably everybody had seen it. A bunch of girls freaked out and had to be sent home. Father Gonzales tried to put some fires out and is supposed to have an assembly about it tomorrow. Anyway, it is a huge deal at school."

Molly and Brooks looked at each other. Molly spoke first. "We had hoped that this horrible thing got under control before it started to affect our community." Brooks was about to add his thoughts, but James beat him to it.

"Let me give you my opinion. ISIS and other like-minded people are already here in our community. And if you think that they don't already have big plans for us, you are nuts! All you need to do is drop by UTSA and look at the growing numbers of protesters who are proud to tell you that they are happy to see their so-called enemies beheaded. They are close to crossing a line where people who have been peaceful and tolerant and welcoming their whole lives are going to cross that same line and go after them!"

Brooks didn't like his son's tone. He had never heard anything like it come from him. Something different was happening to his eldest. Brooks had a brief thought about James' great-grandfather. Was history somehow going to repeat itself?

Brooks and James locked their eyes. "And what exactly does that mean?" As soon as he said it, he remembered that he had repeated just that to a miffed, dark-eyed naked woman earlier that day.

"It means that the raghead bastards would be well served to never harm anyone that I care about!"

Molly gasped. The younger brothers looked at each other, knowing intuitively that the shit was about to hit the fan.

"Outside! Now!" demanded Brooks. On the patio, Brooks questioned his son. "What the hell are you thinking, talking like that around your mom and brothers?" James did not respond. "Now is not the time to go silent, badass."

After a pause, James asked, "Have you seen the videos?" Brooks shook his head. "Well, you better get a look at what Andy has already seen, and what Zane will probably see soon enough."

"Okay, I'll give you that one. But your mom doesn't need to hear some Rambo bullshit coming out of you. That terrifies her. And besides, where do you think you have the kind of skills to go after protesters and terrorists?"

James stared out across the family pool. "I learned everything I need from you, Dad."

Later, in their bedroom, Molly asked, "What's with James? Where did that kind of talk come from?"

"I don't know. Late adolescence thing? Maybe he's been more affected by the ISIS thing than we want to admit. I realize that I didn't take it as seriously as I should have. I think I dropped the ball with the boys. I should have known that some little shit at school would be digging around the deep web and doing some show-and-tell. It must be horrible."

"Oh, you have no idea. I asked Andy how bad it was. He asked me if I *really* wanted to know. He handed me his laptop and said I would be sorry." Molly went to the desk in their bedroom, retrieved the laptop, queued up the clip, and turned it toward Brooks. When it came to its hideous end, Brooks grimaced and looked into Molly's deep blue eyes.

"Now that takes a seriously deranged mind." After a moment of deeper thought about James, he added, "That could make some otherwise normal young men become very angry and do some very out-of-character things."

"You mean like all the young men that joined the military after 9/11?"

"Yeah, like after 9/11," Brooks replied in the affirmative, but he was really thinking about his own son in much darker terms... like going out and killing a bunch of raghead protesters. Brooks' detached-sounding voice suddenly made Molly angry. When there was a significant family problem, he would detach himself from it, dive into his work, and let Molly take care of it. It was his growing flaw.

"Well, Brooks, he's just like you. Warts and all. You are his father; you better address his flaws before he does something stupid."

With that, she fluffed her pillow and got under the sheets with her back to Brooks. After twenty years of marriage, Brooks knew that meant Molly cared for neither further discussion nor the feel of any part of his body.

Brooks turned off the light and put the bedroom into darkness. Sleep escaped him for a long time while he pondered his flaws and sins. Flaws and sins...inexorably related...you cannot have one without the other. Brooks had a sudden epiphany. If you are an accomplished sinner, you have mastered the skill of ignoring your own flaws, which makes continued sinning so easy. It is the ultimate positive feedback loop. But if you are a half-assed sinner, your flaws will always come back to get you.

Around 2:00 a.m., Brooks decided that the problem with James would probably take care of itself. He was busy keeping up with seventeen hours of coursework. If nothing untoward happened to family or friends at the hands of ISIS, then his bravado talk would be just that...bravado. Besides, he might get lucky with the braless blonde from the student union.

Tina, however, was an entirely different sort of problem. Brooks remembered a long-ago discussion with his father about the folly of having a mistress. His father warned that what starts out as a casual little side thing goes way south when the mistress falls deeply in love with the cheater. That is when the demands begin.

Tina's demands were entering into threat territory. If she made good on her threats, life as old Brooks Davis had come to know it would come crashing down. The thought of blowing up his family made his belly ache. He thought of Molly...his life partner...his "till death do you part" partner. Now, the ache moved from his belly into his chest.

Somewhere around 3:00 a.m., Brooks started dreaming about the smell of perfume. Was that Molly's scent or Tina's? Brooks propped himself up and looked at the foot of the bed. There sat Molly and Tina. They were both naked and casually brushing out their hair. They smiled at Brooks seductively and said simultaneously, "Well, Honey, what's it going to be?"

Brooks gasped himself awake and sat up panting. Molly was startled awake and touched Brooks.

"Are you okay, Honey?"

The term of endearment stabbed Brooks in the temple. He exhaled deeply and laid back down.

"Bad dream?"

He couldn't answer.

Molly moved closer and put her hand on his chest, forgetting that she went to bed mad. "Everything will be fine," she murmured.

After a long pause, he whispered, "Yeah, sure."

CHAPTER FOUR
The Davis-Epstein Kidnapping

February 17, Ash Wednesday, 10:30 a.m.

Brooks Davis stood at a contractor's table studying the blueprints of a 10,000-square-foot Mediterranean-style villa that he was constructing on ninety-five acres of pristine Texas hill country ten miles north of the town of Boerne, a northern suburb of San Antonio. He was nursing a venti-sized cup of French roast from Starbucks. His contractor's table was set up in the skeletal great room of the mansion. Subcontractors were pulling cables through wall studs as part of the electrical rough-in chores.

Davis was smiling. He could not help himself. He was three weeks ahead of schedule and everything was perfect. Perfect...that was a great description for the whole event. He was sure that this job was a once-in-a-contractor's-lifetime sort of project.

His client, Raymond Epstein, was an uber-wealthy international investment banker. Most wealthy people could be painfully demanding when building a dream mansion, but Epstein was different. He did not split hairs on costs, had impeccable good taste, and was wide open to the suggestions and advice of the design and construction people. The impossible bonus was that his beautiful, Tel Aviv-born wife, Rona, was the same. Yes indeed, once in a lifetime.

Abu Ramadi sat in the passenger seat of the nondescript white Ford van and peered through the eyepieces of the 10-power Nikon binoculars. He scanned the mansion that was under construction from a standoff position on a hill 400 meters away.

Seated to his left, behind the wheel, was his twenty-two-year-old nephew, Lodin Ramadi. When Lodin was three, his father was killed by a missile fired from a Predator drone while his father and four colleagues were planting an improvised explosive device (IED) on a road near Kandahar. At the same time, his uncle Abu was settling with his wife in San Antonio.

Trained as a petroleum engineer, the elder Ramadi was recruited by Valero Energy Company as a liaison between Valero and its expanding offshore operations. He led a quiet suburban life with his wife and his two American-born children. He was well-liked by neighbors and co-workers. The Valero executives held him in the highest esteem because he was consistently willing to put in the hours and go the extra mile for the company. He was the perfect deep plant for a terrorist organization. Ramadi had waited for a mission of this caliber for fifteen years.

The third man of the team was Rom al-Kahat. He was clearly anxious about the mission. He rechecked the weapons and other gear vital to a successful kidnapping for the tenth time. Like Abu Ramadi, he was a deep plant with a sterling record. He was set up as the owner of a small computer repair business. Unlike Ramadi, he was not married, and he had a very dark secret side. He was not content to wait for the leaders to call for his services. Unknown to the leadership, al-Kahat would periodically test his nerves and create small missions for himself. He would take time off from his business and travel outside the state where he would select a victim, plan, and execute a kidnapping, then kill the victim. He wanted to be sure that when it came time for the real thing, he would not hesitate to slice the victim's throat with surgical precision. His murderous excursions were carried out in seven different states. To date, there had never been any suspicion by police that his killings were in any way connected.

Abu lowered the binoculars and checked his watch.

"He should be arriving at any time," remarked the cell leader.

"Praise Allah!" replied the nephew.

"Allah Akbar!" added al-Kahat.

"Everything prepared?" asked the leader.

Al-Kahat dropped the magazine of his .40 caliber Heckler & Koch P30 and checked the stack of fat 180-grain bonded hollow-point rounds.

"Everything is perfect," he replied.

Four minutes later the sleek black Mercedes CLS 550 sports sedan arrived at the construction site. Abu pointed to his nephew, who, without a word, started the engine of the van and dropped it into gear.

Davis turned at the sound of a car arriving in the porte-co-chère and recognized Epstein's Mercedes. The banker entered the great room and greeted his contractor.

"The roof is coming along nicely," said Epstein as he offered his hand to Davis.

"You bet. Chuck Garza has his best tile guys on it. I've been up there checking on things. We are both going to be dead and gone a long time before anyone is going to have to work on that roof."

Epstein glanced at Davis' forehead, thinking that he had a small, dark smudge of dirt. On a second look, he recognized the Lenten ashes on his contractor's forehead.

"I didn't know that you were Catholic, Brooks."

Davis smiled and nodded. "Born and bred mackerel snapper." Both men laughed.

The sound of an eighteen-wheel stone hauler off-loading several tons of Sisterdale limestone momentarily overpowered their discussion.

"The stone masons will start the day after tomorrow. I've got two crews ready to go," said Davis.

"Are they the same subs that did Jeremiah Fellows' house?" asked the banker.

"Yes, same guys."

Epstein smiled and nodded. His wife had fallen in love with the rockwork of the home of one of the San Antonio Spurs basketball players.

Davis and Epstein stepped up to the contractor's table and began to review blueprints and the latest change orders. While client and contractor discussed the blueprints, a nondescript white van pulled up to the front of the house. Thinking that it was just another subcontractor, they paid little attention.

The terrorists had donned black ski masks as they entered the construction site. The younger Ramadi remained at the wheel of the van while the other men quickly exited the vehicle and walked directly into the massive foyer. They each wore a sidearm and carried an MP5 assault weapon.

They approached Davis and Epstein from behind. The finely tailored suit gave their target away. Ramadi flicked off the MP5's safety and fired a short burst into the ceiling. The effect was immediate. Davis, Epstein, and the electricians all ducked and turned toward the terrorists to find the weapons now leveled at Davis and Epstein.

The contractor's eyes went briefly from the terrorists to the ceiling to assess the damage. His eyes narrowed and turned back to the intruders. He took one step forward and was met with a blow across his face with the MP5 in al-Kahat's hands. Davis went to a knee. His cap was knocked from his head. He shook off the stars and fought to remain conscious. Al-Kahat stood above him with the submachine gun pointed at his forehead. Davis stared into his black, hate-filled eyes and spoke up.

"Why you common bastard! Who the hell are you?"

Al-Kahat raised the MP5 for another stroke, but Ramadi stopped him. He spoke to the other men still standing.

"Get on your knees, now!" Calmly he added, "Get out your cell phones."

He nodded to al-Kahat, who reluctantly took his eyes off Davis and then went to gather the phones.

At that moment, another burst of machine gun fire echoed from outside, followed by a dull thud from near the front door. The young Ramadi could be heard ordering the remaining roofers off the roof. In a few moments, he brought the roofers into the great room. He addressed his uncle.

"One of the men was making a call on his cell phone."

Ramadi nodded and motioned for him to add his prisoners to the electricians. The surviving roofers were pale and shaken.

Ramadi produced a pair of handcuffs and a black hood. He hooded Epstein and handcuffed his hands behind his back. Al-Kahat returned his attention to Davis. He grabbed his hair and jerked the contractor's head back. He pointed the barrel of the MP5 at the ashes on Davis' forehead. In Arabic he addressed Ramadi.

"This one is a Christian dog. We should take him as well."

Ramadi paused for a moment, aware that the clock was ticking. The plan called for the operation to take less than two minutes. Before he could decide, al-Kahat added, "He may serve as insurance." He was thinking that two beheadings would be twice as much fun as one. With some reluctance, Ramadi acquiesced. He tossed al-Kahat a second hood and pair of handcuffs.

In a matter of ninety seconds, Brooks Davis' life was irrevocably changed.

CHAPTER FIVE

The Long Ride into Hell

Davis and Epstein were led to the van and roughly pushed through the side door. Neither man had uttered a word since Davis' opening tirade that resulted in the rapidly growing bruise that started above his right temple and spread across half his forehead. The younger Ramadi put the van in motion and headed quickly for the prearranged second vehicle. The uncle handed al-Kahat the prepared injection. He stabbed it through the leg of Epstein's pants deeply into his thigh and pressed the plunger. For the first time, the banker spoke.

"Damn! What the hell was that?"

In a calm, almost soothing voice Abu Ramadi replied, "Not to worry, Mr. Epstein, just a little something to make your trip a little easier."

From under the hood, he asked, "Who are you? What do you want?"

Ramadi paused for a moment. "Who do you think we are, Mr. Epstein?"

It was Epstein's turn to pause. Davis beat him to an answer.

"You are a bunch of fucking Arabs!"

"Why do you think we are Arabs?"

"Because whatever your asshole partner said to you back at the house sounded like Arabic!"

Al-Kahat glared at Davis while he prepared a second injection of sedative. He jammed the needle into the contractor's leg and sent home the anesthetic. A deep, burning throb radiated toward his groin. As the versed-pentobarbital cocktail began to take effect, Davis' mind was trying to make sense of what had happened. He could see tiny dots of light through the weave of the hood. Soon the dots began to spin. He was no doctor, but he knew that soon the blackness would set in and then be complete. His last thoughts were about why. He briefly thought of the recent kidnappings by ISIS. He realized that Epstein would be a good candidate for any number of Middle Eastern shit lists. But why a country boy contractor from Uvalde, Texas?

The phone rang on the desk of FBI Special Agent Martin Collier, the head of the San Antonio regional field office. He was studying the daily intelligence dispatches that were growing in volume each day since the beheadings had begun. During his weekly meetings with his Counterterrorism group, he had always punctuated the meeting with the admonition to be hyper-alert for any indicators that something was brewing in their region and to pray that ISIS would not find any high-profile targets in South Texas. Their group prayers were about to be in vain. The chief of the Communications section was on the line.

"Sir, we have an alert from the Kendall County Sheriff's Department of a murder and double kidnapping north of Boerne. Sounds like the subjects fit the profile. Three men, black ski masks and automatic weapons."

Collier ground his molars together.

"Time?"

"Nine minutes ago. Kendall County is in route to the scene. I've put our first two counterterrorism units, four men, moving in that direction."

"Do we have victim IDs?"

"Yes. The murder victim is a Chuck Garza. The kidnapped victims are one Brooks Davis, a contractor who is building a house for the other victim, one Raymond Epstein."

Collier's gut knotted. *Epstein...Jewish! Shit! This is it!*

"Do we have any background on Epstein?"

"No. We are talking to Agent Dayton over in Counterterrorism right now and tasking him with collecting initial victim profiles."

"Vehicle description?"

"White Ford van. No license from witnesses. We've already put out a four-county APB for the vehicle with an approach with extreme caution."

"Air assets?"

"Our guys are getting airborne. Bexar County and San Antonio Police are alerted, and their assets are either in route or getting airborne. A total of ten choppers are organizing for a code five radial search pattern."

Collier got right to his initial orders. "I'm going mobile and heading to the site. Insert location data into my vehicle GPS. Broadcast a general alert to all agents. I want everybody in vests now. If the subjects are using automatic weapons, I want everyone with AR-15s at the ready. I'm authorizing weapons free for anybody who confronts people in black ski masks. I do not want any of my people hurt today. Remind everyone that the first thirty minutes are critical."

Tina Landry knew something very bad had happened at the construction site when she was still a quarter of a mile away. She counted at least seven police vehicles all stationed around the front of the house with every possible red and blue light flashing. An EMS bus was loading a body cloaked in yellow plastic. She saw Brooks' Ford truck and Epstein's Mercedes parked in the porte-cochère. As she pulled up as close as she could get to the house, she scanned the crowd. She could not see either Brooks or Epstein. A painful knot started to form in the pit of her stomach. She felt short of breath. The Kendall County deputies were busy stringing yellow crime scene tape.

She approached the first subcontractor she recognized.

"Bill, what the hell is going on?"

"Oh shit! Three guys kidnapped Brooks and Epstein and they fuckin' killed Chuck! Shot him right off the fuckin' roof!"

"Kidnapped? Who would kidnap...?" She stopped in mid-question as her mind flashed to the latest news stories about the ISIS terrorists. Her mind also went to her recent tryst with Brooks. Her mother's most frequent admonition was to be careful about what you wish for. This felt very bad, but like it or not, she was going to have to talk to Molly...today.

Agent Timothy Dayton was just nine months out of Quantico. He was thirty-one years old and was a high school math teacher in his previous life. Five years of teaching in an inner-city Baltimore high school finished off any illusions about helping the culturally deprived. The second death threat from a twenty-year-old sophomore convinced him that federal law enforcement was a far more noble way of putting one's life on the line for a career.

Though he really wanted organized gangs and the Chicago field office for his first assignment, he had grown quite happy with Counterterrorism and San Antonio. He felt it was a perfect fit and a tribute to the Bureau psychologists who evaluated him for assignment suitability.

As soon as he was tasked with initial victim profiles, Dayton could feel the excitement building. He had a pang of guilt about being excited about someone being killed and others being kidnapped, but this was exactly what the Bureau was all about.

Dayton sat in his office cubical and input the names of Davis and Epstein of San Antonio on split screens. He pressed enter, picked up his coffee mug, and took a sip while the FBI computers in the sky decided who the victims were. Before he finished the sip, the split screens were already displaying information. Dayton marveled once again at the power of the Bureau's databases and search engines.

As he was reading the background information, his phone rang.

"This is Agent Dayton."

"Dayton, this is Collier. What do you have on the kidnap victims?"

Dayton was glad that the computers were fast. He shuddered to think of telling the big boss that he had nothing.

"The contractor, Brooks Davis, is a forty-five-year-old resident of Leon Springs. No military, government, or political background at all. The other man was the obvious target. Raymond Epstein is a fifty-six-year-old international investment banker with Chase Manhattan here in San Antonio. He is married to an Israeli national who was a former intel officer in the Israeli Army. He has spent significant time in Israel and apparently came back with strong anti-Arab sentiments. He is a big-time contributor to Israeli causes and is vocal about his feelings. He would be on a top ten list of local targets for Arab extremists."

Collier paused for a moment in thought. The junior agent knew better than to interrupt.

"Alright, Dayton, I have two jobs for you. First, until further notice you are going to be my personal information specialist on this case. I want you to stay on top of all incoming data, sift through it, separate the wheat from the chaff, and keep me appraised of everything I should know real-time. I will notify your boss that you will be assisting me and let the department heads know so that you will be able to move freely throughout the house gathering my data. I will get you set up through communications so you will be able to reach me twenty-four-seven. And Dayton..."

"Yes, sir?"

"Consider this a test. Do you follow me?"

Dayton's heart rate kicked up. "Yes, sir." Dayton had heard rumors of the big boss picking a first-year agent for a special assignment as his way of mentoring up close and personal. The veterans liked to tell young agents that following such tests the newbies would usually be reassigned and never heard from again.

"Secondly, have you checked off notification of next of kin yet?"

"No, sir."

"Well, you are today. Find Mrs. Davis and give her the bad news."

This was a reference to a famous checklist of required actions that every first-year agent was required to complete to pass the probation period.

"What about Mrs. Epstein?"

"I want someone more seasoned to handle that. Keep in mind that she is former Israeli intel. She has plenty of sensitive information that will have to be carefully extracted. You worry about Mrs. Davis. Do you have any questions?"

Dayton had plenty but was too fearful to admit it.

"No, sir. I'm on it."

Dayton entered the GPS data for the Davis home near Leon Springs, a western suburb of San Antonio, and left the FBI office on Interstate 10. The GPS computer reported that the Davis home was only seven miles away. He hoped that Mrs. Davis was home, eliminating the necessity of tracking her down. In this kind of case, time was precious.

As he drove down the long Davis driveway, he was relieved to see a forty-ish woman unloading groceries from the family Suburban. As Dayton approached, the smile on her face told him that she was unaware of the horrific news to come. Dayton presented his badge.

"Mrs. Davis?"

Molly glanced at his badge but continued to smile.

"I'm Special Agent Timothy Dayton of the FBI. I need to talk with you, ma'am. Is there a place where we can sit down?"

The smile began to fade.

"I suppose so. Would you mind helping me with these groceries?"

"I would be happy to, ma'am."

As they carried groceries from the porte-cochère to the kitchen, Molly's mind was trying to anticipate what an FBI agent would want to talk about to her. For a moment she wondered if one of Brooks' subcontractors was using illegals and now her husband was in some kind of trouble. The rational part of her mind said that would garner a visit from the Border Patrol or the INS, not the FBI.

"Can I offer you anything, Agent Dayton?"

"No, ma'am, thank you. Could we sit down? I'm afraid I have some very bad news about your husband."

The final remnants of her smile evaporated like a lone raindrop in a cloudless Texas sky in August.

"What has happened to Brooks?"

"Approximately thirty minutes ago, Brooks and another man, Raymond Epstein, were kidnapped at the construction site."

Molly inhaled deeply and her hand went to her mouth. She could not speak.

"According to witnesses, they were taken by three armed men. The method of the kidnapping leads us to believe that they were possibly taken by ISIS terrorists."

Molly squinted her eyes shut and her lips began to quiver. After a long moment, she found her voice.

"Please tell me you are not talking about the men who are taking people and...and..." She could not say the words.

"That is what we fear, ma'am."

"Well, it just can't be! Those people wouldn't take a contractor, a man that just builds homes for people! It just doesn't make sense!"

"At this moment we don't know why they took your husband. Mr. Epstein, however, is an influential investment banker with ties to Israel. We believe at this early juncture that Mr. Epstein was the real target, and, for some reason, Mr. Davis was also taken. Taking a second victim is a departure from their previous mode of operation."

As soon as Dayton said the word "victim," Molly could no longer hold back, and the tears came in torrents. The young agent felt sick for Mrs. Davis. His own parents were not much older than Brooks and Molly, and he could only imagine how his own mother would handle such horrible news.

Dayton spent time describing all the local, state, and federal assets that were being brought to bear in the search for the van. Dayton suggested that Molly start calling family and friends to gather at the

Davis home for support. Within the hour, Molly and her sons were surrounded by loved ones, and the long wait began.

As family and friends began to gather, Dayton was replaced by a pair of agents who were tasked with monitoring the Davis household. They were there to provide security and to attach recording and trace equipment to the household phones. In case this was a double kidnapping not related to the other ISIS actions, the FBI wanted to be able to record and possibly track the kidnappers should they call and make ransom demands. The FBI was, however, not optimistic that Davis and Epstein were taken by garden variety kidnappers.

Dayton was ordered to the scene of the crime where he met up with Collier to report on the activities at the Davis home. As Dayton approached, Collier asked for the punch line.

"Let me guess. Davis has no enemies, only builds perfect custom homes, pays his taxes on time, and is close to mastering walking on water."

Dayton chuckled. "I don't think you need me at all, sir." He opened his notebook and went to work trying to demonstrate that he was able to investigate autonomously.

"I contacted the team from the Behavioral Analysis Unit at Quantico and gave them everything we've got so far. Their opinion at this hour is that the kidnapping of Davis along with Epstein is an aberration. When ISIS starts a game plan, they stick to the playbook. So, they think that somebody on this team is freewheeling, possibly someone with a personal agenda. That's what is making them think outside the ISIS box."

Collier scratched his chin. "I smell a loose cannon in the group. If it is the cell leader, then things will get ugly."

"Speaking of the cell, the BAU people think that we should be looking for local talent. Common wisdom is that this many kidnappings and killings spread out all over the country means that the composition of the kidnap teams is most likely deeply planted Middle Easterners. They recommend that we start mining our local Arab database looking for model citizen immigrants who have been in the country for more than ten years and who are twenty to forty-five years of age."

Collier thought for a moment. "That's what I want you to concentrate on. Compile a list that fits the BAU profile and then start calling them at work if possible. Don't identify yourself as FBI. See if any of them have recently gone on vacation. If you find two or three that have taken off at the same time, then I want tactical teams assembled ASAP. One team for every suspect."

Collier wanted to test his young agent to see if he understood the logic. "Now Agent Dayton, why would we want to do that?"

Without hesitation, Dayton responded, "The kidnapping teams have thus far consisted of three men. If we find three men that fit the profile that are not at work for whatever reason, we will want the tac teams to hit their residences simultaneously so no one can tip off the other suspects."

"Very good, Agent Dayton. Head back to the office and get on it. Get Agents Dominguez and Wheaton to help you. If there is a very large list, call me and I will get you more help. Time is of the essence here. If we don't physically put our hands on them soon, we probably won't."

Agents Dayton and Dominguez were in the same class at Quantico. Agent Wheaton was three months greener. They were the best of friends. They shared the unbridled zeal for the job that only first-year agents could have. Over drinks, they secretly admitted to one another that they loved everything about the job *and* they were allowed to carry guns! In a moment of strict confidence, Wheaton confessed that he would probably work for half the pay.

By 3:00 p.m. that first day they had already identified thirty-two men of various Middle Eastern extractions who fit the profile that lived in San Antonio. If they expanded the search parameter to a 200-mile radius, the number jumped to 356. Dayton and Dominguez started with the San Antonio list while Wheaton began to slog through the wider list.

By 4:10 p.m. Dayton and Dominguez found two men who were reported by co-workers to be on vacation and unavailable for a week or more. One was a petroleum engineer working for Valero Energy, and the other was the owner of a small computer business. The rapid acquisition of two such promising suspects had the young agents nearly panting.

"I've got to get this to Collier right now," said Dayton.

"Damn! Those BAU guys are mystics. They called it right on the money. How do they do that shit?" replied Dominguez.

At that moment Wheaton joined his colleagues.

"Look at this! On the Austin list, I've got a Lodin Ramadi. Didn't you have a Ramadi?" They compared lists and their collective heart rates jumped fifty beats.

"What does your Ramadi do in Austin?" asked Dayton.

"Student at UT," replied Wheaton.

"Check the INS database for the Austin Ramadi," suggested Dominguez. Wheaton input the information. The response arrived in forty-five seconds. The young agents read the Immigration and Naturalization Service information simultaneously. Dayton read the fastest.

"Holy shit! They are related!" exclaimed Dayton. "I'm calling Collier. Go ahead and alert the tactical commander and tell him to get ready for orders."

Dayton gave Collier the results of their efforts. Collier was frankly shocked at the efficiency of the young agents but would not let on to his junior G-men.

Nonchalantly he remarked, "That's good work, Agent Dayton. Pass my kudos to your partners. How are you going to handle the second Ramadi in Austin?" asked Collier.

"There was no answer on his phone, so we are going to have the people from the Austin office do the *Domino Pizza guy trying to deliver to the wrong address* ploy to see if anyone answers the door."

"That sounds good. Tactical teams?"

"Dominguez is talking to the tac commander now, letting him

know what we have and that your orders will be forthcoming."

"What can we expect from our suspects as far as families are concerned?"

"The San Antonio Ramadi has a wife and two kids. The other men are single, and we think that they live alone."

"Okay. I'll call the tac commander and finalize the details of the operation. I want you at the San Antonio Ramadi location. Dominguez and Wheaton should accompany the team at the al-Kahat residence."

"Sir, do you think that Epstein and Davis will be at one of the residences?"

"Oh, hell no!" replied Collier emphatically. "Only really stupid guys would go back home with their victims. Our best hope is that there might be some helpful forensic material or if the San Antonio Ramadi's wife is at home for questioning."

"When do you think we should raid the residences?" asked Dayton.

"Dinner time. Precisely 6:00 p.m."

At precisely 6:00 p.m., the tactical commander gave the go to the three teams via radio. Much to the chagrin of the young agents, by 6:02 p.m. all the residences were declared unoccupied and turned over to the forensic teams.

Dayton really wanted to be involved in a very high-profile take-down. He queried his boss for new orders.

"Should we go back to the expanded list and keep looking for people not at work?"

"We will spend only one hot body on the expanded list. This is just too sweet a coincidence. We will put most of our assets into locating these three men and Ramadi's wife. I feel confident that is the place we will score. If this trio is not vacationing at Disney World, they are probably chin-deep in this mess!"

Tina had just finished identifying herself to the FBI agent stationed outside the Davis home and stood nervously at the front entry, rehearsing what she would say to Molly. James opened the door.

"Oh, hey, Tina. Come on in. Mom is in the kitchen."

Tina asked, "You guys hanging in there?"

James shook his head. "Zane is too little to fully understand. Andy is upstairs, puking. Mom and Aunt Sylvia cracked out the Glenlivet when the Feds didn't find them at six o'clock. Everything is just peachy."

When Tina entered the kitchen, Molly looked up and saw Tina. She knocked back the last of her dose of scotch and got up to greet Brooks' second in command. Molly tearfully embraced the young woman.

"Oh, Tina, what did we ever do to deserve this?"

Tina gave the question a long moment of thought. "You didn't do anything." She separated herself from Molly and held her at arm's length. "Listen, Molly, I'm not going to hang around. You need to be with your family right now. I just want you to know that I'm a phone call away. I'll keep things going with the business for you until this works itself out. I'll take care of everything, put it out of your mind right now."

Molly dabbed at the tears on her cheeks. "Brooks always said that you were a good, good friend that he could count on when he needed to get things done. If he wanted something done, he said he could always rely on you."

Tina gave her a whimsical smile, tilted her head, and nodded in the affirmative. As she turned to go, she thought, *And Honey, you have no idea of some of the things that old Brooksy-boy wanted done.*

Brooks' mind slowly returned to function. It was difficult to know whether he was awake, dreaming, or dead. The blackness was complete, but his other senses were slowly coming back online. He could feel the vibration of a vehicle in motion. He could also feel a cool breeze of fresh air, for which he was very thankful. His hands were still handcuffed behind his back. He was painfully stiff. When he tried to move his feet, he found that he was bound at the ankles as well. When he moved his feet, they bounced off a padded surface in any direction. When he tried to sit up, he got a sudden understanding of his confinement. He was in a padded, coffin-like box.

Davis was never even minutely claustrophobic historically, but a padded black box will compromise even the strongest of wills. By reflex, he tried to call out only to realize that his mouth was taped shut. The claustrophobia tripled instantaneously. He struggled in panic for a long moment but soon realized that would only lead to insanity or death in short order.

He focused on the breeze from the invisible fan. He let his muscles go flaccid and thought only of the cool breeze. His mind rationalized that if the volume of air being pumped into the box exceeded his metabolic needs and was somehow being evacuated out, his exhaled carbon dioxide would not build up and asphyxiate him. For a moment the rational part of his brain demanded that he should think of a plan to end his dilemma. But just as quickly the more spiritual part of his mind overrode his first impulse. He remembered his mother's answer to everything bad. He started to say the Rosary.

"Hail Mary, the air is cool, full of grace, the air is cool, the Lord is with thee, the air is cool..."

The total darkness and the mantra of the Rosary made time irrelevant. Periodically, Davis would adjust his position to try to relieve the pain and discomfort but was rarely successful. He may have slept but was not sure. Now and then he could feel the rhythmic alterations in momentum associated with gear changes. Once, when the vehicle came to a stop and restarted, he counted at least ten gear changes. He quit counting when he was certain that he was somehow concealed in an eighteen-wheel type truck.

It was becoming steadily more difficult to extinguish the ember of panic that was glowing brightly in the pit of his stomach. He wondered if Epstein was similarly trapped and how he was holding up. He thought briefly of his wife of twenty years, but the pain was just too great. He turned his face toward the invisible conduit of fresh air and inhaled deeply.

"Hail Mary, the air is cool, full of grace, the air is cool..."

Epstein was not holding up well at all. He was in a similar box on the other side of the truck. Unlike Davis, he was very claustrophobic. As soon as he realized that he was bound and in a padded box, his panic crescendoed. In his panic, he never realized that the box was being more than adequately ventilated. He tried vainly to smash his head against the side of the box to induce unconsciousness, but the padding buffered the blows enough to only induce a terrible headache.

In his agony, he thought about his wife and lamented the pain that she would be suffering. For a moment he recalled her repeated admonitions about keeping a lower profile concerning his political stance. She had always warned that the enemy never forgot anything. He now understood her wisdom completely. He cried and prayed but nothing helped with his abject misery. His pain was so complete that he was totally unaware that he had now missed three doses of his beta blocker and afterload-reducing medications that his sick heart needed so badly. He just thought that the dull pain in his left arm was the result of his horrible confinement.

Davis' mantra was finally interrupted by the feel of the truck coming to a stop and the sounds of distant voices and the movement of equipment. The sounds of hands on the box signaled that the box was about to be opened. With the hood still in place, he could not see a thing. He realized that the absence of the fine dots of light through the weave of the fabric meant that it was probably night. He heard voices speaking in Arabic. He was reasonably certain that it was the voices of the kidnappers. They said nothing to him. He was suddenly administered a second injection, and the box was immediately re-closed. Davis did not know whether to rejoice or despair. After a moment of contemplation, the thought of the painless blackness of anesthesia sounded pretty good.

When the second injection was administered, the flatbed eighteen-wheeler carrying 34,000 pounds of water purification equipment and two unconscious kidnap victims was forty-five miles from the international bridge between El Paso and Juarez, Mexico near the tiny town of Acala, Texas. Since the truck was outgoing to Mexico it received only cursory attention on the American side. Since the Mexican crossing authorities were all handsomely bribed, the truck and contents were virtually ignored and sent south down Mexican Federal Highway 45.

After administering the final sedative, the kidnap team backtracked twenty miles on Interstate 10 to a nondescript ranch road west of Sierra Blanca. They followed the road into the Quitman Mountains to a ranch that was only nine miles from the Rio Grande. The ranch was 26,000 acres and was owned by a famous Hollywood actor. He visited only when time permitted. For him, it was a high desert retreat and a great tax write-off. He had no idea that in a secluded valley deep in the back of the ranch, a well-organized group of ISIS terrorists had set up a command post.

The command post was a Spartan hunting cabin. The only sign that it was anything special was the Bell Jet Ranger helicopter that was parked next to the cabin and hidden under camouflaged netting.

The kidnappers met with members of their exfiltration team. The team was composed of the pilot of the Jet Ranger and two of a six-man team tasked with keeping track of the locations of Homeland Security and US Border Patrol surface and airborne assets. The helicopter was prepped and ready to fly at a moment's notice. The kidnappers reviewed the current positions of all federal assets within fifty miles of the cabin. The absent team members were at different locations monitoring electronic surveillance of Homeland Security and Border Patrol radio traffic. They were also equipped with the latest version of Chinese ultra-high-speed encryption radios that could send coded location data to the team members on the ranch. Their transmission bursts could be measured in milliseconds and could not be tracked.

The closest US airborne asset was a Homeland Security helicopter thirty-five miles away. There was one Border Patrol surface vehicle between the cabin and the river and could be easily skirted. With only nine miles to Mexican airspace, the terrorists could get airborne, skim the surface under border radars, and be safe in Mexico in less than four minutes. US authorities would be helpless to stop the terrorists, and short of a chance view from a surveillance satellite, they would not be able to trace them back to the hunting cabin on the movie star's ranch.

The system was complicated, but necessary. If exfiltration and infiltration after completion of a mission were conducted through a regular international border crossing, there would be an in-depth digital and paper trail. Such records would make it more difficult for terrorists to slip back undetected into American society.

CHAPTER SIX
Welcome to Hell

Davis did not know it, but he had been without food and water for nearly thirty hours. He also did not know that he had been delivered to an isolated ranch in the mountains of the Mexican state of Chihuahua, 180 miles south of the border. What he did know was that he was struggling to regain consciousness. He swam in and out of brief snippets of light and dark. He was extraordinarily tired and was more comfortable in the dark.

During one moment of consciousness Davis became aware that Epstein was present in the same room. He was shackled to a small bed across the room. He had lost his suitcoat and wore only an undershirt and trousers. The contractor was glad to see that he had made the journey thus far. However, something about Epstein was not quite right. Davis struggled to focus on him and realized it was his breathing. Each ragged breath sounded of someone near drowning. The effort to study his fellow victim was too arduous, and Davis slipped back into darkness.

The next time that he came back into the light he could feel a palpable air of tension. The kidnappers were hovering over Epstein and were speaking in rapid-fire Arabic. The elder Ramadi was pushing rapidly on his chest while his nephew was periodically lowering his face to Epstein's. It took a moment for Davis to realize that they were administering CPR to a ghostly pale banker.

A burst of adrenalin poured into Davis' circulation, driving away the fog. He tried to rise, and for the first time he realized that he was also shackled to a bed. All he could do was watch the frantic but vain attempts to save the dying Epstein's life. His mind went to the repeated doses of sedative and remembered that Epstein had mentioned his cardiologist on a couple of occasions. He realized that the rigors of the kidnapping were too much for his client.

After twenty minutes Abu Ramadi called off the effort and said something in Arabic. To punctuate the comment, al-Kahat spat on the dead banker and murmured his own epithet. Davis studied the three men and realized that he was seeing them without their ski masks, but they seemed not to care. He had a sure feeling that was not a good thing.

The terrorists were five minutes into their postmortem discussion before the younger Ramadi noticed that Davis was awake and observing the proceedings. He touched his uncle's arm and nodded in the contractor's direction. Abu made eye contact with Davis and gave a quiet order to the others. While they carried the body out of the room, Ramadi stepped over to the bed and spoke to Davis.

"It appears that our guest of honor is unable to attend."

Davis tried to reply but his mouth was too dry. Ramadi smiled and left the room. He promptly returned with a small glass of water. He lifted Davis' head and helped him drink. He was grateful for the water but confused by the terrorist's kindness. With difficulty, he cleared his throat. In a horse whisper, he asked, "Why me?"

Ramadi reflected for a moment and then replied, "Allah works in mysterious ways."

Davis had no illusions. He understood ISIS was on a rampage and that Epstein was Jewish and very anti-Muslim. From the news reporting, the other kidnappings were always single. Why did they vary from their usual plan? The contractor asked again, "But why me?"

This time Ramadi smiled grimly and traced the remnant of the Lenten ashes still on Davis' forehead. Without a word, he left the room.

In a quiet voice, Davis mumbled to himself, "Well shit! I guess I was just begging to be a martyr."

With the sip of water, he was now significantly more coherent. He took inventory of his surroundings. He was in a small room with two single metal beds. He was face up with his hands handcuffed together with the handcuffs attached to the headrail above his head with a second pair of cuffs. He was barefoot with his ankles shackled in a similar way. He gave his bonds a brief tug only to find them solid.

To his right was a window. He stretched his neck and could see the view outside the window. He could see that he was in mountainous country. The cabin sat on low ground in the valley between two hills. A narrow dirt road led away from the cabin and wound its way down the valley.

The cabin smelled old, and the bed was very musty. The walls of the room were unadorned except for an advertisement for Federal Premium hunting ammunition showing a beautiful female in camouflage saying that she never leaves home without her 165-grain Sierra Boat Tail bullets. There were two doors in the room. Both were open. Beyond the first Davis could see a kitchen table and an old gas range. A propane tank sat next to it on the floor. The other door led to a very rustic bathroom.

Davis' eyes went back to the window. The geography reminded him of a hunting lease he once had in West Texas. He decided that he and Epstein must have been taken somewhere in West Texas. After a longer moment of contemplation, he realized that it could be anywhere in the desert southwest of the United States. His eyes studied the sides of the hills. He recognized prickly pear cactus, ocotillo, mountain sage, bee brush, and others. He exhaled heavily. The reality of his situation was that he could be just about anywhere in a million-square-mile area. He was the needle in a very dangerous haystack.

Davis' mind began to play back the whole event over in his mind. He could remember the arrival of the terrorists in detail but that was it. He concentrated for a bit and could faintly remember the sounds of the truck and the claustrophobic box, but the memory was very dreamlike. He looked at the now empty bed across the room. A deep pang of sorrow for Epstein's wife and children suddenly hit him. Just as suddenly a jolt like electricity hit him when he thought of his own wife and family. He reflexively pulled at his bonds only to be reminded of his hopeless situation.

He stared at the ceiling for a long while, gathering his thoughts. He began to envy Epstein. His misery was over, and he had cheated the terrorists of the beheading that they so dearly wanted. Again, the jolt like electricity hit him like a hammer. It would now be his head that would show up on the Internet. For the first time, a brief snippet of Tina's thinly veiled threat to have a discussion with Molly if something bad happened to him flashed through his mind. Well, it didn't get much worse than this. He told himself to concentrate on his current problem.

He had no idea of the time, but eventually the sun began to set. As the shadows lengthened outside, Davis knew one thing for certain. Short of a miracle or the cavalry arriving, he was shit out of luck.

By the beginning of the third day, the San Antonio field office was shifting from the active search mode to the far more tedious and far less satisfying deep investigation mode. They were entering the same phase that the San Deigo, New York, and Phoenix field offices had been in for weeks. They were doing a lot of looking but absolutely no finding. No headless bodies had turned up, with nasty notes from ISIS attached.

Collier was very frustrated. The very quick work of his young agents that had seemed so promising had stalled dead. The FBI director ordered all other field offices to begin a similar program of watching for target groups of Middle Eastern immigrants to see if they could pinpoint suspects that may have been on vacation or otherwise away from their jobs during the time frames of the previous kidnappings. They found seven promising absentees in the New

York area and two each in the San Diego and Phoenix areas. Fearful that if they rounded up the men it would tip off the terrorists, they chose to place them all under general surveillance.

In a proactive approach, the FBI quietly began to question employers of men who fit the profile across the country. They sought to find out if any of their Arab employees had applied for vacation time in the near future. Three were found in the San Francisco-Oakland area and two were found in the Denver area. These five did not know it but they were going to be followed by undercover agents from the moment they went on vacation.

In San Antonio, Mrs. Epstein and her grown sons and their families kept vigil with the support of their friends from the congregation of Temple Beth-El. In Leon Springs, Molly and her sons began the long wait with similar support from family, friends, and their church.

From the second day on, Molly and her family would shudder every time the phone rang. Was this the horrible news that they dreaded? Molly forbade her sons from using their computers. The Internet was considered the portal into hell. She kept Andrew and Zane at home. Her eldest son was a completely different story. When the FBI said that there was a low probability of being in immediate danger, he immediately said that he would be continuing with school. When Molly objected, he got in his car and said he would see her for dinner. With so much gut-wrenching fear consuming her and her younger sons, Molly could not focus on the continued deterioration of James' personality. She did, however, confide in Special Agent Dayton that her oldest was a bit of a hothead and she was fearful that he might say or try to do something that would not be helpful. Agent Dayton said that he would try to keep an eye on him for her.

CHAPTER SEVEN
The Cavalry Arrives

The next day was strangely quiet. The terrorists had apparently stayed out of the cabin and dealt with Epstein's body. In the evening, they returned. They conversed freely in Arabic, knowing intuitively that the Texan would not be able to follow. They prepared a meal of freeze-dried camping rations. They brought a stout wooden chair into the room where Davis was held. They uncuffed his hands and feet from the head and footrails and pulled him into a sitting position and placed him in the chair.

Abu Ramadi spoke to Davis in a quiet voice that was his hallmark.

"We will release your left hand so that you can eat and drink. Be aware that if you cause any trouble, your food and water will be withheld for forty-eight hours. Do you understand?"

Davis looked at Ramadi and his partners. He nodded in the affirmative but said nothing. He wanted the water badly and thought that once he got his fill, he would be more talkative.

A small bedside table was placed in front of Davis on which they placed a plate of some sort of pasta and chicken and a tall glass of water. He went at once to the water and drank the entire glass. He held the empty out at the elder Ramadi.

"May I have another?" After a pause, he added a reluctant, "Please."

Ramadi nodded at his nephew, who left to retrieve a refill. Davis tested the food and found it edible. He ate quickly and then took his time with the second glass of water. He flexed his stiff muscles. Ramadi addressed al-Kahat in English.

"When he finishes, leave him cuffed to the chair for a while."

Al-Kahat glared first at Davis then at Ramadi. In Arabic, he replied, "Why coddle the dog? He won't be here for long."

Ramadi switched back to Arabic. "No decisions have been made."

Al-Kahat let out a disgusted grunt. He was clearly less interested in providing creature comforts for their prisoner than getting to the stroke of the blade through the infidel's throat.

They left Davis and adjourned to the kitchen and continued discussions in Arabic. Davis stretched and flexed as much as his seated position would allow. He could feel that the cuff securing his right hand was attached to the seat back. His ankles were bound together and then to the cross member under the seat.

Ramadi allowed him thirty minutes in the chair. He and al-Kahat returned to the room.

"Do you need to go to the bathroom?" inquired Ramadi.

Davis shook his head. "I must have sweated all the water out of me during the trip. Maybe later. I'll let you know."

"We are going to put you back in the bed. Do I need to explain how sorry you will be if you try something stupid?"

Davis shook his head. "No. I know futility when I see it."

"That is good. Things will go much easier for you if you cooperate."

By the time they re-shackled Davis to the bed, it was dark. The terrorists again adjourned to other parts of the cabin. One of them would look in on him at irregular intervals. Davis presumed that it would go on like that all night. Once, when Ramadi checked on him, Brooks thought he would throw out a test question.

"Hey, chief, you never told me where you've taken me." Ramadi recoiled a bit. He smiled and chuckled. After a pause, he replied, "I bet you were a big hit at open mic night at the comedy club."

Fed, watered, and fully awake, Davis took stock of his situation. Any way he looked at it, things were grim. He was held captive by Arab terrorists who were likely aligned with other terrorists who had already captured and killed at least four other Americans. He revisited the question of why. He did not fit the profile. He was not a prominent American. If they killed a contractor from Texas, very few people would think twice about it. He recalled the one who was the clear leader tracing the ashes on his forehead. That could not possibly be the reason. Arab terrorists hate Jews, not Catholics from Texas.

Davis decided to not waste any more time on the why. His ass was wedged very deeply in the proverbial crack. He needed to think of how to extricate it ASAP.

In his mind, he made a list of the things that he knew for sure. First, he did not know exactly where he was. That did not bother him much. He was an avid outdoorsman who was at home in the wide-open spaces. He had never been lost and always managed to find his way home. Second, he was confident that Epstein, not he, was the real target. The unplanned death of Epstein had upset their plan. His role was not yet defined. Third, the apparent leader spoke to one of the other men in English. He would assume that they all spoke English. The leader's English bore almost no accent. He might have been in the US for a long time. Fourth, the youngest man bore a strong physical resemblance to the leader. Could he possibly be the son of the leader? Fifth, the third man was the scariest of them all. He had a particularly evil look. Was it he who had dealt the blow that Davis had absorbed? He remembered vividly how it felt looking down the barrel of the submachine gun. Davis was sure that if the leader had not stopped him, his present circumstance would be moot.

Davis' mind reverberated with these points, but he was far more troubled by what he did not know. He wondered how his family was holding up. He presumed that the kidnapping and the killing of one of his roofers had been quickly reported to the Kendall County authorities and then the FBI field office in San Antonio. Davis knew that all law enforcement agencies were on high alert and that the federal police would have tremendous assets at their disposal to try to catch up with the terrorists.

He tried praying himself to sleep, but he was too wired. His mind was spinning in a vortex of anxious thought. He replayed his situation repeatedly, trying to formulate a plan or course of action that might result in his release. Should he try to persuade his captors that he was a nobody and that his death would probably yield little or no political capital? Should he caution them that his death might have precisely the opposite of the desired effect? Would the senseless killing of a harmless husband and father so polarize the nation that the act would in essence become the Pearl Harbor of an all-out, no-holds-barred war on Islam?

As he considered how he would present that thought to the terrorists, the third man, the scary one, entered the room and roughly shook his binds and glared hatefully at his captive. The look was a portent of the future. As Davis watched the man leave the room, a clearer, more certain thought centered itself in his mind. "That son of a bitch doesn't like me! I better just figure out how the hell to escape!"

After that first restless night, Davis began what would become the routine activity of his captivity. He was allowed to use the bathroom twice daily. He was given a late-morning and early-evening meal of the freeze-dried camping rations with two glasses of water with each meal. When he was not in the bathroom or seated for a meal, he was shackled to the bed.

Once, he was unshackled and ordered to strip and take a shower and shave. The operation was conducted at gunpoint. He was given clean clothes. He was then seated in a chair against a bare wall and photographed under a banner with Arabic writing. He was then re-shackled to the bed.

That night it struck Davis that for February, it was not as cold as he thought it should be. The idea that he might not be in West Texas momentarily crossed his mind. Since they offered him no blanket, he was just glad that he was not freezing to add to his misery.

The next morning the sound of a heavy truck and other vehicles snapped Davis' attention to the window. In a moment a Humvee followed by a large troop truck could be seen working their way up the valley. A huge burst of elation hit Davis when he realized that they were military vehicles. The cavalry had just arrived! He could hear the terrorists conversing in Arabic, but their tone was nonchalant. His elation turned to panic. When the terrorists realized that they were surrounded they would probably kill him outright, shackled to the bed before they could be neutralized.

The vehicles arrived at the front of the cabin and the engines stopped. The vehicles and their contents were outside of Davis' field of view. He could hear the terrorists get up to face the new arrivals, but there seemed to be no urgency. Davis' panic became confusion.

Davis then heard the leader greet the new arrivals in Spanish. Years of contracting in South Texas had made Davis fluent in Spanish. He was completely dumbfounded.

"Good morning, General. I trust your trip was uneventful?" asked Ramadi.

A new voice replied, "Yes, it is a good morning. Are you ready to conduct business?" Major General Francisco Gomez De La Garza, the commander of the Mexican Army's 24th Division headquartered in the state of Chihuahua, had no time for niceties. He was a very busy man. He had to maintain a delicate balance between his powerful positions in the Army with his responsibilities to his colleagues in the Juarez Cartel. It was the cartel that arranged for the safe house that the ISIS teams were taking their victims for final disposition. For the general it was just one more activity on a colorful and very lucrative business resume.

Ramadi and a swarthy man in a meticulous uniform of the Mexican Army met at the kitchen table. Ramadi placed a metallic briefcase on the table, opened it, and turned it toward the general. Davis could see the proceedings from the bed. He was dumbstruck. Visions of rescue disappeared in an instant.

The general picked up a stack of the neatly banded American $100 bills and fanned through them. He studied the case for a moment, then threw the bills back in the case. His eyes narrowed and he cast a sideways glare on Ramadi.

"This is for one. You changed the deal to two men."

Ramadi and his colleagues were taken aback. Al-Kahat's eye went to the AK-47 in the corner of the room. Ramadi warned him off without a word. He addressed the general.

"The original deal was for one; however, our initial target had a less than normal heart and died before we could carry out our mission that we did contract with you. The second man is simply a backup."

Without so much as a pause, De La Garza dismissed Ramadi.

"Two men is twice the price. No discussion."

"But, General…"

"No discussion."

Ramadi paused a moment in thought. Al-Kahat scanned the troop truck outside, trying to judge how an armed confrontation with the Mexicans might go. He quickly counted a dozen dismounted troops, all with automatic weapons. He and Ramadi made eye contact. They would have to pay up.

"We will need a few days to secure more funds," said Ramadi reluctantly.

The general smiled and quickly closed the briefcase. "We are reasonable people."

He investigated the bedroom for the first time. He picked up the briefcase and entered the room. He approached the bedside and studied how Davis was shackled. Still in Spanish he asked the contractor, "Do you speak Spanish?"

Davis studied his nametag and his two-star rank and thought fast. He gave the general a quizzical look.

"Ah…me no hablo Spanyo. Do you hablo English?"

De La Garza gave Davis a disgusted look. He turned and re-entered the kitchen.

He addressed Ramadi. "Does he have any idea what you have in store for him?"

"He is not an ignorant man. He will be in the negotiating mode soon."

The general made his way to the front door. He stopped short for a final comment. "Remind the others that if they want to continue to use our facilities for your paramilitary activities, the fee is for each man. We have a long and profitable business history with your Taliban brothers buying the fruits of their poppy fields. We would not want to jeopardize our relationship over something as trivial as this cowboy, now do we?"

On his way out he issued an order to his second in command, who gathered some troops and headed for a second building that Davis had yet to see. He addressed Ramadi again.

"We do not want anyone killed until your fee is paid in full. We will take your recording equipment until things are settled. It would be very unfortunate if you thought that you could kill your friend and leave us unpaid."

With his insurance policy in effect, the general and his troops saddled up and left.

Davis lay in stunned paralysis. In less than five minutes many mysteries were revealed, and many questions answered. The question of where was no longer unknown. Mexico. Davis' first thought was that he must have been drugged longer than he suspected.

In rapid order, several concepts became crystal clear. They were going to cut his head off, and were it not for accounts in arrears, it would be sooner rather than later. ISIS was apparently bringing all the kidnap victims to this ranch for termination. If such a high-ranking Mexican military official was in league with ISIS and the cartels, then he was without an ally. He knew from the news reporting out of Mexico that corruption was rampant in the state and federal police and military. Because the Army had the greatest assets, they could easily force their will on lesser organizations. It suddenly struck Davis that there was no one he could reliably turn to for help. And most important of all, they would soon cut off his head!"

CHAPTER EIGHT
The Litany of Goodbyes

At noon, Ramadi and his nephew left the ranch house for a trip to Monterrey to contact his ISIS controllers to request more cash to pay off De La Garza. The trip and acquisition of the funds would take two or three days. As the men were leaving, Ramadi gave al-Kahat very definitive instructions.

"It goes without saying, do not let him escape. More importantly, do not kill him prematurely. The entire relationship with the Army and the cartels is at stake."

Al-Kahat only grunted his acceptance of the orders. Ramadi studied al-Kahat's face and eyes. There was a level of hate there that could jeopardize the operation.

"Don't disappoint me," was his final admonition.

Davis' will was decaying by the hour. With each passing minute, the certainty of his impending death grew in the void left by his vanishing hope. He prayed for a while, but the monotonous litany of spiritual invocations soon stopped having an effect. Instead, Davis began a new litany, a litany of goodbyes.

He thought about his immediate family and decided that they should be last. Instead, he began to think about all the other people that meant something in his life. He started with old friends and distant relatives. He conjured up their images in his mind and relived good and bad times. Those who did good things for him, he thanked one last time. For those he may have hurt in some way, he asked for their forgiveness.

So it went throughout the afternoon. The sun was getting low in the sky when he finally got to Molly. He relived a long sequence of firsts. The first time he laid eyes on her. The first time they spoke. The first date. The first time he held her hand. The first kiss. The first time he touched her. The first time they made love. The wedding. The birth of each of their children.

Then his mind settled on Tina. The radical difference between the sweetness, purity, sincerity, and completeness of Molly's love and the simplicity, unbridled, no-holds-barred physicality that was Tina's specialty made Davis' heart burn. The guilt he felt was terrible, but the fact that he had been able to ignore it for so long made it much, much worse. He wondered if this was how a death penalty prisoner felt the night before execution.

Davis marveled that each vision was so incredibly crisp and clear. There was no patina of time distorting the images. It finally struck him that the clarity was because his subconscious was aware that the end of the memories was near.

An unexpected aura of calm descended upon Davis. He said his goodbyes and felt that his thoughts to his loved ones were a fitting farewell. He was now content to let the situation play itself out in whatever way that God had ordained. He made a promise to himself to only think of his loved ones when God himself intervened and spoke to him out loud. It was a proper promise because any more thoughts about his loved ones would be just too painful. He had achieved a state where the world was occupied only by himself and his captors, with God as the referee.

CHAPTER NINE

Dayton's Investigation

Agent Dayton was tasked by Collier to monitor the activities of protesters on the campus of UTSA. When the anti-US, anti-Israel, pro-Palestine, pro-Hamas, pro-Hezbollah, and pro-Iranian protesters were lumped together, there was no shortage of protesters for Dayton to monitor

Because Dayton was a very youthful-looking FBI agent, all he needed to do to camouflage himself on campus was to wear ragged jeans, a UTSA sweatshirt, and the mandatory backpack. What no one realized was that the backpack held an old textbook, compact binoculars, a notebook, and a .40 cal Glock model 22. He looked so much the part that as he sat in the quad outside the student union, more than one co-ed sat down and started to chat him up. One flirtatious redhead offered him her phone number, which he took just to make things look real. Dayton was starting to like this undercover thing.

Dayton was on the fifth level of one of the campus parking garages, about to call it a day. From that elevation, he could see the roofline of several of the campus buildings. The movement of a person across a roofline caught his attention. The motion was like someone not wanting to be observed. Dayton focused his binoculars on the person.

The image was just beyond the useful limit of the compact binoculars so he could not make out much in the way of facial details. The person was probably male, athletic build, light brown hair covered by a black baseball cap with a round medallion, standard gray, long-sleeved sweatshirt with the UTSA logo over jeans. The subject was very interested in a group of protesters who were milling around preparing for their nightly gathering. He was studying them through his own binoculars.

Dayton felt like he knew the subject. He wished he had his 20-power spotting scope. He checked his watch. He was supposed to check in with the overwatch people at the Davis house so they could get dinner.

At the Davis home, he checked in and decided to see how Mrs. Davis was doing and if there was anything he could do for the family. They met in the kitchen.

"Your offer is very kind, Agent Dayton, but there's not much anyone can do. It's the not knowing that is killing us...it's very tough right now."

"I can't even imagine. My mom is not much older than you. If my dad were missing..." His voice trailed off. "If there is anything that the Bureau can do for you, or I can do for you personally, please let me know."

At that moment James came in and dropped his backpack on one of the island barstools. He affectionately gave his mom a prolonged hug and a kiss on the forehead.

"Are you hanging tough, Mom?"

Molly sighed audibly and waggled her hand, indicating that it was iffy at best.

"You're tougher than nails, Mom. If anyone can stare down the ragheads, it's you."

"I don't feel like nails. Now get your filthy backpack out of my kitchen, go round up your brothers, and get washed up for dinner." He kissed her once again on the forehead.

All during the mother-son interchange, the FBI man was studying James and thinking, *Male, athletic build, light brown hair under black baseball cap with round center medallion, gray, long-sleeved UTSA sweatshirt over jeans. I wonder if there are binoculars in that backpack. So, who do we have here that is so interested in the campus "ragheads"?*

As James turned, he greeted Dayton for the first time. "Anything new on the investigative front?"

Dayton arched his eyebrows. "There's always a little something that pops up. But never fear, the FBI follows up on everything…and not much gets past us."

CHAPTER TEN
Friend or Foe—You Pick

James unlocked his car and tossed his backpack into the passenger front seat. He got behind the wheel, closed the door, and was about to start the car when there was a powerful rap against the driver's side window. He was startled and made a grab for his backpack and tried to see who he was about to face off with. Special Agent Timothy Dayton stood outside the window with a smug smile and slowly shaking his head.

"Get out of the car, James."

James slowly complied while catching his breath. "You scared the shit outta me!"

"Calm down. I just want to talk to you for a bit."

"About what?"

"About you planning to do something really stupid."

James recoiled a bit in surprise.

"What are you talking about?"

"Bring your backpack. We'll sit in my car and have a discussion all about it."

James eyed his backpack and wanted to leave it in his car. Dayton started to move toward his vehicle and called over his shoulder, "And don't forget your backpack."

James reluctantly complied but was already formulating a reason for not showing Dayton the contents. When they were settled in Dayton's car, James tucked the backpack on the floorboard next to his feet.

With his best bravado, he quizzed the Fed. "Okay, so what's this all about? Why are you following me around?"

Dayton looked at young Davis out of the corner of his eye but didn't answer right away. He retrieved a tablet computer and queued up a password-protected photo file.

"What's this all about, you ask? I like you, James. I feel sorry for you. I see a bit of a younger me in you, James. I've decided to do you a favor...a huge favor...a favor at *my* own risk."

"I didn't ask for any favors."

"You can thank me later."

"Dream on, G-man."

Dayton arched his eyebrows and nodded marginally. "Yeah, a bit like a younger me." He handed the tablet to James. "Flip through these photos, chief."

The first photo was of a group of protesters in front of an identifiable UTSA building. The second was a clear image of James on the top of a building observing the protesters. Each photo was time and date-stamped.

As James scrolled through the photos, he could see that Dayton was following him around and recording his activities via telephoto lens. It was clear that Dayton had accumulated multiple days' worth of evidence of his interest in the "raghead" protesters. When he finished the file, he handed the computer back to Dayton.

"So, you're telling me that there's a federal law against being on the roof of a public building, on a public university campus, observing First Amendment-protected activities of a bunch of lunatics?"

"No, James, no federal laws against that. But you might want to do some careful study about when simple observation may slip across that delicate line into conspiracy to plan to commit a felony. It's that conspiracy thing that the dumbasses always forget about. That's when we get them. So, James, are you the scholar that your mother thinks you are, or just another dumbass?"

James was silent, thinking about his mother.

"So why are you doing this? What's your interest in me?"

"For now, it's because I feel like it. But that could change. Let's see what's in your backpack."

James thought fast. "Let's see your warrant."

"I don't need a warrant. I've got probable cause."

"Bullshit! You don't have probable cause!"

"Oh, yes, I do! I tap on your window, you go for your backpack like there's a weapon in there, so you gave me all kinds of probable cause. That's how I'll write it up. Who do you think the judge will believe in a high-threat environment? A federal officer or a dumbass? Dayton waved his hand, indicating that James should hand over the backpack. James did not move. Dayton thought for a minute. "Okay, James, we can do this another way. I'm going to ask you if you have a gun in the bag. But first, I'm going to tell you that if you lie to a federal officer, it is a felony with mandatory jail time. So, if you tell me yes to the gun question, I will know it is the truth and you will earn special consideration. If you answer no, then you are going to have to prove it, but you get no special considerations. If you make me take the backpack and I find out you are lying about a gun, it will take me hours to write up all the charges. And then I'll have to call your mom and tell her the horrible news that James is not a scholar."

James thought for a bit. "And what would be a special consideration for telling the truth?"

Dayton slowly nodded. "In this case, I would tell you to take it home, lock it up, and only use it in the defense of your mother and brothers. But be aware, I will be surveilling your ass from now on. And trust me on this, Boy Wonder, the FBI has assets that you can't even dream of." After a pause, Dayton asked, "So, what's in the bag?"

James took a deep breath and slowly exhaled. "Colt Commander, .45 cal."

"Uh-huh. Great gun. Take it home and lock it up."

James looked at the agent. "That's it? You don't want to see it?"

"Not really…. You see, James, you and I have entered into a desperate agreement. Your freedom is in my hands. So don't you dare ever forget it."

CHAPTER ELEVEN
Extreme Prejudice

Darkness claimed the little valley of his captivity. When he finished his goodbyes, Davis was spent of emotion. He lay shackled to the bed but was not aware of the cuffs. He finally fell asleep. At some point, the lights in the room went on and al-Kahat entered. Davis absently thought that it was time for his evening ration. The terrorist unlocked the cuffs at the head and foot of the bed and roughly pulled Davis into a sitting position with his feet on the floor. Al-Kahat grabbed Davis by the hair and gave him a shake and a warning.

"Do not move!"

He turned as if to return to the kitchen, but instead spun and struck Davis with a powerful blow to the jaw. Davis' vision went from white to complete blackness.

Davis began the arduous task of climbing back into consciousness. Before his vision returned, he became aware of a sizzling pain in his jaw. For a while, the pain was all that he could focus on. He slowly became aware that he was shackled in a different position. There was uncomfortable pressure in his midsection. He focused on his hands and found them no longer handcuffed together to the head of the bed, but to either side of the bed frame side rails. The pain in his midsection resulted from being draped over the bed's footboard. His feet, like his hands, were fastened to some part of either side of the bed he could not see. He struggled against his binds, but he could not move out of the painful position. He felt cold. It took him a moment to realize that he had been stripped of his clothes. Gut-wrenching panic suddenly replaced all his pain.

Al-Kahat stepped into the doorway and looked at his captive. When he recognized that Davis had regained consciousness, an evil grin formed on his face. He knelt at the bedside and looked closely into Davis' face. He did not want to miss a moment of his captive's desolation and despair.

"I want to tell you a story, Mr. Davis. Not a fairy tale, but a true story. It is a story of good people and bad people. This is the kind of story you Americans love."

Davis looked back into al-Kahat's eyes and could see a combination of hate and insanity that was tangible.

"The good person in this story was a beautiful young woman named Nameem. She was seventeen years old and a true believer in Islam. And like all good Islamic young women, she was a virgin. She led a good life until her homeland was invaded by a massive force of heathen non-believers. The bad people were bent upon the destruction of all the people like Nameem and their one true religion.

"One day Nameem's city was assaulted by the Army of heathens. They indiscriminately bombarded parts of the city and destroyed the city's water system. Nameem was hiding in a basement with other women and children. They ran out of water, and after two days the children were dying of thirst. Nameem left the basement in search of water. She was captured by a squad of the heathen soldiers.

"Nameem was one of the most beautiful young women in Iraq. I know she was beautiful because she was my younger sister. The soldiers of the Great Satan took her to an abandoned building. There they stripped her and took turns ravishing her until they all had their fill. Instead of mercifully killing her, they set her free to wander the streets naked.

"She was eventually found by mujahedeen and taken to the hospital. She was physically ruined and mentally destroyed. The next day she left the hospital and found an uncle and described what had happened. Not able to exist after her ordeal, she asked him for his pistol. He gave it to her, and she shot herself in the mouth."

Davis grimaced at the story's climax. Al-Kahat laughed and said, "I told you it was not a fairy tale with a happy ending."

The terrorist got up and moved to the end of the bed and loosened his belt and dropped his pants. He began to stroke Davis' buttocks.

"You see, Mr. Davis, I want you to leave this world knowing first-hand what this true story is all about. Feel free to scream all you want. No one will hear you here in the middle of nowhere. Only I will hear you. And I want you to scream long and loud."

With the first thrust, Davis bit a hole in his lip and screamed into the mattress. Al-Kahat made it last almost an hour. He released Davis and threw his clothes at him and ordered him to redress. He kept his pistol aimed at him to discourage any retaliation. He then re-shackled Davis to the bed. When the terrorist left the room, he was sure that he had exacted all the revenge he had ever dreamed of for his sister. What al-Kahat never realized was that revenge, that all-powerful of motivators, never dies. It only passes on to the next man.

CHAPTER TWELVE
The Power of Motivation

There was no sleep for Davis that night. As the rising sun began to lighten the eastern sky, his mind was occupied by only one thing, how to get out of the handcuffs.

At 9:00 a.m. Davis could hear al-Kahat in the kitchen preparing the morning rations. He brought the food and set it before Davis as always. Neither man said a word. To al-Kahat's enjoyment, Davis moved like an obedient and thoroughly beaten animal.

The food looked and smelled disgusting to Davis. He tried to eat, but a wave of nausea washed over him. He retched and nearly vomited. Then a pain began deep in his belly. For a moment he thought that it was somehow related to damage caused by al-Kahat's assault of the night before. The pain was soon accompanied by loud bowel sounds. The sensation of impending diarrhea became overwhelming. Davis knew that he could not hold on for long. He called to the other room.

"Hey, man! I'm about to have diarrhea in here!"

There was no response from al-Kahat.

"I mean it, asshole! If you don't hurry and let me go to the john, you are going to have to live with the smell of the results!"

Since there was a good deal of logic attached to Davis' threat, al-Kahat moved to the bedroom and removed the shackles. Without waiting, Davis made for the bathroom. He struggled to lower his pants and then sat heavily on the toilet. He made it with not a moment to spare. He doubled over and moaned out loud. The wave of nausea crescendoed. He retched and grabbed a small waste basket next to the toilet. Since he had no meal the night before, there was little to throw up.

Since there was no way to fake such impressive gastrointestinal signs, al-Kahat was satisfied that it was the real thing. He pointed his pistol at Davis and ordered him to re-cuff his feet together and then his hands. With the next rush of diarrhea, al-Kahat laughed and chided Davis. "I thought you Texans were smart enough to know better than drink the water in Mexico."

As he left his captive to his misery, Davis retched again and understood his problem.

"The fucking 'tourista!' Just what I don't need right now!"

Davis soon began to develop a fever with the protozoal infection and began to sweat profusely. He mopped his brow with the back of his cuffed hand. The sweat trickled down under the handcuff and disappeared under the cuff of his sleeve. Davis stared at the moisture for a moment and then rotated the cuff around the circumference of his wrist. He tried moving the cuff toward his fingers. The cuff appeared too snug to slip over his hand. He tried more sweat, then saliva, but it was still too tight. The toilet sat next to the bathroom lavatory. Resting there was a bottle of pump hand soap. He picked up the bottle and added the slippery soap to his sweaty wrist. With a great deal of effort, he could move the cuff a little further toward his fingers. Davis raised his left sleeve and applied a generous amount of soap to his arm and then replaced the sleeve.

Later that night al-Kahat moved Davis back to his bed. Davis objected, saying that he felt that more diarrhea was still a strong possibility. Al-Kahat dismissed him, telling him that he did not care if he fouled his bed.

Davis' sick bowel made it through the night. He slept only briefly while putting together his plan. He knew that his only possible avenue of escape was while he and al-Kahat were alone. When the other terrorists returned, all was probably lost. He decided that there was only a narrow window of opportunity for escape, and having the "tourista" might play to his advantage.

At mid-morning al-Kahat brought a plate of food and a cup of water and placed them on the small table. He placed Davis in the chair and fastened one of his ankle cuffs to the cross brace under the seat. His hands remained cuffed together so that he could feed himself. Al-Kahat studied his captive. He was satisfied with the pallor of his face and the beads of perspiration that ran across his forehead. He fantasized for a moment about stroking the razor-sharp blade across his throat. As he turned to leave the room he mumbled, "Soon, very soon."

Davis found it hard to eat. He was not hungry and very weak from the intestinal infection. However, he knew intuitively that he needed energy for what he was about to attempt. He forced the food down. He rested for thirty minutes, gathered his wits, and put his plan in motion.

He raised his sleeve and gathered the soap that he had placed on his forearm. With a few drops of water, he began to work up a lather under the cuff. The right cuff was tighter than the left, so he concentrated on moving the left cuff. He struggled for twenty minutes but could not get the cuff past the wide part of his hand. He was growing more desperate. He studied his hand for a moment and finally realized that his only hope was to dislocate his thumb. The certainty that death was close made impossible actions distinct possibilities.

Davis listened carefully and tried to determine al-Kahat's location in the house. He placed the collar of his shirt in the corner of his mouth and bit down hard. He placed the outer edge of his left hand against the seat of the chair between his legs. He took several deep breaths and concentrated on not making a sound. With a single violent application of pressure with his right hand against the base of his thumb, he dislocated the digit.

He could not stifle a deep groan, but it was not loud enough to garner al-Kahat's attention. Davis looked down at his hand. The thumb was in a grotesque position, but the width of his hand was visibly narrower. He let the pain slowly subside before he tried to remove the cuff. He reapplied a layer of soap and slowly wound the cuff toward the tips of his fingers. The pain was intense, but he persisted, and the cuff finally slipped off. Davis looked up to try to once again assess al-Kahat's position. He could hear faint sounds of movement from somewhere on the other side of the kitchen. He looked at his hand and tried to assess if he could flex his fingers. The pain from his disjointed thumb made his left hand very nearly useless. He carefully wiped the thumb free of the soap to ensure traction. He forcefully grasped the digit and pulled it away from his hand until it popped back into place. Again, he groaned with the pain but was now able to flex it enough to make it usable. He rested for a while and mentally formulated his all-or-nothing plan.

Davis rotated the left handcuff so that he was able to grasp it with his right hand, not unlike a set of brass knuckles. He put his hands in his lap and gathered his strength. He called out to al-Kahat. He made his voice as plaintive as possible.

"Hey, man, I need to go to john. Please. Can you help me?"

Al-Kahat entered the room. His Glock was tucked in his waistband. He glanced momentarily at Davis, who had his head bent forward slightly. The terrorist thought that Davis looked properly submissive. Al-Kahat picked up the small table and moved it to the side. When he turned back, Davis coiled all his muscles for one massive release. He came to a standing position and grabbed al-Kahat's shirt with his injured hand while simultaneously loading everything he had into his right. He brought the handcuff down on the bridge of the terrorist's nose. Al-Kahat was stunned and tried to push away from Davis with one hand and attempted to draw the Glock with the other.

Davis hung onto al-Kahat tenaciously and quickly struck his face with three more blows in rapid succession. On the edge of unconsciousness, al-Kahat started to fall backward. Davis hung on and followed him down. He managed to raise the knee of the leg not handcuffed to the chair. When al-Kahat's back hit the floor, Davis' knee was planted just beneath his breastbone. Davis focused all his 212 pounds on the terrorist's midsection, knocking every bit of al-Kahat's breath out of his gaping mouth.

Davis aimed a powerful right at the terrorist's jaw just below the bottom of his left ear. Al-Kahat was just seconds away from blackness, but Davis did not pause in his attack. He rolled the man over on his belly and grabbed a handful of his hair and slowly pulled his hand backward. When al-Kahat tried to resist the motion, Davis suddenly reversed the motion, smashing the man's forehead into the floor.

Davis positioned his right knee in the center of al-Kahat's back and reached over his head and found his eye sockets with his middle and ring fingers. He pressed his fingers into the sockets like he was picking up a bowling ball. The fingers of his left hand found al-Kahat's chin. With all his remaining strength, Davis snapped the man's head back and to the left.

Al-Kahat's third and fourth cervical vertebrae ground together in a complete, comminuted fracture. When the neck broke, Davis was surprised at the sound. Al-Kahat went completely flaccid.

Davis gathered a few ragged breaths and rolled al-Kahat onto his back. His eyes were open, and his mouth hung agape. Davis looked closely into the terrorist's eyes and noted that his pupils were not yet dilated. He was still alive. On the outside chance that the paralyzed man could still hear him, Davis put his face close to al-Kahat's and addressed him in a controlled tone.

"Listen up, Ali Babba. I just want to let you know that you really picked the wrong guy to fuck." Davis patted al-Kahat's cheek softly.

"And I want you to know one other thing. Where you're going, asshole, there ain't no seventy virgins waiting for you. There are seventy more cowboys just like me. And don't forget, hell lasts an eternity."

With that, al-Kahat's pupils dilated to the maximum and his tongue began to turn blue-gray.

Davis rolled off al-Kahat and sat heavily on the floor just a few feet away. As his breathing and heart rate returned to normal, his eyes never left the inert form of al-Kahat. With his tormentor dead, Davis started to think of his next course of action.

He crawled back to the body and rifled through his pockets and found the key to the handcuffs. Once completely out of his shackles, he stood up only to find that his knees were shaky. He found al-Kahat's pistol and studied it in his hand. He found great comfort in being armed. He dropped the clip and noted that it was full of .40 caliber rounds. He partially opened the slide and verified that a round was in the chamber. He walked into the kitchen and got his first look at the rest of the small ranch house.

Davis glanced out the window of the main room and could see three other buildings. One was a large barn-like structure and two smaller outbuildings. Everything appeared deserted. In the corner of the main room was a gun cabinet with several weapons lined up at the ready.

He walked back into the kitchen. He opened the door of the rusty refrigerator and found bottled water and bottles of some sort of green-colored drink. The label was in Spanish, but it was clearly the Mexican equivalent of Gatorade. He helped himself to a bottle and took a long drink.

He sat down at the kitchen table and gathered his thoughts. On the table was the camera that they used to photograph their captives. As he sipped his drink his eyes went to the doorway to the bedroom where he was held captive. Al-Kahat's body lay motionless on the floor. Davis could not believe that he had just killed a man and was now sipping a sports drink. Molly had always said that he was a lover, not a fighter. Davis grimly thought that being raped certainly had a way of turning that around.

His mind reviewed his current situation. He was somewhere in Mexico. The terrorists were in league with the Army, the cartels, and probably others. It made for a very short list of people in the area that he could turn to for help. He was in the deepest dilemma of his life. He thought briefly of waiting in ambush for the other terrorists to return and ridding the world of them as well. But then what? He would have the blood of three dead terrorists on his hands, but would then have to face whatever authority, probably corrupt, that would show up. And what if the terrorists showed up in the company of De La Garza and a truckload of infantry types? That would be a suicidal ambush.

It did not take Davis long to conclude that his mother was right when she preached that God helps those who can help themselves. If he was ever going to see American soil again, he would have to do it on his own.

CHAPTER THIRTEEN

Getting the Hell Out of Dodge

Once his decision was made, Davis began to worry that he needed to be as far away as possible, as soon as possible. He began a systematic search of the cabin for equipment and supplies. His first thought was weapons and ammunition. He went to the gun cabinet and took inventory. His attention was drawn to two rifles. One was a Chinese-made AK-47 assault rifle. The other was a custom hunting rifle. He removed the custom rifle from the rack and studied the engraving on the barrel. It was made by a gunsmith in Boulder, Colorado and was chambered in 7mm magnum. The barrel was carbon graphite and was designed for very long-distance precision shooting. Mated to the rifle was a 5-by-20 variable power telescopic sight by Huskemaw Optics. As a lifelong hunter, Davis knew a great rifle when he saw one. He just could not believe that anyone would leave such a prized weapon in a dusty old hunting shack. He decided that these weapons would serve well for both close-in and long-distance fighting. He prayed that he could find ammunition. In a closet near the gun cabinet, he hit the mother lode.

The closet was full of not only plenty of ammunition but all sorts of hunting and camping gear. He began carrying weapons and ammo to the kitchen table. He found a well-used Eberlestock backpack with a built-in rifle scabbard for the long rifle. He found a belt and holster for the Glock that he had taken off al-Kahat.

Davis began to think in terms of a long survival hike. As a Boy Scout, and later as a Scout Master for the troop that his sons were members, there were many such preps. He scavenged the closet and brought items to the kitchen table for arranging and stowing in the pack.

Within an hour, Davis had assembled a wide array of equipment that would allow for an extended hike in unknown territory. He packed heavily with rifle and pistol ammunition. He found and loaded four long, curved thirty-round magazines for the AK-47. He also found three six-round box magazines for the 7mm magnum. Additional boxes of rifle and pistol ammo were placed in the bottom of the pack. He also found three one-liter plastic water bottles, a large, heavy-gage plastic tarp that could be used as a ground cloth and to catch rainwater, a Browning hunting knife, an insulated sleeping bag, a pair of 10-power Nikon compact binoculars, a rain poncho, and a camouflaged hat. He almost passed up a six-foot by ten-foot piece of camouflaged netting, but after a moment of consideration, he added it to the equipment. Similarly, he thought about the camera and added it as well.

In the kitchen cabinets, he found more of the freeze-dried camping rations and packages of dried fruit and nuts. The fruit and nuts were two years beyond their expiration date, but he took them anyway. He found a small frying pan in which he could heat food and water. He found ancient silverware and took one spoon and one fork. In another drawer, he found two Bic lighters. Under the sink, he found a half-full quart bottle of Purex bleach that would kill any Giardia protozoa in any water he might find. He searched the bathroom medicine cabinet and found aspirin, a tube of antibiotic ointment, and a prescription bottle of tablets. In Spanish, the label advised to take two tabs twice daily for diarrhea. Davis had no idea what Metronidazole was, but he took two tabs and pocketed the rest. He said a short prayer that it would kill the "tourista."

He found and packed a change of clothes and a hooded parka. When he awoke after the kidnapping, he was barefooted. His Red Wing boots were somewhere between San Antonio and Mexico.

He first tried al-Kahat's Nikes, but they were hopelessly too small. With a rising panic, he tore the cabin apart looking for any kind of shoe that would fit. He knew that having no shoes was the same as a death sentence. In the very back of the equipment closet he found a very well-seasoned pair of hunting boots of an unknown brand that were only one or two sizes too large.

Davis neatly stowed everything in the pack and tested its weight. He guessed the pack weighed fifty pounds. A new sense of urgency struck him in the pit of his stomach. He had a suffocating premonition that the others would return soon.

He took a last look at al-Kahat. He felt no remorse for having killed him. He remembered how the terrorist had spat upon Epstein's body for having the audacity to die from a heart attack. Davis was not motivated to spit on al-Kahat, but he had a strong urge to send a message to his terrorist colleagues. Davis went to look for paper and a pencil.

Five minutes later, Davis shouldered the pack and walked out of the house. The February Mexican air was quite sweet and cool, buoying Davis' spirits. He stood in front of the house for a few minutes thinking of where he should go. He did not know where in Mexico he was, but the one sure constant was that the US border was somewhere to the north. With the setting sun on his left shoulder, Davis started the hike of his life.

CHAPTER FOURTEEN
The Infidel's Revenge

That first night Davis maintained a steady pace but did not rush. The night was clear with a half-moon that provided more than enough light to allow for relatively unimpeded travel. He headed north into mountainous terrain. He once again thought that the Mexican geography was very similar to that of his Trans Pecos hunting lease in West Texas. He hoped that it meant that he was not too far south of the border. From his high vantage point, he never saw the lights of a town or village. He hoped that was a good omen.

As he hiked, he had plenty of time to recall everything he knew about northern Mexico. He remembered that west of Monterrey the country was mostly mountainous and high desert. He knew that the westernmost reach of the Rio Grande was just west of El Paso. Having made many float trips down the Rio Grande over the years with the Boy Scouts, Davis felt sure that he would recognize it when he saw it. That would be his goal. He would find the Rio Grande, cross it, and surrender to the first border patrolman he found. If he could stay out of sight and keep moving north, he might just pull it off.

He stopped and rested occasionally and ate one package of dried fruit and nuts during the night. With the weather cool but not cold, he needed to drink only sparingly. At sunup, he was tired and hungry. He stopped and gathered a small amount of wood for a fire to heat water for a beef stew breakfast. Being free and in the wide-open spaces and not in immediate danger made him feel reasonably well. The stew tasted good. He continued to take the Mexican diarrhea pills, and his dysentery was quickly coming under control.

He found a secluded spot in the brush at the bottom of a ravine and prepared his sleeping bag. He knew that lack of sleep could kill you as readily as dehydration and starvation. He wanted to be as sharp as possible mentally if trouble showed up. He was glad that he brought the piece of camouflage netting. He wove grass and brush into the netting and suspended it above his sleeping bag. From the air, it would be very difficult to spot him.

At noon, the day after Davis' escape, Ramadi and his nephew returned to the ranch house with a new briefcase full of money for General De La Garza. When they pulled up to the house, the younger Ramadi noticed that the door was standing open. Without a word, they both drew their sidearms and carefully exited the vehicle. They entered through the kitchen door. Ramadi immediately noted that drawers and cabinet doors were standing open. He signaled to his nephew to go left as he went right toward the bedroom.

Ramadi approached the edge of the bedroom doorframe. A pair of legs were stretched out on the floor. He came around the doorway with his Glock at the ready and stopped cold at the sight. A body was propped in a sitting position with feet toward the center of the room. The head was twisted 180 degrees and was facing the wall. A note was attached to the chest that read, "You've picked the wrong cowboy from San Antone to fuck with!"

Ramadi left the ranch house and stood in the yard and activated his satellite phone. He notified his ISIS superiors in remote Pakistan of his newest complication. He requested more funds because he was certain that the general would demand much more for the kind of help they would need to reacquire Davis. The funds were approved, and Ramadi was warned about the consequences of continued failure. The ISIS brass indicated that they did not care if Davis' death had any propaganda value so long as he was killed before he could reach the border and tell his story.

He made the call to De La Garza. The general was highly amused at the new turn of events. With the promise of more money, he was happy to assist in the search for the upstart American. Ramadi keyed off his phone and looked at his watch. The general promised help by 2:00 p.m.

Davis was awake at mid-morning, feeling rested. He was always good to go with three or four hours of sleep. He repacked his gear and prepared to move out. He was worried about being spotted as he hiked in daylight. He cut a slit in the center of the camo netting and placed it over his head, turning it into a makeshift ghillie suit. If he saw or heard anything that put him on guard, he could push into the brush and become almost invisible so long as he did not move. Davis traveled without problems and stopped in the early afternoon for another snack. While he ate, a light aircraft flew over at an altitude too high to be in search mode. Though he had little to fear, the sight of the aircraft was unsettling.

Shortly after 3:00 p.m., Ramadi heard the distinct sound of a helicopter approaching the valley from the south. Moments later the UH1 Huey landed near the ranch house. It was manned by a pilot, co-pilot, and crew chief/gunner. The crew chief jumped out of the aircraft and approached Ramadi.

"Do you know how long the head start?"

"No. We picked up some footprints heading that way, but lost track in the rocks," replied Ramadi.

The man looked north in the direction indicated by the terrorist.

"That is the way I would go if I were the American. Mount up."

Ramadi and his nephew joined the crew chief in the open bay of the Huey. They buckled in the jump seats as the pilot pulled pitch and lifted off. They hugged the mountaintops and flew a three-mile-wide east-west search grid that progressed northward. The crew chief sat behind an M-134 minigun that was mounted in a multi-directional pivoting gun mount. The gun was fed by a motorized belt feeder that was attached to a 5,000-round magazine box. The side of the box was stenciled "1:4 tracer," indicating that every fifth round was tipped with a tracer bullet.

The sun was starting to get low to the west when Davis first heard the rotor beat of the helicopter. He was just crossing the high point of a mountain when his attention turned south. He froze so as not to attract attention by being in motion. He carefully retrieved the binoculars from a side pocket of the pack and focused on the helicopter in the distance. When he recognized the Mexican Army insignia on the tail boom his heart sank. He watched as the Huey flew briskly back and forth on the search grid. He tried to estimate how long it would be before they would reach his position. He hoped that they would break off and head in another direction, but they continued on a bearing that would put them right over his position in a few minutes.

At that moment, the helicopter came to a hover and the gunner fired a burst of tracer fire into a valley in the distance. The minigun's rate of fire was so high that tracer rounds produced a solid beam of red light probing the valley. The phrase "reconnaissance by fire" popped into Davis' head. He had seen films of soldiers who had been raked by minigun fire. He removed the long rifle from the scabbard and focused on the helicopter. He dialed up the 20-power objective and focused on the open bay of the Huey. Even at the great distance, Davis could see Ramadi and his nephew in the open bay of the helicopter.

The small feeling of elation he felt earlier in the day evaporated into despair. Davis looked around. He thought that he would never guess that he would die in such a place. He thought for only a moment of the long litany of goodbyes to his friends and loved ones. He thought one last time of Molly. She was a fanatic about justice. She was a force to be reckoned with anytime she saw injustice. At that moment Davis decided. He would go down fighting. He would fight like Molly righting an injustice.

Tina then crowded her way into his thoughts. His mind conjured up the memory of the dream of Tina and Molly sitting together, naked, at the foot of the bed, brushing their hair. The soul-crushing guilt he felt about his affair felt like a knife thrust into the liver.

He clearly remembered that it was he who cast the first flirtation her way. He also clearly remembered how she volleyed...sly smile... slightly arched eyebrows...no words. Damn! It was the no words! She was so young, but so perfectly effective. She dissected Davis like a master swordswoman. And now, she will do it to Molly. And the penalty for Davis' mortal sins was death on a Mexican hill and being helpless to prevent it.

He slipped out of his pack, laid the long rifle down, and picked up the AK-47. He camouflaged himself as effectively as he could and checked the long, curved thirty-round magazine. All that was left was to wait for the right moment.

Ramadi was growing more anxious by the minute. The sun was sinking rapidly and would set in less than an hour. He feared that Davis would elude them in the darkness. He continued to scour the landscape out the port side door while his nephew scanned from the starboard.

The helicopter completed the eastbound leg of the search pattern and was slowly traveling up the spine of the hilltop. The aircraft was on a head-on course with Davis' hiding place. Davis watched through the brush as the windscreen of the Huey grew closer. He could now make out the shapes of the heads and shoulders of the pilot and co-pilot above the instrument panel. Davis estimated 100, then seventy-five, then fifty yards and closing. He flicked the selector switch from safe to fully automatic.

At twenty-five yards, Davis rose calmly out of the brush, shouldered the assault rifle, drew a bead on the center of the pilot's outline, and squeezed off a long burst of fire. The full metal jacketed rounds stitched a line of holes through the windscreen and then into the pilot's face. In a death spasm, the pilot's hands pulled back on the cyclic and collective controls. His left boot fully depressed the left rudder pedal while his right boot spasmed off the right. The nose of the Huey was pulled radically skyward. At the same time, the helicopter rolled dramatically to the port side. Because of the aberrant maneuver and the low initial altitude of the aircraft, the rotor blades bit into the side of the mountain and exploded into a shower of jagged fragments. Centrifugal force did the rest. The Huey slammed into the ground and began to roll down the mountainside. It came to rest upside down about halfway down the slope. Fuel began to leak from ruptured fuel tanks.

Davis stared in stunned paralysis as the Huey rolled down the hill. When it came to a rest he moved in the direction of the doomed chopper. With the AK at the ready, he studied the crash site. He could see the co-pilot struggling to free himself from his safety harness. There was also motion in the open cargo bay. At that moment the scent of the spilled aviation fuel reached Davis. Without hesitation, he sent another burst of automatic fire into the ruptured tank. With a loud "whomp," the fuel ignited.

Davis kept his distance but watched to see if anyone escaped the wreckage. He thought that he heard the muffled cries of one or more of the crew, but the sounds were soon overwhelmed by the explosions of the machine gun ammo cooking off in the heat of the fire. Davis stood there paralyzed until the wind brought the distinct smell of burning flesh to his nose.

He quickly returned to his hiding place and gathered his gear and left the scene. He moved out once again to the north. He never looked back.

CHAPTER FIFTEEN
The Platoon

The sun went down, and the sky transitioned to a star-filled winter night. Once Davis left the scene he never stopped moving. He ate and drank only while on the move.

His mind was in constant motion, trying to be alert for the arrival of other threats. He played the surrealistic images of the shootdown of the chopper over and over in his mind. He could not believe that one burst of machine gun fire neutralized the gunship and the other two terrorists.

He felt sick to his stomach with fear. He realized that he had just upped the ante in a terrible game that he had no desire to play. ISIS had lost three of its soldiers with untold numbers of replacements ready to take their place in the mission to hunt him down. And now he had offered an irrevocable challenge to the corrupt Mexican authorities. Davis' sick stomach told him that they would now come after him in force.

After De La Garza's air traffic controllers lost contact with the Huey on the "special surveillance mission," they notified the general. He angrily sent a second chopper to the location where contact was lost. The second chopper had no problem finding the smoldering remains. They reported details of the crash site to the general and added that there were no apparent survivors. Because it was already dark, De La Garza ordered his crash investigators to be at the site at first light.

The next morning, the general watched over the investigators from atop the crest of the mountain. As troops collected shards of shattered rotor blades, De La Garza was able to discover the gouge marks and could visually trace how the aircraft had rolled down the slope. As he strolled about the hilltop, his eyes were drawn to a metallic glint on the ground. He approached and found fifteen spent 7.52mm brass casings scattered in a small area. He picked up a casing and sniffed the open end. It was freshly fired. At that moment his investigators called via radio to report on the presence of bullet holes in the instrument panel and part of the airframe. De La Garza shook his head and spat on the ground and said, "Pendejo Americano!" As he boarded his personal helicopter, he began issuing orders to one of his captains. It was time to get serious about this troublesome foreigner.

Davis did not stop until mid-morning on the second day after the shootdown. He was totally exhausted and knew that he needed rest and a reasonable amount of food. He chanced the heating of water to prepare a meal. Immediately after the water was hot, he stamped out the small fire for fear of the smoke attracting attention from the air. He once again found a secluded, brushy spot, set up his camouflage net, and retired to his sleeping bag. Davis was indeed exhausted, and he slept all day.

While Davis was sleeping, De La Garza had assembled a platoon of his Special Forces troops at the crash site to begin the pursuit of Davis. The soldiers were special not in the sense that they were highly trained elite troops, but rather because they were like the general, on the payroll of the cartel. They were thugs and killers, but not very good soldiers. The platoon was led by a first lieutenant who was also a first cousin of the general's wife.

De La Garza had contacted ISIS and reported the continuing debacle. He demanded reimbursement for the lost Huey and a very large bonus to put the problem to bed. ISIS realized that if Davis was somehow actually successful, their operation would be blown, and any positive propaganda gains would be lost. The terrorist organization leaders gave the general carte blanche. They just wanted Davis to cease to exist, whatever the cost.

Another helicopter arrived at the crash site and delivered a man in civilian clothes and a pair of bloodhounds. The handler and dogs were taken to the spot where Davis had fired on the Huey. The dogs immediately keyed in on the scent and went to the spot where Davis had lain in the brush. His scent was much more concentrated there. The dog's olfactory lobes were now locked and loaded. There was nowhere that Davis could hide.

The special platoon was to travel fast and light. Their goal was to kill Davis' head start as quickly as possible. The platoon had one radioman with GPS capabilities. They would be re-supplied by air whenever necessary. They loaded light packs and left the crash site at 4:00 p.m. and planned to travel all night with the bloodhounds leading the way.

Davis awoke with a start. It was completely dark. He froze in his sleeping bag and listened intently. He was rewarded with only the sound of the wind moving the brush. He felt well-rested and hungry. He did not chance a fire and ate only dried fruit and nuts. He finished his first container of water.

It was overcast and it made the night particularly dark. He was forced to travel more slowly than he liked. He was content, however, because he felt that he could move with impunity in the darkness. It was the coldest night that he had experienced thus far. The physical exertion of the hike kept him warm enough. He thought briefly about his good fortune that his ordeal did not occur in the summer. Summer in Mexico was rattlesnake time. Davis hated snakes.

The next day was more of the same. As he hiked, a thought kept resurfacing in his mind. How did they know where to search? He could have struck out from the ranch in any direction. Davis had been careful to stick to very rocky ground as he left the terrorist hideout to avoid leaving footprints. He asked himself, "So how did they know what direction to go?" The answer was so obvious it was painful. It made Davis stop in his tracks. What direction would a dimwitted American go? North! They were just following the obvious.

When he reached the crest of the next hill, Davis stopped and studied the landscape for 360 degrees around his position. He could still see no signs of civilization. He sat down for a little water and a lot of thought.

It was now clear that he needed to change the direction of his travel at irregular intervals to make it harder for them to track him. He wished desperately for a map, but that was a waste of effort. The only constant was that the US border was somewhere to the north. He thought of his problem in the most fundamental of geographic terms. The US border with Mexico was comprised of the southern borders of California, Arizona, New Mexico, and Texas. To the east was the Gulf of Mexico, and to the west, the Gulf of California. From El Paso eastward, the Texas border dipped farther and farther south. Because of the mountainous terrain, he knew that he was at least in the central or western part of Mexico. If he went west, he would remain in the mountains. If he went east, he would eventually walk out of the Sierra Madre Occidental as it transitioned into the Gulf Coast plain.

Davis picked up a stick and drew a primitive map of the US southern border. He arbitrarily put an X in north-central Mexico since the geography looked too arid to be consistent with the wetter, more temperate highlands of central Mexico. It did not take a National Geographic explorer to see that the deep southward bend of Texas would be the shortest way home. It all seemed so simple now. He worried for a moment that it was so obvious that the Mexicans would think of it as well. Maybe having started off due north would actually play in his favor. If they continued to look due north, he could put some serious distance between himself and his pursuers if he headed east for a day or two and then proceed on alternating day-long treks of either due north or northeast. In that manner, he would be closing on the Rio Grande at the best possible pace.

Davis stood and adjusted his pack. With a final look at his rudimentary map, he used the toe of his boot to erase any sign that he had made a strategic decision. He turned and headed due east for a day.

It had been twelve days since the kidnapping, but Davis had no idea of the exact date. Sedations, stress, illness, rape, and fighting for your life tend to make a lot of bad days run together. To Davis, it seemed like months since he had seen Molly and the boys and felt the comforts of home.

At midday, Davis was near the crest of a particularly tall hill, taking a break and warming some rations, when he heard the distinct beat of helicopter rotors. He immediately stamped out the remains of the little fire and scattered the ashes. He found a clump of brush that offered some cover. He retrieved the Nikon binoculars and scanned the distant hilltops to the west and finally picked out the image of the Huey as it flared for a landing about two miles away.

Davis studied the helicopter to see how many men would exit. To his surprise, no one exited the craft, but a line of men approached the aircraft from lower on the hill. Not satisfied with the low magnification of the binoculars, he switched to the 20-power scope on the custom rifle. The view threatened to make his meal come up.

The men who were already on the ground met the helicopter and began to unload some sort of cargo. They were all wearing similar military-style utility uniforms in a desert camouflage pattern. All of them carried assault rifles slung over their shoulders. As soon as the cargo was unloaded the helicopter took off and headed southwest.

Through the powerful scope, Davis watched as the soldiers broke down the cargo and began distributing supplies of food and water. More soldiers joined the first group until Davis could see more than a dozen men milling around and gathering supplies.

With rising panic, Davis wondered how they knew to follow his track to the east rather than continue their previous northerly pursuit. At that moment, a man not wearing a military uniform with two large dogs on long leads came into view. After a moment of study, Davis recognized them as bloodhounds. Things had just gone from bad to much, much worse.

Davis watched the men for a few minutes and then scanned all the other hills in the distance to see if he could pick up any other search parties. With nothing obvious in view, he quickly packed up, donned his makeshift ghillie suit, slipped over the crest of the hill, and headed northwest. He moved as fast as he could on the downhill sides of the mountain slopes where his movement would be blocked from view. He moved more stealthily on the uphill slopes where he could possibly be picked up by an observant soldier. Each time he crested a hill, Davis took some time to see if he could catch a view of his pursuers on an exposed hillside. By the time night fell, he had not seen the search party again. Davis never stopped moving. He knew with sickening certainty that they would move behind the dogs all night with only small rest breaks.

The night was overcast, and the visibility was poor. Davis stumbled several times during the night. Each time he cursed because he had no choice but to slow his pace. He just hoped that he could maintain the two-mile separation. Unknown to Davis, his pursuers were all equipped with night-vision goggles and were able to close the distance during the night.

At mid-morning Davis caught a glimpse of the column of soldiers. Only three ridgelines separated them. Despite ever-increasing fatigue, he picked up the pace of his escape. He ate and drank only sparingly and always while on the run. As he crested ridgelines, he now plotted the fastest track to the next ridge, not sticking to a persistently northeasterly heading. Distance to the Rio Grande took second place to distance between himself and the enemy.

At 4:30 p.m. the next day, Davis knew that he was spent. Despair was growing by the hour. He knew that he could not physically keep it up much longer. Once again, the certainty of death loomed in Davis' gut.

As the sun was setting on his back, he crested a ridge and began to look for the best route across the next valley. The sight stopped him cold. The downslope of the ridge he was on was not steep and very wide open. Brush and cactus were relatively sparse and there were few boulders. The far slope was diametrically opposite. At the bottom of the ravine was a sheer drop-off, roughly fifteen feet deep. Across the ravine, the slope rose acutely, forming a very steep hillside. The hillside itself was a tortuous pile of broken boulders and clumps of dense brush.

Davis sat down and studied the opposite side of the valley while he caught his breath. He did not know if he had enough energy left to make the arduous climb. The feeling that a desolate, unnamed little valley somewhere in Mexico would soon be the place of his death returned. He started calculating how many of his tormentors he could take with him. He squinted at the far side of the valley. It suddenly struck him that if he could get up the opposite slope and find an adequate hiding place, he would have a significant tactical advantage. The enemy would be spread out on a relatively bald slope with no cover, and he would have the advantage of the high ground if any of the soldiers tried to assault his position.

For a moment he wondered if he could cheat death a third time. He thought that the odds would be astronomically slim, but for the sake of his family, he would keep trying.

Davis looked back in the direction of the platoon of soldiers. He could not see them, but he knew that they were coming. He stood and thought about the bloodhounds. Maybe he could use their talents to his advantage. Davis unzipped his pants and urinated on the ground. He then walked in the puddle, saturating his scent on his boots. He gathered his equipment and marched on a straight line down the slope through an area with little or no cover. At the bottom of the slope near the edge of the sheer drop-off, he urinated again.

Davis struggled up the steep hillside in the gathering darkness. He was approximately three-fourths of the way up when he found a good spot for a hide. On a narrow, flat saddle, two large boulders were separated by a space of perhaps eighteen inches. On the downhill side of the boulders, dense brush grew in perfusion. Davis dropped his gear and began clearing a shooting lane through the brush. Just before last light, he placed the barrel of the 7mm magnum rifle on his backpack. He lay behind the rifle and sighted in on the opposite slope and panned the barrel left and right. Satisfied with his field of fire, Davis placed the camouflaged netting so that both he and the rifle were hidden from view. He unrolled his sleeping bag and moved small rocks so that he would be as comfortable as possible. He ate a small leftover portion of one of the dehydrated meals and ate the last two bags of dried fruit and nuts. He did not worry much about running out of food and water because he thought there was a better than even chance that he would be dead by the next day anyway.

As the sun rose behind him, Davis marveled that the Mexican troops had not shown up during the night. The sky was clear, and the air was very crisp and cool. There was no wind. He thought of many mornings identical to this one that he had spent waiting for four-legged quarry. He was suddenly aware how similar the feelings of anticipation and tension really were. What he felt while waiting for four-legged quarry was anticipation. Two-legged quarry gave rise to a similar but much more intense feeling of tension. He watched as the shadow line slowly worked its way down the opposite slope as the rising sun cleared the crest behind him.

Davis heard something in the still morning air. He strained his ears and could make out the unmistakable baying of the bloodhounds. Though he could not yet see them, the platoon had just cleared the second ridgeline to the west. He estimated that they would be topping the ridge to his immediate front in less than twenty minutes.

Davis picked up the first of the three six-round box magazines and locked it into the receiver of the rifle and chambered the first round. He placed the other two magazines within easy reach to his right. He placed the AK-47 and spare magazines to his left. He opened his third water bottle and took a long drink. With nothing left to do to prepare for battle, Davis took a deep breath of the sweet morning air and waited.

The volume of the baying of the hounds suddenly increased as they topped the far hillside. Davis' heart rate accelerated. He pressed the stock of the rifle into his shoulder and looked through the scope. The image of the dogs appeared huge at 20-power. He dialed the variable scope back to 12-power and widened his field of view. The dog handler came into view behind the dogs and then the soldiers in a single file. He studied the dog handler. He carried no weapon. He wore a harness-like device to which the lunge lines to the dogs were attached with large D rings. When the dogs found the spot where Davis urinated their baying intensified noticeably. They placed their noses on the damp ground and paused for a long moment, absorbing every molecule of the man's scent. With a sharp tug on the lunge lines, the dogs headed downhill directly on Davis' trail.

For the first time, Davis had the opportunity to observe the soldiers up close. As each man topped the ridge, Davis counted them and assessed what kind of weapons they carried. Davis could see at least two kinds of assault rifles. The seventh man in the column wore a smaller backpack and carried a very compact submachine gun. He also wore sergeant's stripes on his sleeves. To Davis' surprise, no one wore a combat helmet. Instead, they wore soft baseball-type caps.

When the twelfth and thirteenth men came over the hill Davis began to panic. He thought that he had seen perhaps a dozen men the first day as they unloaded supplies from the helicopter. Now, the column seemed to never end.

When the seventeenth man topped the hill, he was wearing a backpack-style field radio with a long flexible antenna. Following the radioman was the eighteenth and final man in the column. Like the platoon sergeant, the last man carried the compact weapon. Davis was sure that he was the platoon leader.

Eighteen men. Davis thought about the three magazines for the 7mm magnum. He slowly shook his head. He had better make it good. He was pretty sure that after he emptied the third magazine there would be no time to reload them. That meant changing to the AK-47 for more close-in fighting. Davis thought, *If these guys are any good, I will probably never get to the AK.*

As the column worked its way downhill, Davis realized that he really did not have a definitive plan. He began to perspire even though it was quite cool. As the dog handler reached the bottom of the slope, the dogs stopped to examine the spot where Davis had urinated the second time. Davis scanned the length of the column. The dog handler was perhaps 200 meters downhill from Davis' hide. The platoon commander was closer to 300 meters and on an approximate level with Davis. He suddenly realized that he had never fired the long-range rifle. If the scope was not zeroed in at the customary 200 meters, then the next few minutes were going to get very ugly.

From nowhere the words "the road to Basra" flashed in Davis' mind. A plan materialized and he flicked off the rifle's safety. He prayed that the rifle was sighted in properly. The reticule of the Huskemaw scope had crosshairs with sets of horizontal and vertical mil dots. If the rifle was properly sighted in at 200 meters, the mil dots would allow for accurate holdover for greater or lesser distances.

Davis centered the crosshairs on the center of the dog handler's chest and squeezed off the first round. The 165-grain Nosler Partition bullet ripped through the handler's heart and spinal cord, knocking him flat and instantly dead.

Davis cycled the rifle's action and moved to the top of the column of men. At the first shot, every man in the column ducked and went to a knee, and brought their weapons to bear on the eastern hillside. Two natural phenomena came into play in Davis' favor. First, the sound of the cross-canyon shot started an echo that reverberated in both directions up and down the valley, making it very difficult for the soldiers to locate the source of fire. Secondly, the sun had risen into the eyes of the platoon on the east-facing slope, making it even more difficult to locate Davis' position.

Before the echoes of the first shot dissipated, Davis located the platoon leader in the scope. He was holding out his hand, trying to accept the radio handpiece from the radioman. Davis placed the first mil dot on the man's face and squeezed off the second round. The second Nosler caused the lieutenant's head to explode in a red mist. Davis cycled the bolt and shot the radioman through the chest and radio. Davis' mind registered a large electrical spark as the bullet also killed the platoon's radio.

Though no one put a stopwatch on it, the first three shots were accomplished in six seconds. In those six seconds, Davis' three shots had accomplished in his small personal battle exactly what the Air Force fighter bombers accomplished on the road to Basra in the first Gulf War. The head and tail of the enemy column had been killed and communication with the outside world was cut off. He had accomplished the primary tenet of warfare. If you kill your enemy's forward observer, command, control, and communications and fix them in a poor defensive position, then the battlefield is yours for the taking. All that remained for Davis was to kill the rest of the column before they could get organized.

After the third shot, the platoon sergeant who was now in command gathered his wits and sprayed a fully automatic burst at the eastern slope. None of his bullets came even remotely close to Davis. The sergeant screamed at his troops to lay down suppressive fire. His burst of fire and screamed orders got Davis' attention. As the sergeant was replacing a spent magazine, Davis placed the crosshairs on the man's head and squeezed. Again, a red mist filled the morning air.

As the panicked troops crawled for whatever cover they could find, they started to return fire in earnest, but their fire was ineffective.

The men closest to the downed dog handler tried to edge back up the slope. Davis refocused his attention to the top of the column of men. He started with the troop closest to the dead radioman and put a round in his neck. After his sixth shot, he pulled the trigger on an empty chamber. The misfire startled Davis for a moment, but he quickly recovered and changed to his second magazine.

Davis systematically fired on each troop, one after the other down the slope. Soon, the outgoing fire from the platoon diminished and then stopped altogether. Six minutes after the opening shot, the only sound coming from the valley was the sound of the baying bloodhounds. After pulling the body downhill for a short distance, the dogs simply sat down and continued to bark at the chaos.

Davis finally raised his head from the rifle stock and stared at the killing ground. He could not believe the sight of the bodies sprawled across the hillside. Had he killed them all? Had he just killed eighteen men? Davis found himself short of breath. He lowered his head and took several deep breaths. His eyes focused on the spent brass lying on the ground next to him. He slowly gathered them up and lined them up in a row. Each casing represented a dead man. Almost as an afterthought, he counted the casings. Sixteen. Not eighteen, but sixteen.

Davis remounted the rifle and focused the scope on the dead lieutenant at the top of the column. The exploded head was clearly visible in the scope. The radioman was also clearly dead. He slowly scanned downhill, stopping at each man and making sure that each body was bloody and not breathing. He stopped at the twelfth man. He could not see any blood. He dialed the scope up to 20-power. He stared at the man's chest and could finally see the rhythmic rise and fall of his breathing. The man's head was turned away from Davis, but he could tell that his jaws were slowly moving as if he were talking to someone nearby. Davis scanned the bodies near the man. One was obviously dead from a massive wound in the neck. The second man was facing downhill with his eyes open. While Davis watched, he blinked several times and then mouthed some words to his fellow faker.

Davis placed the intersection of the crosshairs over the man's right eye and squeezed the trigger. With the shot, the last man jumped to his feet, abandoning his weapon, and started running uphill. As Davis recycled the bolt, he wondered why the man chose to run uphill. He would have obviously had a better chance running downhill or across the face of the slope. Running uphill was his final mistake. Davis put the crosshairs on the back of his head and dropped the round right between his shoulders.

Davis checked the rest of the men in the doomed platoon and verified them all uniformly dead. He lay motionless in his sniper's hide for a long time in a sort of physical and mental paralysis brought on by killing so many men. Only his eyes were able to move, repeatedly scanning the far hillside and visualizing that the dead men would soon resurrect and become a platoon of unkillable wraiths that would march across the valley, tearing him to bits. The mental image made him scream and cover his eyes.

"I can't do this anymore! Leave me alone! Let me go home! I just want to walk home and not hurt anyone else!"

The bloodhounds continued to prevent the quiet from returning to the valley. The sound of their baying caused tears to roll down his cheeks.

"I'm sorry I had to kill your handler. He was probably your friend and raised you since you were puppies. I know that you were doing what you were born to do. You probably thought this was just a great adventure. You are just too good at what you do...and I have such a long way to go." Davis reloaded one of the box magazines and locked it into the rifle's action. He shot both dogs and then he wept for a long time.

Davis packed up and headed northeast. He felt like he was in slow motion. He knew that he needed to put some real distance between himself and the carnage in the little unnamed valley, but it was as if the dead were tied to him, trying to prevent his escape. As he hiked, one overriding thought reverberated in his mind. Someone would certainly find the dead platoon, and whoever had sent them on their mission would be very angry. Davis knew without a doubt that you can't kill that many people without setting off an even greater effort to find and kill the man responsible.

CHAPTER SIXTEEN

Fox News Alert

7:30 a.m. ET

We have a Fox News Alert. It has just been verified by Fox 43 in Topeka, Kansas that shortly after 1:00 a.m. Central this morning, Kansas Lieutenant Governor David Whittier was kidnapped from his home. The method of the kidnapping makes it appear to be the work of ISIS terrorists. The lieutenant governor's wife was witness to the kidnapping and was handcuffed but otherwise unharmed. She was found at 6:30 a.m. local time by a maid. Mrs. Whittier reported that the kidnappers shouted "Allah Akbar!" as they left with the lieutenant governor. Members of the Topeka office of the FBI are on scene and collecting evidence at this time.

San Antonio FBI Field Office, 9:15 a.m. Central

Collier entered the Counterterrorism Department conference room with a stack of the latest dispatches from Washington and Topeka. The brief was intended to keep his counter-terror troops up to speed on what Washington was thinking.

"The tea leaf readers at the BAU feel certain that something new is up. Well, duh! There has been too much time since the Epstein-Davis kidnapping with no gory internet show. Big difference...*too* big. Therefore, we should be alert for changes in the ISIS modus in our area."

Dayton raised a pencil in the air, which Collier acknowledged. "Any ideas or intel on what we should be looking for?"

"The lieutenant governor is not wealthy, not powerful, not well known. I mean, before today, how many of you could actually name the guy? He's a nothing burger for God's sake! Why would ISIS even bother? Is he going to just disappear like Epstein and Davis? Then why all the Allah Akbar shit? Something is up. They have either intentionally changed their modus, which means they are vicious and smart, or maybe they have been forced to change their modus."

"Which means?" asked Agent Wheaton.

After a moment of contemplation, Collier replied, "It may mean that they aren't as vicious and smart as they think they are, or somebody may have got their number."

CHAPTER SEVENTEEN
Avoiding Civilization

When the dead platoon missed the second scheduled radio check at 4:00 p.m., the general sent the scout helicopter on a search. When one of his captains commented that they were probably in some kind of trouble, De La Garza exploded and said that it better be a bad radio.

Davis' luck was holding up and darkness fell before the search helicopter could find the right valley. At first light, the search resumed. At 10:45 a.m. the search pilot reported the carnage. De La Garza was dumbstruck. He could understand the escape, he could even understand the American getting lucky and shooting down the helicopter, but the loss of nearly two dozen of his best killers was impossible. He ordered up his own helicopter and went to the scene.

The scene was even worse than he'd imagined. Because the head of his wife's cousin was nearly gone, it took a while for De La Garza to determine which body was his. One of his captains commented that the American must be shooting hunting ammunition rather than steel-jacketed-type military rounds.

From the top of the ridge, the general could look downhill and see the trail of bodies ending with the dead bloodhounds. It was clear that the American had ambushed them while in column. De La Garza looked across the valley and could see why the American chose his ambush spot. He turned to his captain and pointed across the valley and said, "Get some men up the far slope on this line and find his ambush spot."

Once across the valley, it took only five minutes for the troops to signal that they had found the location of Davis' hide.

The general crossed the valley. He counted the twenty spent cartridges. The twenty cartridges represented eighteen men and two dogs. All dead. He thought that whoever this man from Texas was, he never missed. This man would take special handling. The name "El Serpiente" flashed in his mind. If anyone could defeat the Texan, it was the serpent.

The general looked at the sky. Dark clouds were gathering in the northwest. The chance of rain was becoming a real threat. He turned to his second in command.

"Find more tracking dogs and get them here before it is too late."

As the captain issued orders to the radioman, De La Garza activated his satellite phone and dialed the number of an intermediary in Monterrey.

"This is De La Garza. I have a priority for "El Serpiente.""

The second night after the ambush, a cold rain began to fall. As the weather front moved through, the intensity of the rain increased until it fell in torrents. The plastic poncho helped, but Davis was soon soaked to the bone and suffering. Even though he was exhausted he was too fearful to stop for a rest. He knew that if he stopped moving without real shelter, hypothermia would stealthily kill him. He tried eating a freeze-dried meal without reconstituting. He chewed the crunchy material and drank water and hoped for the best.

At midday, it was still raining, and he had run out of bottled water. He stopped and stretched out the plastic tarp and tied the four corners to some brush. The rain quickly collected on the plastic and Davis was able to refill all three of his plastic bottles. He then drank his fill as the rain accumulated in his cooking pot.

While he rested, he began to think about the obstacles he was facing. First, there was the matter of all the people who were on his trail bent on killing him. He quickly did the math. He had already killed twenty-four men. No one was going to let that go. He was as fully committed as a man could be. It was an elementary equation. Cross the Rio Grande and live. Failure to make Texas was a death sentence.

Food was soon going to be a problem. He rifled through the pack and found that he was down to three of the freeze-dried meals. He realized that he would soon be in hunting mode. He had seen two mule deer and a group of javalinas so far on his trek. He decided that he would take the next deer that he saw and harvest some venison. He liked venison rare, but he had never eaten it raw. After the heavy rains, it could be days before he found any dry firewood. He was very glad that he had the containers of salt and pepper that he'd scavenged from the cabin. The spices would help preserve and season the meat. He hoped that the temperature would stay cool. He would be okay with food for about three days, but after that, he had better find some meat.

While Davis was cold and miserable because of the rain, there was an unrecognized blessing in the clouds. His scent trail from the ambush site was washed away before the general was able to enlist the services of more tracking dogs. The Mexicans were now at best only able to guess what direction the American was heading. As a result, Davis was putting more distance between him and his pursuers each day.

Disgusted with the rain, De La Garza thought of other options to reacquire the surprising American. He decided that he needed more eyes searching for the man. The next day his troops were posting wanted posters in every town and village north and east of the ambush site for fifty miles. Since he was spending ISIS money, he thought that the one-million-peso reward would enlist many more eyes.

Davis had seen no signs of civilization since the escape. The rain had stopped, and he was making good progress. He estimated that he was traveling between eight to ten miles each day. The march was becoming routine. Davis' only concern was food and water. He was down to one liter of water and his last freeze-dried meal. Just before dark one evening, he surprised a mule deer. It ran 200 yards and then stopped and looked back at Davis. He killed it with a single well-placed shot. He collected the tenderloins, backstraps, and the hams and left the rest for the coyotes. That night he had thin slices of tenderloin. In the dark it was easy to tell himself that it wasn't raw, but just very rare. It was the first fresh food he had since his breakfast on the day of the kidnapping.

Davis was on a northeastward leg of his trek. Water was now a serious problem. He was now eating cactus pears and peeling and chewing cactus pads to supplement his fluid intake.

At mid-afternoon, Davis was approaching the crest of a ridge when he thought that he heard the faint sound of a train's air horn. He topped the crest and peered into the valley beyond. The mountainous terrain made a sudden change. He now faced a broad, flat valley. A mile in the distance was a small, paved road running roughly east-west. The road was paralleled by a railroad track. For its size, it was a busy little road. Davis could see cars and trucks moving up and down the road. The train was moving away to the east.

Davis sat with his binoculars and spent an hour scanning all the visible countryside. To the east, he could see a small town that sat astride the highway and the railroad tracks. To the north, he could see an even smaller village. The towns had one thing in common. Water towers. While Davis was loath to approach the towns, his dire need for water was about to force the issue. Davis used the 20-power rifle scope to read the name stenciled on the side of the tower of the smaller village. Sierra Mojada. Davis smiled. You could not ask for a more fitting place to look for water. Sierra Mojada. Wet Mountain.

Davis began his approach to Sierra Mojada at midnight. By 2:00 a.m. he was close enough to see that the only gas station on the west end of town was his best bet to find water and not be observed. He was within fifty yards of the building when two dogs began to bark. Davis froze and prayed that he had not been discovered. After ten minutes the sound of the barking seemed to be diminishing to the south.

He approached the station from the rear. He hoped that there would be a water faucet on the back wall, but the wall was void of any plumbing fixtures. He glanced down each side of the station and again came up blank. The front of the station was lit by two bare lightbulbs. He hated the idea of exposing himself to the light, but there was no choice. He slipped out of his backpack and gathered his empty water bottles. He checked the pistol and re-holstered it. He left the rifles and backpack on the side of the building and moved quietly to the island where the gas pumps were located. At one end was the requisite air hose to fill tires and water hose to fill radiators.

Davis uncapped and filled the bottles as fast as he could. He drank his fill from the hose and then headed back to the side of the building. On the front of the building was a community bulletin board of sorts. As he walked by, Davis glanced at the flyers posted there. He stopped in midstride and stared at the poster placed prominently in the center of the board. There was a photograph of his face. He realized that it was taken by the terrorists on the second day that he was held at the ranch house. In bold print in Spanish, it read:

One Million Peso Reward
For information leading to the capture
Of the North American
Brooks Davis
DEAD OR ALIVE

At the bottom of the poster was the phone number of the Army's 24th Division Headquarters.

Davis pulled the poster off the bulletin board and retreated to the side of the building. He repacked his water and folded the poster and placed it in the side pocket of the backpack. He then melted away into the night and out of the town as quickly as possible.

Davis knew that the ambush of the platoon was going to be viewed as a gauntlet dropped. The one-million-peso reward was an indication of just how serious the Mexicans were about picking up the gauntlet. The "dead or alive" admonition was indicative that they were not keen on wasting time on a judicial process. As Davis slipped back into the hills, he knew that his fight was plain and simple, a fight for his life. The terrorists and their Mexican colleagues had taken the gloves off. With grim determination, Davis knew that his gloves were off as well. He now had a new understanding of his uncle's comments after he returned from a tour in Vietnam. When you are out in the bush, you shoot first and ask questions later. He also knew that to get to the Rio Grande, more people were likely to die.

CHAPTER EIGHTEEN
The Women at the Well

Davis continued his march in alternating northerly and northeasterly increments. As the terrain allowed, he moved primarily at night. The weather was cool and clear, and the countryside had become less mountainous. He was fearful that any serious airborne search would likely spot him. During the bright part of the day, he was content to hide under the camouflaged netting and move only during darkness. Even though he tried to ration his water supplies, he was once again getting critically low.

Three days after Sierra Mojada he crossed a north-south leg of the railroad that he had previously observed. He was now seeing more small dirt roads meandering through the countryside. He was forced to change his direction more frequently for fear of someone traveling the ranch roads spotting him.

As he moved out of his hiding place in the late afternoon, he topped a hill. In the distance, he could see a windmill. Needing water, Davis headed in that direction. He passed small groups of goats as he arrived at the well. The water trough was full and reasonably clean. Davis dropped his pack and rifles against some brush near the trough and gathered his water bottles. He dropped a small amount of bleach in each container and filled them. He was thirsty but he knew that it took thirty minutes for the bleach to do its job on the bacteria and protozoa in the water. He planned to wait, then drink his fill, then refill the bottles a second time.

While he waited, Davis wondered how many days had passed since his last bath. He had no clue but felt grimy and knew he smelled bad. He took off his shirt and splashed the cool, slightly green water on his face and upper torso. He did not know if he was getting any cleaner, but it made him feel better.

A sound made Davis freeze in place. It was the sound of a voice. He slowly looked to his left. Standing in a goat path, twenty-five yards away, were two women. They were dressed in peasant clothing, and both were carrying machetes. They stared at Davis and were quietly talking to each other. Neither Davis nor the women moved. After a long moment, Davis picked up his shirt and quickly slipped it on. His eyes flickered to his backpack and rifles lying in the brush fifteen feet away. The women's eyes followed his and made note of the man's belongings.

Davis did not know what to do. His mind was flying through the possibilities, and all were bad. He looked at the older woman. Her fist was rhythmically gripping the handle of the machete. She was not smiling. She was saying something out of the corner of her mouth to the younger woman, but he could not make out the words. Suddenly, he did hear the word "Americano," to which the younger woman nodded. Both women broke into a run toward Davis with machetes raised above their heads.

Davis called out, "Alto! Por favor!" as his hand went for his pistol. The women did not stop. He cleared the holster and thumbed off the safety, hoping that the sight of the weapon would stop their charge. It did not faze them. Davis repeated his plea to no avail. At eight feet he shot the older woman twice in the chest. The younger woman screamed but kept coming. Davis dodged the arc of the blade and pushed the woman away forcefully. She raised the blade again for a second thrust and Davis shot her once in the chest.

Davis was gasping ragged breaths as he gathered his gear and hurried away from the well. It all happened so quickly. He chastised himself for not studying the area around the windmill before committing to collecting the water. A terrible, sick pain formed deep in his chest. As he jogged away from the scene, he retched and vomited.

A quarter mile away he stopped long enough to finish redressing and donning his ghillie suit. He looked to the west and knew that there was at least an hour before darkness. He wondered if there was anyone nearby who had heard the shots. If no one had, how long would it be before the women were missed and their bodies were found? His situation had just gotten terribly worse.

Davis moved nonstop through the night and stopped only when it was too light for safe travel. He burrowed deeply into the brush and made himself as invisible as possible. He tried to rest but sleep eluded him. His mind was in constant motion. He did not know how he could have done things differently. Davis was now acutely aware of a striking paradox. It was one thing to kill terrorists or armed military men who were out to kill you, but quite another thing to kill a woman. His mind once again focused on the idea that once you kill, how easy and how quickly you turn to the ultimate of all solutions.

CHAPTER NINETEEN

Father Coyote

Fatigue like Davis had never felt finally drove him to a stop. It was night when he found himself on the top of a bald, little hill, literally in the middle of nowhere. He shed his backpack and rifles and took his hat off. After a moment of staring forward, unblinking, he found and opened one of his water bottles and had a short drink. He rolled the water around his dry mouth for a moment before he swallowed.

He looked up into a sky that looked like a black, velvet cloth that someone had spilled a bushel basket of diamonds upon. He slowly performed a left-to-right, 180-degree scan around the hilltop and saw nothing but stars and a hint of the horizon.

He spoke out loud. "Hey! Any more bad guys out there?" Then, a bit louder, "I'm right here. Come and get me. What's the matter? You scared of a little ol' white boy from Uvalde?"

Off in the distance, a lone coyote responded to the sound of his voice traveling through the still night air. Davis chuckled and took another swig of water, rolled it around his mouth, and then spat on the ground. He addressed the invisible animal.

"Well, since it's just you and me, I guess you are stuck with hearing my confession."

Davis went to his knees, made a hugely exaggerated sign of the cross, and then spread out his arms like he was about to be nailed to a cross.

"Bless me, Father Coyote, for I have sinned. I don't know how the hell long it has been since my last confession, but you're not supposed to hold that against me!" Davis paused and looked in the direction of where he last heard the coyote. After a moment, the coyote responded with a short yelp.

"Oh good. I thought you might have nodded off there, Father C. Okay, let's begin. When I say I've sinned, I'm talking a shitload of sins...big-ass sins...first-degree mortal sins...go to hell, straight to hell, do not pass purgatory sort of sins."

"Now I'm not going to bore you with ALL my sins, because that would take too long, and I know you have to go catch and kill your dinner. But on top of all the sins against Molly and the boys, I'm now a killer...a serial killer. I've killed more than TWO...DOZEN... MEN and NOW...WOMEN! I told myself it was kill or be killed, but it was TOO MANY and TOO EASY!"

Davis threw his head back and shouted the last again, as loud as he could. "IT WAS TOO MANY AND TOO EASY! DON'T YOU UNDERSTAND? THAT'S WHAT MAKES IT MORTAL IN THE FIRST DEGREE!"

Father Coyote spoke once again, granting absolution, and telling Brooks to recite an Act of Contrition. Brooks broke down on the barren hilltop in the dark of night and wept. He folded his hands in prayer.

"Oh my God... Oh my, Molly...I am heartily sorry, for having offended thee..."

When he finished his Act of Contrition, Davis sat down heavily and stared unblinkingly at the dark, distant horizon for a long time. His mind tried to piece together how long it had been since the kidnapping. The days and nights were a jumbled blur, and he just couldn't be sure. Home could have been a week or a lifetime ago. He just couldn't be sure. But what he was feeling surer of was that it had been long enough that Tina had already told Molly that she was the wife of the devil himself. If Molly already knew the truth, then his Act of Contrition was too late and therefore meaningless.

Davis entertained another, darker thought. It would be better for Molly and the boys if he just never showed up again. Father Coyote spoke again, reminding Davis that there was one more step in the confession rite.

"Oh yes, for my penance." Davis's hand slowly went to the butt of the pistol and removed it from the holster. He flicked off the safety and ran his fingers over the barrel of the gun. Brooks wondered if he should end everyone's misery on top of this miserable hill in this miserable country. Should he offer Father Coyote the opportunity to invite all of his friends over to the hill to share in an unholy communion? Waste not, want not. Scatter the bones, hide the evidence that the serial killer, serial cheater ever existed. Not a bad idea. Environmentally wholesome!

Davis's subconscious suddenly conjured up the dream image of the naked Molly at the foot of the bed. The thought shocked him back to the reality of the barren hilltop.

"Why do I keep thinking about that dream? And why no Tina to torment me this time?" Davis heard no answer from nature. He closed his eyes and the vision of Molly returned.

Molly suddenly stopped brushing her hair and gave him one of her patented combos of exasperated head tilt and death ray stink-eye. That was followed by the don't make me say this twice advice: "Is *that* what Father Coyote said was your penance?"

Davis opened his eyes. Nothing had changed...black star-filled sky...gut-wrenching fatigue and guilt...hopelessness. He listened for the voice of the coyote for a long time but only heard a freshening wind. He looked to the far-left horizon and saw the first flashes of lightning of a brand-new weather front that was forming in the distant west. He wondered if it was a sign that a righteously angered God was preparing to mete out his just punishment.

He looked down at the pistol in his hands and flicked the safety back on. As he re-holstered the pistol, he quietly mumbled, "Maybe Molly will hear my confession."

Davis gathered up his gear and moved out in the dark, moving roughly northeast. He knew he was somewhere in Mexico and was heading somewhere in the general direction of Texas. What he did not know was that he was going to have to go through a lot more purgatory to get there.

It was a day and a half before the general got word of the killings of the women. He smiled grimly. He now had a new point of departure for the American. During the time between the ambush of his platoon and these latest killings, De La Garza had gotten an idea of how to find Davis more quickly.

The general called the director of the regional Narco Police and described his problem. An ultra-violent cartel assassin had killed several of his troops and was at large somewhere in the triangle bordered by Sierra Mojada, La Esmeralda, and Sabaneta. The Narco Police were in a joint program with the American Drug Enforcement Administration to utilize the DEA's unmanned surveillance drones for interdiction missions south of the border. It was one of President Martinez's first cooperative programs with Mexico in their war on the drug cartels. The drones could be vectored to an area to fly grid searches and use ultra-high-resolution infrared scanners to pick up the body heat signatures of unsuspecting criminals from 10,000 feet in the air. The Narcos were only too happy to cooperate with the Army in removing such an unsavory killer.

De La Garza was terribly amused at the irony of the situation. He was about to get American high-tech help in finding and eliminating one of their own. The general thought it was so fitting considering the amount of trouble that the American had caused.

That night the unmanned drone flew the mission 110 miles south of the nearest US airspace. The controllers were working out of Laughlin Air Force Base in Del Rio. The drone controller set the flight computer to fly the search pattern on autopilot. When he picked up a hot spot, he would manually lock on the target, then zoom in on the image and rapidly determine if it was an animal or a human on the prowl.

Shortly after 2:00 a.m., he zoomed in on a clearly human hot spot in the hills east of Sabaneta.

"Got ya, you cartel bastard!" exclaimed the drone pilot. He immediately reported the GPS coordinates and direction of travel to his superiors at the DEA. They immediately forwarded the intel to their counterparts south of the border. Within six minutes the general's phone rang and woke him up. His only order was, "Send Serpiente."

It was 3:30 a.m. and Davis was making good progress through the hills. The further he got away from the place where he had killed the women, the lighter the weight of his terrible burden seemed. He had plenty of time to reflect on the event. He had come to the rationalization that they had attacked him with the intent of collecting an unjust reward. It was clearly self-defense. Or was it? He longed to find the Rio Grande. It had become the most important river on the planet.

In the distance, he heard helicopter blades beating the night air.

CHAPTER TWENTY
The Serpent

Davis could hear the helicopter but could not see any running lights. As he listened, he could visualize the chopper coming to a hover but not actually landing. Only a moment later the RPM of the rotor blades increased, and the aircraft turned and left the area.

Davis was certain that the Army was back on his tail but was confused as to why there was only one helicopter. And how could they unload and depart so quickly? He strained his ears for the sound of dogs, but there was only silence. Whatever their plan, Davis was certain once again that bad things were on the horizon. He gathered his gear and set his mind to the task of putting as much distance as he could between him and his pursuers.

El Serpiente was in his element. He was a former Colombian Special Forces troop who got into trouble in Colombia and found refuge with the northern cartels in Mexico. He was the consummate killer. He was at home in any environment. His contracts had taken him all over Central America. He had gained a reputation for hunting down people who knew that someone was out to kill them. They could try to run and hide, but the serpent always found and killed them anyway. He had learned his tracking skills from his father in the Colombian jungles. He was extraordinarily calm and patient, just like his namesake.

He had the helicopter drop him off at the highest point north and east of Davis' last GPS location. As he unpacked the infrared spotting scope, he thought about his latest quarry. This American was unusual. There were men who were natural killers. This man killed with his hands, and he killed with weapons at short and long range. He knew how to evade, spring an ambush, and live off the land. The American had field skills just like El Serpiente himself. But what set this quarry apart was the women. Many excellent killers could not pull the trigger on a woman. It was a fatal flaw that separated the wheat from the chaff in the world of uncommon killers.

He powered up the infrared scope and started a systematic scan of the darkened hillsides. He took his time. He was confident that he would find the American, and once he did it was just a matter of time. Every man, even the most careful man, leaves a trail. And once he was on the trail, the quarry rarely escaped.

In the distance, he caught a glimpse of a bright spot in his scope. He focused the scope and adjusted the magnification to 30-power. He saw the bright silhouette of a man with a backpack and two rifles. El Serpiente got a compass fix on the spot and casually packed up his gear and moved out. He wanted to be closer at first light.

At first light, Davis was on top of a hill that offered good conceal-ment. From 3:30 a.m. on, he had thought of nothing but the arrival and quick departure of the helicopter. He knew intuitively that they had somehow changed their tactics, but he could not quite figure it out. He reasoned that only a small group of three or four men could have been delivered by only one helicopter. He also knew intuitively that these men would be different. They would be much better sol-diers. And good soldiers were not likely to fall headlong into a trap.

Davis was using the binoculars and had not picked up anything of interest. He decided to pack up and move out to the north in the direction of better hills that offered more opportunity for concealment. As an afterthought, he used the long rifle with its more powerful scope to scan a distant ridge line. He almost missed it at first. With a second look, he saw the movement. Davis dialed the scope to 20-power. From two miles away it looked like a bush magically moving across the crest of the hill. He then realized that it was a man in a very effective ghillie suit slowly moving in his direction.

Davis watched motionless, waiting to see if there were others. After five minutes he was sure that the man was alone. Davis was morbidly fascinated. When the man stopped moving, he blended in with the hillside so well that he seemed to disappear. As he watched, the man continued to move precisely in his direction. Davis was suddenly sure that the man knew where he was. The thought set Davis' heart racing. He was certain that the terrorists or the Army or the cartels had sent a single man, a specialist, to track and kill him. Davis found the thought considerably more frightening than his previous encounters. His enemies had upped the ante once again and Davis knew that there was now no room for any error at all.

Davis waited as the apparition of a man went out of sight in a valley and then moved out of his position. He donned his makeshift ghillie suit. Having just seen what the real thing looks like, he knew that his suit was a poor substitute for the camo worn by his opponent. He prayed that his suit was good enough.

His plan was to move at maximum speed when he was on the downhill side of a hill situated between him and the sniper. When he crested the next hill, he found a well-concealed spot and started to scan for his adversary. Once again, he almost missed the motion. He watched the man as he produced some sort of optical device on a small collapsible tripod. The man scanned in Davis' direction. Davis froze. Eventually, the man scanned left and right of his position. After fifteen minutes, the spotting scope disappeared under the man's ghillie suit. He then moved out on a line that would bring him straight to Davis' position.

When Davis moved out for the second time, he was troubled. The man always seemed to know precisely where he was.

El Serpiente had quickly guessed that the man from Texas was on to the fact that he was being tracked. This fact did not bother him at all. He smiled when he realized the fact. It just made the exercise more like a chess game. And like his chosen profession, El Serpiente never lost a chess match.

Davis made up his mind to concentrate on moving as fast as he could. While he moved, two questions kept rolling through his mind. First, how was it that the helicopter dropped off the sniper in the dead of night in such close proximity to his position? Second, how did the sniper know exactly what direction to travel that put him on the exact path of Davis' travel? The thought that his adversaries must be able to see in the dark crossed Davis' mind. He decided that they must be using some sort of night-vision technology. He realized grimly that he could run but not really hide. The result was that he was going to have to face this man just like all the others.

Davis kept pushing all day. He ate a small amount of the ripening venison and drank only sparingly, always while on the move. He wanted to keep the distance between him and the sniper as great as possible. He remembered reading about how military snipers routinely make thousand-yard shots. A mile was more than 1,700 yards. If he could keep the distance at least a mile or more, he felt that he had a chance. At the same time, Davis also realized that at some point he would have to stop for a rest. But his next thought was that the sniper would have to rest as well. He caught himself watching the sun sinking in the west and hoping for the comparative safety of darkness. Then he remembered that if his adversary had night vision, darkness would be no safer than noon.

Once, just before sundown, he caught a brief glimpse of the sniper. He was always very careful as he crested a hill. The man spent time studying the opposite hillside before he moved out. Davis realized that the man was fully aware of how he pulled off the ambush of the platoon.

The moon was nearly full, and Davis was making progress, but fatigue was slowly dragging him to a halt. At some point during the night, he knew that he would soon have to stop for some real rest. At about midnight, he found a spot on a hillside where he would be able to hear anyone climbing the hill. The position would at least give him the advantage of high ground. He stopped to rest. As he settled in, he began to try to visualize exactly what he would need to do to deal with the sniper. He quickly realized that if he was going to be successful, he would have to change his modus operandi or it would boil down to a duel with a seasoned killer.

At 2:30 a.m., Davis decided. He rationalized that if the man already knew his approximate position and direction of travel, he could call in the Army at any time. If the Army arrived in strength, then there was little hope of survival. Davis was certain that his only option was to eliminate the sniper now, rather than to try to outrun him. His plan called for a different type of ambush. He crossed the valley and ascended halfway up the eastern slope and then turned and traveled some distance parallel to the long axis of the ridge. He then re-crossed the valley and re-ascended the western slope and found a secure hiding place. The moonlight was bright enough for Davis to find a spot in the brush and rocks that he hoped would be both safe and offer a good view of the eastern slope. He settled in under his camouflaged netting with the 7mm magnum resting on his backpack. He took a long drink of water and began the wait.

El Serpiente had moved hard through the night. He once caught sight of his quarry through the night scope as the man crested a hill. He had closed the distance to just over a mile. He felt confident that sometime during the coming day he would possibly be in range for a high-probability shot.

At first light, he found the spot where he had seen the Texan when he crested the hill. The sniper carefully approached the crest and began to study the opposite slope. The slope was relatively bare of vegetation with only a few rocky outcroppings that could afford the man a hiding place. The sniper spent twenty minutes studying the hillside through binoculars and decided that it was not a good place for an ambush. He crept forward and studied the hillside that he was on to his left and right. Again, nothing set off alarm bells. He moved out to cross the small valley.

As he moved downhill, he picked up other evidence of his quarry. Here and there the man's boots were making scuff marks that were easy to follow. He thought that it meant that the man was becoming exhausted. El Serpiente smiled again, more confident that today would be the day. It never crossed his mind that the man might have left the scuff marks intentionally.

The sniper crossed the ravine at the bottom of the valley and started up the opposite hillside. When he reached the midpoint of the slope, the Texan's tracks indicated that he had made an abrupt change of direction. El Serpiente went to a knee and quickly scanned in the direction of the track as well as the hillside from which he had just come. He saw nothing out of the ordinary, but his instincts told him that something was not right.

Just before sunrise, Davis heard someone moving carefully through the rocks somewhere to his right. He reminded himself to be patient. He knew that it would be difficult to see the sniper until he was much lower on the slope. He reminded himself again that patience was a virtue and the hallmark of the true hunter. He could feel himself transitioning from prey mode to predator mode. He was certain that if he rushed, he would fail. And it would probably be his last failure.

After a tedious twenty minutes, he finally caught sight of the man in the amazing ghillie suit. He was 150 yards away. He watched him with fascination. The man moved slowly and smoothly. His head constantly checked the ground to his front and then left and right. Davis was sure that if he made the slightest sound or movement, the sniper would instantly be aware.

As the sniper moved downhill, Davis mounted the rifle and found the man in the scope. He could hear his own heartbeat in his ears.

The rate was on the increase. He could tell that the sniper was wearing a backpack under the ghillie suit. He knew that he needed to make a one-shot kill. The presence of the backpack precluded a center body shot. He moved the crosshair to the spot where the man's head would be under the ghillie suit. Because his target was on the move downhill and moving over rough ground, Davis found it difficult to keep the crosshairs on target. An ember of panic began to glow in the pit of his stomach.

After a brief pause at the bottom of the ravine, the sniper started climbing up the opposite slope. Davis was still not sure of the shot, so he held off. When the sniper got to the spot where Davis turned and began to move parallel to the long axis of the hill, he paused and studied the new track. Davis flicked the safety off and re-centered the crosshairs on the sniper. Before he could take up the slack in the trigger, the man moved out again. Davis was again facing the moving target dilemma. After the man had moved about fifteen yards, he broke into a run across the face of the slope.

Davis was startled and lost the image of the man in the scope. The sniper dove headfirst behind a large boulder. Davis ground his teeth together when he realized that the sniper was on to his tactic. Davis also realized that he had no shot. He scanned through the scope and could only see a portion of the man's left boot that protruded beyond the boulder.

Davis studied the sniper's hide. It was situated in such a way that for the sniper to get a view of Davis' position, he would have to crawl forward and expose his head from behind the rock. Davis hoped for a shot there, so he positioned the crosshairs on the spot and kept his finger on the trigger. It was 7:50 a.m. when the long wait began.

One hour became two, and then four. With the sun now directly overhead, Davis was becoming dry and hungry. He kept his eye glued to the eyepiece of the scope and scarcely blinked, fearful that he would miss a shooting opportunity. He had a blazing headache. At one point in the middle of the afternoon, he heard the sound of a canteen being tapped against the boulder. He could visualize the sniper drinking comfortably. Davis thought seriously about trying to retrieve a bottle of water for a drink, but he hesitated. He knew that the sniper was only guessing that he was waiting in ambush. If he made a sound, he would be delivering confirmation on a platter. He put the thought of water out of his mind.

What was the sniper waiting for? The man should know that if he bolted downhill he would have a good chance of evading any rounds sent in his direction. Once in a better position, the sniper could level the killing field.

At mid-afternoon, Davis decided what El Serpiente's plan was. Darkness. He would wait until darkness to make his move. The thought of going head-to-head with a professional killer in the dark made Davis' empty stomach begin to churn. He felt that he must somehow force the action.

Davis studied the rock that protected the sniper. His eyes focused on the small portion of the sniper's boot that was visible. Davis turned the variable power knob of the precision scope from 8 to 20 power. The image of the visible portion of the boot grew logarithmically. He thought about the shot. He was perhaps 200 meters from the sniper. It would be a cross-canyon, slightly downhill shot. If he could put the 165-grain bullet through the sniper's foot, he would change the dynamic in his favor. He thought about the incredible accuracy of the rifle during the engagement with the Mexican platoon.

He felt that he could do it, but if he missed, the only trump card that he held would be irrevocably played. He snugged the rifle butt deep into his shoulder and pressed the side of the barrel of the rifle into the rock behind which he had laid for all those hours. The crosshairs were motionless and centered on the boot. As he began to take the slack in the trigger another motion attracted his eye. From the top of the rock the top of the sniper's ghillie suit slowly appeared. Only a few inches became visible, then became still. Davis moved the crosshairs from the boot to the visible portion of the ghillie suit.

Davis blinked a drop of sweat out of his eye and concentrated on the new target. The hood moved slowly left and right and then a little more of the camouflage appeared above the rock. With the additional exposure and the 20-power magnification, Davis could tell that the sniper was trying to entice a shot. He was trying the old cowboy trick of using a stick to expose a hat from behind a protected area. Davis began to chuckle. The more he tried not to laugh, the more he wanted to. He thought of the absurdity of it all. Two men were trying desperately to kill each other, and one was resorting to B-movie tactics. Davis whispered out loud, "You just hope that I'm that dumb."

The sniper spent the next forty-five minutes exposing more and more of the hood. Davis began to reconsider the shot at the sniper's boot when the boot suddenly disappeared behind the rock. This perplexed Davis. He had lost another opportunity.

The boot disappeared because the sniper had moved slightly and was trying to get a look at the area on the opposite canyon wall that he had not been able to view from his original position. Davis re-settled the crosshairs on the spot where the sniper's head would appear and waited.

Davis assessed the position of the sun and estimated two more hours until sundown. Just when he was sure that the sniper would remain in place until dark, he suddenly raised his head momentarily above the rock. It was just a brief flash, but Davis got a look at him. He appeared middle-aged and had a prominent mustache. Davis' mind flashed to the last two men he had killed when he ambushed the platoon. They wore mustaches as well. The long wait had taken the edge off Davis' anxiety. He was surprised that he felt calm. He was in control and sensed that his long wait was almost over.

El Serpiente raised his rifle to the top of the rock and then quickly scanned Davis' side of the canyon through the scope. Davis froze in place and prayed that he was adequately camouflaged. He was torn between taking a snapshot at the sniper's head or waiting for a higher percentage shot. His quarry continued to scan the opposite side of the canyon with his rifle at the ready to squeeze off a shot at the first hint of a target. Davis whispered to himself, "Patience will prevail."

After a very long three minutes, El Serpiente lowered his rifle and changed to a set of binoculars. Davis remained motionless, waiting. He watched the sniper lower the binoculars and smile and laugh at himself for thinking that the Texan would have the expertise to catch the serpent in an ambush. Convinced that he had wasted a whole day of the hunt, El Serpiente stood up.

Davis marveled at the man's misguided confidence. He centered the crosshairs on the center of his chest and fired.

The sniper collapsed instantly. As the sound of the shot echoed and then died in the mountains, Davis quickly chambered a fresh round and reacquired the rock behind which the man had hidden all day and behind which his body now lay hidden from view.

Davis did not move for fifteen minutes. He felt confident in the shot, but not being able to see the body had him second-guessing. Was the sniper dead, or was he playing possum? There was only one way to find out. Davis slowly got to his feet. He was weak and had to sit down for a moment to gather his strength. He never took his eyes off the place where the sniper lay hidden.

He made his way across the canyon. As he approached the sniper's hide, he could finally catch a glimpse of his body. He re-shouldered the rifle as he approached. The man lay on his back. A large crimson stain could be seen leaking through the weave of the ghillie suit. Davis watched his chest for a couple of minutes to make sure that he was not breathing. He finally lowered his rifle and approached the dead man. The man's eyes and mouth were open. His last expression was one of profound surprise.

As the sun began to set, Davis began to go through the sniper's belongings. His rifle was a Remington 700 in .308 caliber with a fixed 10-power Zeiss scope. It was the classic military sniper rifle. The infrared spotting scope was of military issue but had no other markings. He carried no identification. The backpack held routine rations and water and little else. Davis marveled that he did not even have a sleeping bag or bedroll. Other than his rifle, the only two important possessions were a satellite phone and a roll of topographic maps.

Davis' attention was immediately drawn to the phone. It was turned off. He wondered if he could turn it on and dial his home phone number and tell his wife not to worry, that he was okay. He hesitated for a moment and then opened the back of the phone. In addition to the battery, there were two small plug-in electronic cards. One was the microprocessor that ran the phone and the second had the letters GPS embossed on it. His initial elation at having the phone was now destroyed by the certainty that if he used it, his precise location would be broadcast to anyone monitoring the phone's use. Even if he destroyed the GPS card, he knew that his position could be triangulated from the satellite's position. With great reluctance, he disassembled the phone and threw the parts into the canyon.

He turned his attention to the roll of topographic maps. A ballpoint pen was clipped to the top page. He studied the page and recognized the sniper's tracking notes. One note written in Spanish read "Women killed here" and included an undulating line that led to the valley in which he died. Davis slowly held the map to his chest. He now knew for the first time precisely where in Mexico he was. The maps would tell him a wealth of information.

He pulled the sniper's body into the brush and carefully covered his equipment and remains with his makeshift ghillie suit. He decided to keep the sniper's ghillie suit for himself. He added more brush and rocks to make it very difficult to observe from the air. He kept the man's food and canteens of water to supplement his own diminishing supplies. He also kept the man's watch and compass. With darkness now upon him, he gathered his gear and moved out to the north. He wanted to be out of the area as fast as possible. He walked all night.

At first light, he stopped and prepared breakfast. He warmed water and even treated himself to instant coffee compliments of El Serpiente. While he sipped the coffee, he studied the topographic maps and the sniper's notes. He was able to piece together that he had started his journey in the state of Chihuahua. The ranch where he was held was north of a tiny village called Santa Elena. The location where he shot down the helicopter was circled and noted, as was the valley where he killed the platoon and the women at the well. To his surprise, he had crossed the boundary into the state of Coahuila. He laid the maps border to border until he found the nearest point of the Rio Grande. Davis's heart sank. He was still over a hundred miles from the US border.

Under normal hiking and camping conditions, he felt that he could easily do ten miles a day. His present circumstance, however, meant that he could not move in a straight line and had to dodge all forms of civilization. The 100 miles were probably more like 150. Davis thought that if everything went perfectly, the remainder of his trip would last two to three weeks minimum.

Davis was not sure how long it had been since the kidnapping. He looked at the sniper's watch, but it did not have a date function. He re-looked at the maps and studied the symbols for rivers, creeks, villages, and towns. It would require a very circuitous route, but he still had a fair amount of ammunition and deer were still abundant. With a huge amount of luck, he just might make it. And if his luck ran out, then he would die trying.

CHAPTER TWENTY-ONE

Point of Never Return

Molly opened her front door to find a solemn-looking Rona Epstein standing there holding a compact briefcase. The women had not seen each other since the horror story had begun. They greeted each other with a warm embrace. A few tears leaked from their eyes.

"We should have gotten together sooner, I'm sorry," said Molly as she invited Rona into the living room.

"There's been too much to do, too many people to talk with."

"Are your sons doing, okay?" inquired Molly.

"They both went home to Israel to rejoin their IDF units. They will be safer in Israel and will be able to get their minds off their father."

"But don't they want to be here with you?"

"They know that their mom can take care of herself and things here."

Rona asked, "What about your boys?"

Molly shook her head. "Not good. The younger two are still home. Andy, the middle child, is old enough to understand. He is doing very badly. James is very angry and is acting very strangely. I'm afraid... well...I just don't know what he is thinking."

Rona nodded her understanding, then put her hand on Molly's.

"Molly, you must understand and accept that it is all over for our husbands. The fact that we haven't seen confirmation shouldn't be misconstrued to give you some sort of misplaced hope. They are gone. ISIS is too vicious. When they take you, you are done for. You must accept it. I accepted it. My boys accepted it. We all agreed that the best option for our family was to leave Texas, go back to Israel, and go back to the war."

Molly stared, unblinking, at Rona. She was receiving advice from a kindred spirit, but she would not willingly take such painful advice.

Rona could see that Molly was entering into a kind of paralysis. She retrieved her briefcase and positioned it on her lap.

"Molly, the main reason I came today was to conduct business before I go back to Israel. The long and short of it is this. Raymond made us very wealthy. I've consolidated everything except the unfinished house that Brooks was building for us, and the land it is sitting on. Technically, you already have a builder's lien on the house, so that leaves the land. I can't take the land with me, and I feel terrible that Brooks was kidnapped along with Raymond for whatever twisted reason. I've signed the deed to all the land and ownership of the unfinished home to you."

Mrs. Epstein opened her briefcase and retrieved a stack of notarized papers and handed them to Molly.

"Take these to your lawyer. He will find that everything is in order. The property is yours. I just wish it was Brooks."

She stood and made her way to the door. Molly followed behind. At the door, Rona turned and embraced Molly.

"Molly, you must be strong for your sons. Part of that is to be realistic. When I get back to Israel, I will use my contacts in Israeli intelligence to try to keep you informed about what I can find out, and what your government may be reluctant to tell you. If someone approaches you and asks, "Is it true that Zane hit two home runs?," it will be safe to talk to them."

CHAPTER TWENTY-TWO

Adjusting the Timetable

It had been a month since Brooks had been kidnapped. Tina had been content to stay in the background and keep the Davis Construction business running in the absence of the CEO. Tina had always thought that Brooks would find a reason to divorce Molly and be done with her. He would buy her out of her share of the community property, and that would free Tina to fill the void. And boy, could she fill the void.

Who would have ever, in a million years, thought that ISIS would screw up a really sweet and simple deal? Now, Tina was forced to go to a much less simple Plan B.

Work was continuing slowly on what was formerly the Epstein project. Molly had notified Tina that Mrs. Epstein had sold back the unfinished home and property. Molly informed Tina that the project was now going to proceed and be finished as a high-end speculative mansion and property. Tina was invited to continue as construction superintendent.

Molly and Tina agreed to meet at the business offices on a weekly basis for progress reports and for Molly to deliver checks that needed to be delivered to subs. Tina decided that before the Widow Davis decided to sell her business to one of the other custom home builders, she had better start making her move. She felt that Widow Davis would be at her most vulnerable now and would be harder to manipulate later.

Tina sat behind Brooks' desk when Molly arrived to hand off checks. The sight of Tina feeling so at home there bothered Molly, but she held off telling her so.

"Are the boys back in school?"

"Yes. Andy has come around and Zane's teacher prepped his classmates to be careful and kind around him for a while."

"That's good. He's still very young. Andy is very smart. He will get through this mess better than the rest of us."

The women made small talk for a bit until Tina brought things back to business.

"Molly, have you made any decisions about the business?"

"Decisions?"

"Yes, like what are you going to do with the construction company?"

Molly stared at Tina for a long moment.

"Well, I'm not going to do anything with it."

Tina rebounded a bit. "So, you are going to try to keep it and try to run it yourself? I thought you were trained as an RN. What do you know about the construction business?"

Molly's first impulse was to tell her to just keep doing her job and not to worry about things that don't concern her. Her second impulse was to keep her talking.

"Well, I learned a good bit about the construction business from my husband of twenty years. Sort of like what you've learned in a small way over the last four years. Brooks is...or was...a great teacher. In any event, I know how to find and hire good subcontractors and superintendents. In fact, did Brooks ever tell you that I was the one who found your application and resume and gave it to him? I was the one who said this gal is young, but you ought to give her a try."

Tina swallowed hard, but Molly missed it. She could see where the discussion was heading. She decided to get back to trying to stay a step ahead.

"Did Brooks ever discuss what his long-range goals for the business were, and where I would fit in?"

Molly tilted her head in surprise. "Long-range plans, yes. Where *you* fit in, *no*! He's not here so I guess you will have to enlighten me."

"Brooks always appreciated my...contributions to the business. We had an unwritten agreement that when he was ready to retire, we would determine the value of the business, and he would sell it to me. He would bank it for five percent for ten years. It would be his... your retirement plan. Win-win."

Molly contemplated Tina's revelation.

"Brooks must have really appreciated all of those...contributions to the business. However, since this is the first I've heard of it, and you are absolutely right about the unwritten thing, I'm going to have to give this a lot of thought. In the meantime, just keep doing your job and get those checks out to the subs."

CHAPTER TWENTY-THREE
The Finite Limit of Luck

He did not know that he had been missing for a month when he woke up that morning. Davis was now in the rhythm of the march, and time was becoming a little less relevant each day. With the compass and maps, he was now able to plot a specific route for each day's journey. He was particularly happy to have the compass. Of only small value by itself, when coupled with the topo maps Davis was able to keep precise track of his location and progress. It also made moving at night much less daunting. When it was cold, he could travel all night and sleep in the sun by day. There had been little rain, but it offered a welcome replenishment to his water supply and was worth the misery of being wet and cold.

Davis could now avoid areas of civilization and plot approaches to water. He had run out of rations completely and was now a hunter-gatherer. A bullet was now his unit of currency, not just a means of self-defense. He decided that it was too expensive to spend a bullet on small game. He killed mostly deer. He would take the carcass apart and try to waste nothing. He cut the meat into thin slices, carefully salted and peppered it, and smoked it dry over a fire, making a quick and tasty jerky. He would not waste the long bones as he had done earlier in his ordeal. He now cracked the bones open and ate the rich, fat-filled marrow.

His backpack began to smell strongly of ripe meat and blood. One sunny day he found a cattle trough in a secluded valley. He stripped and took the most thorough bath he had taken thus far. He washed his clothes. While they dried, he looked at his naked body and realized that he had lost all the excess weight that Molly had nagged him about. He flexed his bicep and slapped his flat, hard belly. He felt ripped, but he could not recommend the radical weight loss program.

By his best calculations since killing the sniper, he had traveled about fifty miles but was only thirty miles closer to the border. Roads and villages were becoming more numerous. He was in constant fear that he would make a mistake and be discovered.

The weather turned ugly, and Davis tried to hike in utter darkness during a rainstorm. He had even warned himself of the folly, but he was cold and by moving he was staying a little warmer. He used a walking stick to try to feel his way, but he stepped off a cap rock, fell ten feet, and rolled down a slope. His knee and ankle were badly sprained but not broken. He lost some of his gear in the fall including his flashlight. He had to spend the night in place in abject misery and wait for light to find his belongings.

In the morning, he recollected the lost items, hobbled down the hill, and took stock of his new situation. He knew that trying to walk would be futile. The knee and ankle needed rest. As much as he wanted to keep moving, he decided that a day or two of rest would be his best option in the long run.

Convinced that walking in the pitch dark was not a reasonable option, Davis decided to don the sniper's ghillie suit and travel by day and sleep at night until the moon was bright enough to ameliorate the danger. He was making only minor progress in his travels. His knee and ankle were still problematic. He ate some of his usual jerky for dinner with aspirins for dessert and turned in early. He went to sleep quickly with his backpack for a pillow.

It had been six days since the male mountain lion had killed his last mule deer. He ate well for two days, but on the third night his kill was discovered by a pack of seven coyotes and he was forced to give it to them. He missed another deer two nights ago. The day before he tried to take a goat from a pen, but the human prevented it. He was now on the move and very hungry. With his nose in the wind, he picked up the faint smell of blood. He turned to the odor and went into hunting mode. As the lion closed the distance, he became aware of other smells. He stopped his approach. His nose identified meat, but it was tainted with the smell of a human. He padded closer. He stopped again when he picked up the sound of rhythmic breathing. The blood and meat smells were wonderful, and his current state of hunger made him more optimistic than cautious. Maybe the human was alive but seriously wounded. Maybe this would be an easy kill. He always wondered what a human would taste like.

When he was within twenty feet of the man, he coiled his muscles and calculated the angle of attack. When he released, he covered the last twenty feet in a single bound. He buried his fangs into the head of the man and tried to do the same with his claws but was prevented by some sort of bag that held the man's body. It was just a matter of hanging on to the head until the man became still.

At first, Davis thought it was just a very vivid nightmare, but soon he realized that the pain was real. He thrashed in the sleeping bag trying to get his hand out. The pressure applied to his head was incredible. He was able to get his left hand to his head and suddenly understood what was happening. His right hand went to his hip and tried to free the pistol from the holster. He became aware of the cat's fetid breath mixed with the smell of his own blood. Despite the darkness of the night, his vision was beginning to white out. He knew that if he could not free the pistol quickly, he would soon be a dead man.

The pistol came free, and he thumbed off the safety and blindly pointed it in the vicinity of his right ear. He forced the barrel rearward until it encountered something firm. With a final prayer that the firm spot was not his own head, he fired.

The explosion so close to his ear was deafening. The excruciating pressure on his head was replaced by the pain of a large piece of his scalp being torn from his skull. The cat screamed in pain, having been shot in the neck. It rolled and pawed at its neck, confused as to why such an easy kill had gone so wrong. Davis kicked his way out of the sleeping bag and turned the weapon on the lion. He continued to shoot the cat until the clip was empty and the animal stopped moving.

Davis collapsed on the hard ground, gasping ragged breaths and trying to stay conscious. After a few minutes, he became aware of the blood running freely into his ears. He struggled into a sitting position and fought off a wave of vertigo. Blood was now running down his face and dripping from his chin. With great reluctance, his hand went to his head, and he gingerly explored his wound. There was a long, full, thick laceration starting in his mid-forehead above his right eyebrow that ascended perhaps five inches into his scalp like a macabre part in his hair. The scalp was pulled from his skull and was bleeding freely. His fingertips found all four of the fang marks. One was in the middle of the torn part of his scalp. He could feel small shards of bone indicative of a focal depressed skull fracture. He assumed that the other three marks were similar and stopped short of further examination.

"Fucking mountain lion! Survive all this shit to be killed by a mountain lion!" He spoke out loud, not caring at this point if anyone would hear his ranting. After a long pause, he shook his head and continued his soliloquy. "Damn it! You better get your act together or you are going to die in this piece of shit country!"

After another pregnant pause, he crawled to the backpack, found his flashlight, and located his meager medical supplies. He found the tube of triple antibiotic ointment and forced the medication into the fang marks and under the flap of skin. The pain was intense, but the thought of a rampant infection in his skull made him persist. He pressed the flap of skin back into place. He cut the sleeve from his extra shirt and used it as a bandage to wrap over the top of his head. He tied it under his chin, applying pressure to the wound in hopes of stemming the hemorrhage. He went back to the medical supplies and retrieved the bottle of aspirin. He shook out four and chewed them into fine particles before swallowing them with a drink of water. He did the same with the antibiotic pills that were left over from his bout of diarrhea. He did not know if they were effective against lion bites, but it was all he had.

He remained awake all night. At daylight, he got his first look at his assailant. Of the fifteen 9mm rounds he fired at the lion, he could only find five bullet wounds. At such close range, he was embarrassed at his poor marksmanship but was thankful that it was enough to get the job done.

Davis was in serious pain and had more aspirins prior to his usual jerky breakfast. As he chewed, he smelled the meat and better understood the attack. He vowed to correct the mistake in the future—if he had a future.

He studied the maps and made a notation of the location of the lion attack. He planned the route for the day's travel. After he packed his gear, he took one last look at the lion. He retrieved the camera and posed with the cat for a photo. He placed the camera on a rock and set the timer so that he could be in the shot. After the timer took the picture, he looked at the photo. The lion was stretched out with his head on a rock. Davis was behind the cat with his pistol drawn and sporting his bloody bandage around his head. It was reminiscent of photos of successful hunters on safari in Africa. Davis mumbled out loud, "I hope I live to show this to the boys." With a thought of the boys and home, Brooks' lips quivered. He choked out a ragged sob and sat down and began to weep. He knew that he had been gone so long that they had all probably given up hope. With gut-wrenching certainty, he felt that Tina had confronted Molly out of sheer spite. If he survived this nightmare, what would he be facing with Molly and the boys?

Brooks looked off in the general direction of San Antonio and studied the horizon for a long time. He stood and gathered his vital belongings. "I've got to get home...maybe she'll forgive me."

With a still sprained ankle and knee, the going was slow and painful. He was forced to stop frequently for rest. At midday, he stopped, removed his makeshift bandage, and lightly touched the long laceration. He wished he could see the wound. Without a mirror, he used the camera to take a picture of his wound. When he viewed the image on the LCD screen, he grimaced. It was gaping open nearly a half inch. Davis wished for a needle and thread so he could suture the wound. After a moment of thought, he remembered reading how Native Americans treated such wounds. He began to search the mountainside for a mesquite tree. He collected several mesquite thorns and used some of the bleach to sterilize them. Working blindly by feel, Davis slowly and painfully used the thorns to cross-pin the wound and approximate the edges together. He used the camera to assess his work. He shook his head and decided not to give up his day job. He applied more antibiotic ointment and reapplied the sleeve to protect the wound.

Davis continued to march toward the border. His vigilance was now doubled. He not only had to worry about people trying to kill him but animals as well. It had been several days since the chess match with the sniper. Davis had frankly expected that the Army would have pulled out all the stops to hunt him down, but he had not seen or heard anything that would indicate that the pressure was being turned up. Could it be possible that they had finally decided that the cranky contractor was not worth all the trouble that he could dish out? Davis told himself that he could always hope.

Two days after the lion attack Davis could feel things starting to go bad physically. He could tell he had a significant fever. His wound was growing more painful each day and he was now aware that he could smell it. He was getting low on meat and was not seeing any deer or anything else for that matter. He knew that he had the lion to thank for that as well. He finally spotted a moving lone mule deer doe at 400 yards, but he missed the long shot. He felt that the fall from the cap rock had probably knocked the scope out of adjustment. He gave some thought to re-sighting the rifle, but he was down to only nine rounds of the 7mm magnum ammunition. He decided to wait for a stationary target to see how badly the scope was off.

The weather had also become Davis' enemy. It had become persistently cold and very windy. The multiple stresses caused Davis to develop a cough and cold. When he coughed, he began to experience chest pains. He was worried that pneumonia was lurking around the corner. He experienced a delirium-filled sleep that night. Though he didn't know it, his temperature had reached 104 degrees.

When he awoke, Davis knew that he could not make much progress that day, so he did not even try. He stayed at the bottom of a ravine under his camouflage and out of the wind as much as possible. He slept a fitful sleep throughout the day. At mid-afternoon, he was awakened by the sound of a light plane. The plane was crossing directly overhead at low altitude. He listened to the sound of the engine. It was idling back and losing RPM. Davis was sure that he had been spotted and that the plane would circle for another pass. He wondered if there would be an airborne sniper who would try to kill him from the air. He prepared the AK-47, making sure that the long, curved magazine was full. He doubted that he could be lucky twice with two different aircraft.

The plane did not circle back. Davis thought that he could hear the plane landing. With no immediate threat, he retrieved the topographic map with which he was currently navigating. He studied the map and pinpointed the canyon in which he was hiding. Just over the hill to his east, the map showed the symbols that indicated two permanent buildings and an unpaved road. The map also showed that the elevation flattened out into a broad valley about a mile wide. He remembered that before the fever set in, his plan was to close on the location because buildings usually meant water.

Davis armed himself with the AK-47 and pistol and carried the binoculars around his neck. He left everything else in his hide and started to climb the hill behind which the plane had disappeared. When he topped the hill and got a view of the valley, his eyes were drawn immediately to the ranch buildings. One was a modest home and the other was a spacious barn. Leading directly away from the buildings were two apparent dirt roads. One was the actual road that led to the house and connected to some other road in the distance. The second was a dirt runway. It started near the barn and ran straight away, parallel to the long axis of the valley. Davis recognized the plane as a Cessna 172. It had landed and was now taxiing toward the barn. Davis found a spot that afforded good concealment and started studying the area with his binoculars.

The plane pivoted and came to a stop facing down the runway. The engine stopped, and the single occupant of the plane disembarked. In a moment, he was greeted by a barking dog. From the house, two boys joined the arrival party. After hugs, the taller boy went to the barn and returned with a pair of tie-down cords. The pilot attached the cords to the underside of each wing and then to a pair of weights made from concrete-filled tires. The man wore a gray shirt with large letters embroidered on the back. With the plane secure, the group adjourned to the house.

Davis spent more than an hour studying the area around the ranch house. The plane seemed so out of place. The house seemed too modest for the owner to also own an airplane. Even though the scene was desolate, the house sported a satellite dish. The ubiquitous pickup truck was parked in front of the house. Davis' eyes kept returning to the plane.

Just before sundown, the man and the taller boy reappeared. The boy went to the barn while the man appeared to be checking the plane. In a moment, a flatbed truck with a large tank appeared and parked next to the plane. It was a fuel truck. The pilot filled the wing tanks of the plane and then finished his essential post-flight chores. Davis noted that the door of the fuel truck had the same letters that were on the man's shirt. Davis theorized that the man worked for some company that required the services of a pilot to fly inspections of pipelines or power lines or whatever their needs. The man and boy returned to the house just before dark.

Davis made his way back over the hill to his hideaway. By the time he arrived, he was shivering with a fever and had difficulty stifling a productive cough. He ate a little jerky and sipped his declining water supply carefully. The wind was picking up and he knew that he was in for a very bad night. He reworked his head wound and then climbed into his sleeping bag with his flashlight and maps. He covered his head to block the wind and any escaping light.

Davis studied the maps for a long time. His best estimation placed him still a minimum of eighty miles from the nearest US border. That was bad enough, but as you neared the border the towns became larger and closer together. The zigzag route that would probably be necessary would add at least thirty more miles. He thought about his present circumstance and slowly shook his head. Images of the snowball in hell came to mind. He admitted to himself that no one could have that much luck in any one crisis. He thought that he had been doing well until the mountain lion. He sighed heavily and coughed painfully. "Fucking mountain lion!"

At 2:00 a.m. he came to a simple, two-part conclusion. First, if he did not get home soon, he was a dead man. Second, the fastest way home was the Cessna on the other side of the mountain. The Cessna was the only answer to his complex, multi-layered problem. However, there was one fundamental but overwhelming problem. He was not a pilot. He would have to somehow press the man on the other side of the mountain into his service.

Davis began to think about what he would have to do. He would have to take the man at gunpoint and make him fly him home. The painfully obvious weak point in that plan was that once airborne, the will of the pilot rules. He would have to take one of his children as the trump card. He would be able to force his will on the pilot if the life of his child was on the line.

He visualized kicking in the door and terrorizing the pilot and his family. In the next instant, he realized that he was getting sicker and weaker by the minute. What if the man overpowered him? Then the man would collect a fat reward, and old Brooks would be back in the hands of the terrorists with his head squarely on the chopping block.

Davis went back to the maps. He drew in a line that represented the dirt runway. It struck him that the runway was pointing northeast. If you extended the line, it would pass just west of San Antonio. He took a sip of water and took more aspirin. He turned out the flashlight and tried to sleep. As he drifted off into a fever-driven delirium, his last cogent thoughts were of the single flying lesson that he had when he was in college.

He awoke before daylight feeling worse than the day before. Every part of him ached. The thought of his rancid jerky made him retch. He forced himself up and repacked his gear. His first goal was to get over the hill and move into a better position to observe the plane and the inhabitants of the ranch. He found a perfect, secluded vantage point about halfway down the slope about 300 yards from the plane. At 6:00 a.m. the lights of the house were switched on around the house. With daylight coming on at 6:45, the woman and the boys left the house and piled into the truck and left. Davis thought that they were probably heading to school and work.

According to the maps, the nearest town was San Melchor, about nine miles away. The pilot stayed in the house until around 9:00 a.m. He did a few chores in and around the barn and spent some time checking something in the cockpit of the plane. He moved in and out of the house erratically until noon when he went in and never came back out. At 4:30 the woman and two boys came home.

When the boys returned, they played outside with the dog. Davis watched them closely and with substantial melancholy. Their actions were so reminiscent of his sons. He looked at the house and could visualize the woman preparing the evening meal. He fantasized about what she made. He fought a deep pang in his chest, wondering what Molly was doing at that moment. Just before dark the woman called the boys in for supper. Their names were Paulo and Xavier.

That night Davis was torn. He asked himself a litany of questions. *How should I proceed? Should I wait until 3 a.m. and then kick in the door and try to establish control with shock and awe? It will be dark. What if I can't get control of the man? What if he sleeps with a .357 magnum on the nightstand? Then he either kills me or I kill the pilot. That would be an all-lose situation. Should I try to go for one of the boys to put the father under my control?* That thought made Davis once again think of his boys. He shook his head. He just could not do that. After all, he now knew their names. He had another, darker thought. What if one of the boys somehow died at his hand? After all, he had killed men, and he had killed women. But the thought of dead children engulfed him in black despair.

The more questions he asked himself, the fewer satisfactory answers he came up with. Davis was tired. He was more physically and mentally beaten than at any point in his life. The more he contemplated terrorizing the man and his family the less he could stand it. He would be no better than the terrorists who had kidnapped him. The parallel of the actions that he was contemplating against this family were the same as what had happened to his own family.

At midnight he thought of a plan that was an incredible long shot. At first, he attributed the idea to the delirium that accompanied the fever. As a second thought, he realized that in his present condition, it was really the only thing that he had left to save himself. The one certainty was that there was no way he was going to make it to the border on foot. This plan would either save him or put a sure end to his misery. It was sort of like involuntary suicide. A strange sort of calm came over him. Historically, he always felt better after he made a very difficult decision. His favorite proverb crossed through his fevered mind. "Desperate times call for desperate measures."

He would steal the Cessna and fly himself home.

CHAPTER TWENTY-FOUR

The Widow's Revenge

Tina's thought-provoking discussion rattled around Molly's brain for two days. The way that Tina had emphasized her "contributions" to the business had finally raised a magnum-sized red flag in Molly's stressed-out brain.

Molly dialed up the personal number of Dwight Lee, the owner of Texas Custom Homes. Dwight was one of Brooks' major competitors, but also a very good friend and golfing buddy.

"Dwight, Molly."

"Hey! How are you guys doing? Please tell me that you've finally thought of a favor that I can help you with."

"We are doing alright, and yes, I have a favor to ask."

"Anything. What do you need?"

"You know, last year when you guys were at the national trade show in Chicago?"

"Yes"

"Brooks' construction super, Tina Landry, was also at the show and had her boyfriend with her...some banking guy...I need his name. Do you know her boyfriend's name?"

There was a long pause. "Are you still there, Dwight?"

"Ah, I'm not sure I remember. Can't you ask Tina?"

Molly squinted her eyes shut and let him stew for a moment.

"It's very important for me to know, Dwight."

"Well...ah..."

"Was his name Brooks?"

Molly could hear Dwight audibly exhale through the phone.

"Molly...honey...I don't know anything for sure. And Susan and I love both you and Brooks. And I sure as hell don't want to say something bad about anybody who is probably dead. Oh hell! I'm so sorry for saying that, but you get where I'm coming from, right?"

Tears rolled down Molly's cheeks. "So, they appeared to be... together, right?"

After another long pause, "If I had to guess. I'm so sorry, Molly"

IN THE LAW OFFICES OF MEYERS, GOLDSMITH & MARTIN

Robert Goldsmith had been the Davis family and business attorney for fifteen years. Molly was proceeding through a small stack of papers and signing each on the line opposite a small, yellow sticky note arrow. When she finished, the lawyer collated the papers into a neat stack and placed them in a folder tagged "Tina Landry."

"Okay, Molly. This should be very simple. You call Ms. Landry and nonchalantly tell her that you need her to come by my office to pick up some papers. When she arrives, I will sit her down and explain that you, as acting CEO, have elected to terminate her employment immediately according to the terms of her employment contract that she probably did not read carefully, and that Brooks was smart enough to let me put together four years ago. She will be given two certified checks. The first will be for her final regular pay, and the second will be for her calculated quarterly bonus. She will be paid in full and can't come back against you on the financial side."

"She will then be served with a witnessed restraining order that prohibits her from approaching within 500 yards of any Davis Construction Company Office or Building Project or the personal or vacation residence of Mr. or Mrs. Brooks Davis or the schools of their children. I will then give her a copy of the statutes and penalties for violations of the restraining order. Finally, she will be asked if she has questions."

"How about you, Molly? Anything you need to add?"

Molly gave her lawyer a glum look. "Other than Brooks is a sonofabitch, I guess not."

The lawyer gave her a fatherly look in return. "Molly, I know you have been through hell. If our worst fears about Brooks are true, try to remember this. That sonofabitch...that randy old sonofabitch...was once, for you, the pick of the litter. And he will always be the father of your sons. My advice, protect your sons from this part of their father. He is still their hero. Give them the image that he probably went down fighting and took a couple of them with him. Do that for the boys."

Molly slowly shook her head as she got up to leave. "I don't know if I'm that strong."

CHAPTER TWENTY-FIVE

Penance Fully Paid

Davis ate one of his last three pieces of jerky for breakfast. He watched as the woman and boys left home right on schedule. He was about to move toward the runway when the man exited the house carrying a small overnight bag. He went to the Cessna, opened the cockpit door, and placed the bag in the back seat. At 300 yards, Davis knew that he could not get to the plane in time. The man made a cursory inspection of the plane and removed the tie-downs from the struts. He climbed into the cockpit and a moment later the engine turned over. He let it idle for a short while and then applied power and quickly rolled straight down the dirt runway. He rapidly picked up speed and halfway down the runway he lifted off and climbed away. Davis watched helplessly as the plane banked east and flew away.

Davis' plan imploded like a house of cards. He had planned to wait until the wife and children were gone and then take the man by surprise. He was going to use the handcuffs that he had carried since his escape to secure the man to some immovable object. He would then study the plane at his leisure until he felt ready that he could fly away to safety or to his untimely death.

He realized that the man and his family could change their routine and add days of waiting. He did not know how many days he could hold on waiting for another opportunity.

The woman and boys did stick to their routine and were home well before dark. However, when night fell the plane did not return. Davis had expected it because of the overnight bag carried by the pilot.

What followed were two more days and nights of ever-increasing despair and diminishing physical stamina.

With food completely gone and only about half a cup of water, Davis thought long and hard about entering the house when the woman and boys were gone to forage for food and water. He felt certain that living in the middle of nowhere would make locking the house unnecessary. He could probably walk in and help himself to what he needed. If he was careful, they would not even know he was there. There was, however, the prospect of two possible complicating factors. The first was the dog. If he was a valiant guard dog, he might have to dispatch him and hide the body. The second was the prospect that as soon as he was in the house, the man could return and force a premature confrontation. Davis decided that if the plane had not returned by the next day, he would enter the house at any cost. That evening the woman and boys returned right on time. Thirty minutes before dark the plane returned as well.

Davis watched closely as the man serviced the plane. With the wing tanks filled and the plane tied down, the man went into the house for the night. As soon as the back door closed, Davis slowly sipped the last of his water and then packed his gear. He tried to sleep but he could not keep his eyes off the lights shining through the windows. By 10:15 p.m. the last light went out.

At 2:00 a.m. Davis moved out. He approached the plane from down runway. The wind had changed in his favor. His scent was blowing away from the dog. He moved slowly, frequently stopping and listening for signs that he may have been discovered.

When he reached the plane, it was 2:45 a.m.. He waited and listened. The only sound was of a dying wind. He felt for and carefully removed the tie-downs from the wing struts and left them on the ground. He felt for the recessed door handle on the port side door. When he located it and applied pressure, it opened with a loud click. Davis squinted in the dark at the sound and clenched his teeth. He froze and waited for the dog to begin barking. He was rewarded with quiet.

He opened the door of the plane and carefully placed the backpack and rifles in the back seat. With a final look around, he slowly climbed into the plane behind the left control column and settled into the seat. He only partially closed the door for fear that he would alert the dog. He decided that if he got airborne without killing himself, he could slam the door shut then.

The night was very dark, and Davis could not make out any of the details of the control panel of the plane. His hands slowly moved over the control column and panel, trying to see if he could identify anything in the blackness. Nothing felt familiar. His mind went back to his short-lived experience with flight school when he was a senior in college. After five ground school classes where he was familiarized with the fundamentals of powered flight and the functions of the Cessna's controls, he and his instructor went for a first flight one hot summer afternoon.

As a confidence-building exercise, the instructor lined the plane up on the centerline of the runway and then gave Davis the controls and told him to apply power and take off. He told him to just keep the control column straight and level and the plane would lift off by itself.

Davis' joy at getting the plane airborne and gaining altitude without crashing in flames was short-lived. As soon as he cleared 500 feet, the buffeting winds began. What followed was the wildest thirty minutes that he had ever experienced in motion. When the seasoned instructor nearly crashed on landing, the confidence of the student approached absolute zero. After thirty minutes of vomiting, a younger Davis vowed to never consider a small plane again. Now, twenty years later he was forced to break that vow.

Davis retrieved the flashlight. He covered the lens with his fingers but let a tiny shaft of light bleed from between his fingers. He slowly studied each of the dials and gauges on the control panel. He was surprised that nothing looked overly foreign. A simple key was in the ignition. After a moment of trepidation, he turned it to the on position. The entire control panel lit up brightly. He checked the fuel gauges and noted with relief that the tanks were indeed full. He quickly turned the key off and returned the cockpit to the comfort of complete darkness.

He checked his watch: 3:15 a.m. He closed his eyes and assessed his physical and mental states. Mentally, he was only a few grades better than coma. Physically, he knew that he was in trouble. The effects of starvation, dehydration, infection, and sleep deprivation were not just additive but were affecting each other in a logarithmic way. It suddenly struck him that this is how someone feels who is slowly dying.

His mind flashed back to each time during the ordeal that he was certain that he was living his final moments. He closed his eyes and relived the feeling behind his heart and in the pit of his stomach that accompanied each event. He opened his eyes and stared at the darkened silhouette of the control panel. With the thought of what he was about to attempt, and the fact that you can successfully dodge only so many bullets, the sickening feeling returned. He took a deep breath, which made him cough. He whispered to himself, "Who knows, maybe God will grant me one last miracle."

By 4:30 a.m. he had carefully reviewed each instrument and control in the cockpit. As he studied the controls, his mind strained to remember what he had learned in ground school so many years ago. He remembered that the instructor had a quirky way of emphasizing a critically important point about flying a light aircraft. He would make a point and punctuate it by saying, "You will want to remember this, because if you don't, it will probably kill you."

Davis was as ready as he would ever be. He resigned himself to wait until he could just see the outline of the dirt runway and then he would start up. He hoped that the family was on schedule, and they would not be up earlier than their usual 6:00 a.m. when there was barely enough light to see the runway.

At 5:45 a.m. it was still pitch dark. He started getting panicky.

What if they got up early? Would he be able to get the aircraft started and taxiing before the man came out shooting? He tried to focus on the eastern horizon and not his watch. Even though it was a cold morning he could feel a colder sweat forming on his forehead. He said an Our Father, a Hail Mary, and an Act of Contrition, trying to get right with God. He remembered that his father always referred to a person's final prayers as "cramming for the final." The desperate feeling in his gut told him that he had not prepared adequately for such a critical exam.

His final prayers brought the image of Molly clearly to the front and center of Brooks' mind. It was as though she was looking at him from the other side of the windscreen of the Cessna, and she was not smiling. Brooks had a sudden, gut-wrenching feeling that Tina had not only told Molly of his indiscretion, but in a spiteful rage, made a scene in front of the boys. Brooks thought once again about the whole concept of forgiveness. A benevolent God can forgive anything, but is it realistic to expect forgiveness from a whole family of broken-hearted humans?

At 5:55 a.m. Davis looked at his watch and gasped. The lights would be coming on in five minutes! It was still dark. The thought of a blind takeoff terrified him. His mind conjured up the vision of a fiery crash. The next moment he had a different thought. He wondered what day of the week it was. He tried to count the times that the woman and boys left, presumably for work and school. What if it was the weekend? Would they sleep in? Would that give him enough time and light for takeoff?

Davis watched the second hand move toward the twelve announcing 6:00 a.m. He glanced at the house. No lights. He invoked the deity. "Please, God, let it be the weekend!"

He looked to the east and could see that the horizon was beginning to lighten.

As he looked down the runway, he was rewarded with the dim but visible outline of the edges of the strip. He was happy to see that it was about the size of a four-lane highway and that the plane was precisely centered for takeoff. It was perfectly quiet with no wind. It was now or never. He closed his eyes, said one more prayer for good measure, powered up the control panel, and hit the starter.

The prop began to spin with the typical stutter of a cold engine start. The sound seemed deafening in his ears. His heart rate jumped from 80 to 150 beats per minute. With no more need for quiet, he cajoled the engine.

"Come on, baby! Start for Daddy!"

After a very long fifteen seconds of rising panic, Davis glanced at the house. No lights. His second plea was less polite.

"Start, you son of a bitch!"

The engine coughed and caught. The prop came up to speed and became invisible. Davis turned his head at the precise moment that the first light came on.

"Oh shit! We gotta go!"

Without benefit of the usual warm-up, he throttled up the engine RPM. The soft balloon tires broke loose, and the plane began to roll. He did not look back at the house because he could visualize the scene.

The man was rocked out of a dream about a mountain lion eating one of his goats. It took a few seconds for all the synapses to close and to realize that the company's Cessna that he was responsible for was currently being stolen. He exploded out of the bed, startling his wife awake. He did not have the .357 magnum on the nightstand that Davis had visualized, but the Winchester Model 94 lever action .30-.30 was in its usual place in the corner of the room. He flipped on the bedroom light, retrieved the rifle, cycled the action, and headed for the back door.

Davis concentrated on keeping the control column forward and level to prevent premature liftoff that would precipitate a stall. He also concentrated on keeping the plane heading straight down the runway. His feet were on the rudder pedals, but he dared not apply any pressure to either one. He prayed that he stayed on the runway until the plane became airborne. Twenty knots became thirty, thirty became forty. Hope and despair battled in his belly.

The man flew out the back door and ran for the airstrip. The plane was already nearly a hundred yards away and near takeoff speed. As he shouldered the rifle and took aim, he knew that it would not really make a difference. The cartel pilot stealing the Cessna must be an expert because only an expert would attempt a take-off without even a minute of warm-up. In anger and desperation, he took a shot at the departing plane.

Davis glanced down at the airspeed indicator. As it touched fifty knots the sound of a loud thump drew his attention to the left strut. The rifle bullet carved a nasty gash in the aluminum wing support. His head snapped back to the front. Davis wondered if there was an official, Vatican-approved patron saint of pilots that he should be presently invoking.

At fifty-eight knots Davis could feel the Cessna go airborne. He resisted the temptation to pull back on the control column and increase the angle of climb. The little aircraft was very well maintained and steadily gained altitude and airspeed without overt encouragement from the amateur pilot. As the Cessna climbed into the cold, dense early morning air Davis remembered his flight instructor's often repeated admonition that airspeed provides lift, lift provides altitude, and altitude usually prevents you from crashing into tall, immovable objects like skyscrapers or mountains.

At that moment he looked out his starboard window and saw the first rays of sunlight peek above the mountains in the distant east. His eyes traced the ridgeline to his front. He was heading across the broad valley to a range of immovable objects that were currently at a higher altitude than the Cessna.

Thus far, the plane had simply flown by itself. But like it or not, Davis was about to be required to get personally involved.

CHAPTER TWENTY-SIX

What Goes Up May Crash

The mountains grew steadily in the windscreen of the Cessna. Davis studied the altimeter. It read 1,500 feet and slowly climbing. He wondered what the altitude of the mountains to his front was and if at his present rate of climb he could get over the top. As he closed on the mountains, he could see that the ridgeline was lower in height to the west. He was tempted to try to turn the plane in that direction, but he was only now getting a little optimistic about flying essentially straight and with a modest rate of climb. He was not yet enthusiastic about trying to turn the aircraft left or right.

He watched the mountains and decided that he would cross them with altitude to spare. In the increasing light, he could now see other mountains in the distance. They seemed similar in height, so his apprehension began to subside. He was still on a gentle climb. The ground was getting further and further away. He could now see the network of small rural roads. To the east, he could make a more substantial divided highway. There was a fair amount of early morning traffic. The cars still had their headlights on.

Davis checked the altimeter. He had just crossed 2,500 feet and was still climbing. He eased the control column forward. The altimeter came to a brief stop and started to reverse with loss of altitude. He worked at keeping the plane at 2,500 feet.

Fifteen minutes into the flight with a glorious sunrise to the east, Davis began to breathe normally. After a moment of reflection, he began to softly chuckle. The chuckle became a full-blown laugh. He shook his head in utter disbelief. He addressed himself out loud.

"Brooks, you crazy son of a bitch! You actually got this thing airborne without killing yourself. I can't believe it! And as a bonus, you are pointing in the general direction of Texas!"

He had a sudden thought. He scanned the instrument panel for the airspeed indicator. He was traveling just under 120 miles per hour. He made a quick calculation.

"I'm moving two miles a minute! If that ranch was less than 100 miles from the border, I could be crossing the Rio Grande in less than fifty minutes! Jesus Christ! Could that be possible?"

He was shaken out of his reverie by a set of flashing red lights just to the right of the nose of the plane. It was an oncoming aircraft traveling at approximately the same altitude. The feeling of rising panic returned. It occurred to him that the man on the ranch certainly called the authorities to report the theft of the Cessna. What would they do? Would they call the military? Would the military scramble some sort of intercept to prevent him from entering US airspace? There were too many questions with no answers.

He strained to identify the oncoming aircraft. It turned slightly on a course that would intercept the Cessna at some distance ahead. With the turn, he could identify the aircraft as a helicopter. His mind immediately replayed the confrontation with the helicopter on the day of his escape. He remembered in excruciating detail how the door gunner sent the stream of tracer rounds to the ground trying to flush him from his hiding place. Davis knew that the little Cessna was helpless. He wondered how they had found him so quickly. The word radar snapped into his mind. At 2,500 feet he was certainly easy to track on radar.

He looked at the terrain below him. The mountainous land had given way to rolling hills and wide areas of flatter ground. He decided he needed to get to a lower altitude. The maneuver would accomplish two goals. First, if the helicopter followed, it would mean that they were indeed on an intercept. Secondly, he would try to get under the radar. With no shortage of trepidation, Davis pushed the control forward and watched the altimeter unwind. He tried to divide his attention between the helicopter and the onrushing ground. He could feel the airspeed rising but he was too frightened to look at the indicator. At some point, he lost sight of the helicopter and just concentrated on keeping his wings level and tail straight. At 500 feet he started to slowly level out. At 300 feet, he was able to reacquire the helicopter off his left-wing tip. It had not changed direction and was still at 2,500 feet. He was traveling, not intercepting.

Davis was elated but there still was the question of radar. He could not remember how low you had to fly to be under the radar. Intuitively he knew that it must be below 300 feet. With rising anxiety, he nudged the control column forward and watched as the ground began to rise.

When the altimeter hit 100 feet, Davis could no longer stand his rising panic, and he slowly leveled out. He seemed to be very close to the ground, and at 120 miles per hour it was scarier than his heart could stand. He knew that at this altitude there was no room for error. He decided that if he was still on the radar screen, he would just have to live with it and pray harder.

Ten minutes later he could see a town approaching in the distance right off the nose of the plane. He glanced at the altimeter and was shocked to see that he had sunk to eighty feet. That was scary, but the fact he was on a straight line with the municipal water tower was much worse. Davis swallowed hard and realized that like it or not, if he was going to remain under the radar, he would have to quickly learn how to turn the nose of the plane, or it was Cessna versus immovable object in less than a minute.

Davis gingerly dipped the right wing and slightly depressed the right rudder pedal. He was rewarded with the plane turning away from the water tower and toward more open airspace. Once clear of the small town he returned to straight and level flight at 100 feet. A few minutes later, he crossed over the runways of a small municipal airport. He swept by before he had time to worry whether he had just violated a traffic pattern. He could visualize the Mexican air traffic controller going crazy trying to contact him by radio. He decided even before he took off that morning that he would not turn on the radios until he was in US airspace.

Flying at such a low altitude kept his mind so completely occupied that when he flew over a river it took him a long moment to ask himself if that might have been the Rio Grande. When he looked at his watch and realized that he had been airborne for forty-eight minutes, Davis began to shout, "Yes! Yes! That's the Rio Grande!"

He was jolted out of his moment of geographic realization by suddenly flying through a rising thermal that buffeted the plane. Davis was in serious need of a safer altitude. He added power and nursed the control column backward. When he got to 1,200 feet he thought of the radio. When he first studied the control panel by flashlight, he noted a piece of tape attached to the panel just above the UHF/VHF radio set. Printed on the tape were the initials USACT and a specific radio frequency. He had bigger problems on his mind at the time and did not give the tape a thought. As he switched on the radio he took a second look at the tape. He stared at the letters for a moment before it hit him. US Air Traffic Control.

Davis dialed the frequency, placed the headset over his ears, and adjusted the voice-actuated mic to the corner of his mouth. He thought for a moment about what to say. He wondered if anyone would respond.

"Ah... US Air Traffic Control this is a Cessna 172 coming out of Mexico on a heading of thirty-three degrees at an altitude of 1,200 feet declaring an inflight emergency. Ah...over."

Davis listened to the background noise in the headphones for a few seconds. He rechecked that he had the frequency dialed in correctly. He was about to repeat his distress call when a clear voice replied.

"Cessna 172 on a heading of thirty-three degrees at 1,200 feet, this is US Air Traffic Control, please state your aircraft identification number and state your emergency, over."

Davis gasped. The sound of a clear, friendly American voice took his breath away. His throat suddenly went bone dry. He tried to make a reply, but nothing came out. The American controller repeated his request for an ID number and emergency. Davis finally got out a reply.

"US Air Traffic Control, I can't tell you how great it is to hear you. Please bear with me and I'll try to explain my situation. I don't know what the ID number is. My name is Brooks Davis. I'm from San Antonio. Maybe a month ago I was kidnapped by ISIS terrorists along with Raymond Epstein. We were taken to Mexico. I managed to escape and have been fighting my way back to the border ever since. Earlier today I stole this airplane and managed to get out of Mexico."

After a pause, the controller replied, "Mr. Davis we have you on radar. You appear to be flying straight and level and in control. Can you state your emergency?"

"Well, the emergency is that I'm not a pilot and I've never landed a plane before!"

"Is Mr. Epstein a pilot?"

"Mr. Epstein is dead."

"So, you are alone?"

"That's affirmative!"

"So, if you are not a pilot, how did you get airborne?"

"I guess the one flying lesson I had twenty years ago must have stuck."

There was a long pause from the controller. "Mr. Davis, just take it easy and try to keep it straight and level. Do not change heading or altitude. That is very important. I'm going to get the word out and clear the airspace in front of you. The next voice you hear will be the station supervisor, Bob Thacker. He will try to make a plan for you. Remember, straight and level and no changes without our permission. Over."

"Great! A plan is just what I need! Ah...over."

Davis checked his heading and altitude and was satisfied that things were stable. He glanced at his watch. It was 6:59 a.m.. He thought that in less than one hour he had escaped a hell of despair. It somehow felt too easy. After all the pain and misery, he was suddenly teleported back to a place where hope was possible. He knew that landing the plane without killing himself was going to take a major miracle, but miracles were already happening this day.

"Mr. Davis. This is Bob Thacker. Are you with me?"

"Call me Brooks and yes, I'm with you. Please tell me you've got a plan."

"We are sure going to give it the old college try, Brooks. You appear to be in pretty good control of that Cessna. And you say you only had one flying lesson twenty years ago?"

"Yes, but it really did not go that well. And I definitely did not land the plane."

"Well, whoever that instructor was, he must have been a genius about take-offs and straight and level flight. How are you at turns?"

"I've made a couple of very small course corrections. They worked out alright, but Bob, I've got to tell you that my confidence level is not great when it comes to turns."

"You flew out of Mexico and you made no turns?"

"Not like a left or right turn. I took off, got to 2,500 feet, had to descend to 100 feet to get across the border, and then back up to this altitude, and that's it. That's the sum total of my flying experience to date."

"Why did you descend to 100 feet? That's very dangerous territory."

"To get under the radar."

Thacker grimaced in confusion. "Why did you want to get under the radar?"

"Because of the fucking Mexican Army!"

Thacker looked at his fellow controllers gathered around the radar scope and shook his head and shrugged his shoulders. "I don't follow, Brooks."

"It is a long, long story, Bob. I'll tell you what. If you figure out how to get me down in one piece, we will get together over as many beers as you can drink, and I will tell you the whole sordid tale."

"I look forward to it with bated breath. You keep flying straight and I'll have a plan for you in a few minutes."

"Roger that, Bob. I'll be waiting."

CHAPTER TWENTY-SEVEN
Conflict with the Home Team

Thacker declared a regional air traffic emergency and started to issue orders.

"Jim, I want you clearing traffic on his heading from the ground to 5,000 feet."

"Already on it," replied the controller who had made the initial contact with Davis.

"Sam, Carol, Ted. Hand your sectors off to your backups and stick with me."

After the controllers handed off their areas of responsibility to other controllers, they gathered around their supervisor for instructions.

"Sam, get Homeland Security on the horn. Tell them what we've got. Let them know where we picked him up and ask what their long-range radars showed. Tell them he either sounds legit or he is a really good actor. It will be their call if they scramble an intercept out of Del Rio."

"Carol, get FBI San Antonio notified. Their counterterrorism group will have a task force active on the Davis-Epstein kidnappings because they are unsolved."

"Ted, on his current heading, what are our options for some nice safe place for the possibility of a less than controlled landing?"

Ted thought for a moment.

"His heading will take him right between the small airports at Hondo and Castroville. Hondo has two north-south runways, and the Castroville strip runs northwest to southeast. To the east of those, you get into the big stuff in San Antonio. San Antonio International, Randolph Air Force Base, and Kelly, USA."

Thacker stroked his chin while in thought.

"If he is legit, he will really need something long and wide. If he is a terrorist with a good Texas accent, hauling a load of anthrax and TNT, Homeland will want to keep him as far away from major population centers at all costs. Since this mess started, they have had their finger on a hair trigger, twenty-four-seven. If they decide that he is a threat, they will probably order a shootdown before he gets anywhere near San Antonio." He turned to Jim and asked, "What is his current airspeed?"

"Ninety knots, steady. No change in heading or altitude."

Thacker did the quick math and turned to Sam and Carol.

"Tell Homeland and the FBI that whoever oversees making big decisions had better be thinking at warp speed. At current speed and location, if he turns toward San Antonio, he will be there pretty quick."

The big decision maker at regional Homeland Security was Gerard Lindsay. When he got the call and was apprised of the situation, he immediately began to earn his pay.

"Tell ATC to vector this guy away from San Antonio. I don't care where, so long as it is west, away from San Antonio. Second, patch me through to the commander of the 228th Fighter Wing at Laughlin in Del Rio."

It took four minutes to get Colonel John Wainwright patched through to Lindsay.

"This is Colonel Wainwright. How can I help you, Mr. Lindsay?"
Lindsay did not beat around the bush.

"There is a possible airborne terrorist threat in a Cessna just coming out of Mexico. He is moving in the general direction of San Antonio. Scramble a loaded interceptor. Instruct the crew that we will want to try for visual confirmation on the pilot. Should the aircraft be deemed a legitimate threat, they should be prepared for a shootdown. Homeland radars will vector the fighter for the intercept."

Wainwright triggered an alert device that he wore around his neck on a chain. It sounded a claxon horn in a special hangar where a fully loaded F-15 fighter was parked. The aircraft as well as the air and ground crews were in a state of perpetual readiness. The claxon also alerted the base control tower that a real intercept, not a drill, was taking place. Their job was to clear the taxi aprons, runways, and all the airspace downrange of the main runway. The time that the horn sounded to wheels-up for the fighter was six minutes.

Lindsay's next call was to his boss, David Ratzner, the secretary of Homeland Security. Ratzner listened to Lindsay's description of the threat and his overall plan. Satisfied, Ratzner gave Lindsay authority to run the operation to its conclusion. He did not have to tell Lindsay to keep him in the loop in real-time so that the White House would also be on top.

"Brooks, we've got the beginnings of a plan for you," said Thacker.

"That's good news, Bob."

"We want you to turn very slowly northwest. Treat this just like the course correction you described before. Slow and easy. You are in charge of how fast you do this so don't rush."

"Where are we heading?"

"We want to put you on a vector for the north-south runway at the Hondo municipal airport. There is a flight school there. We are getting one of their instructor pilots in a similar Cessna to fly alongside you and to talk you down."

"That sounds good. Is the runway plenty long and wide?"

"About average for a small-town airport."

"I hope that is sort of a yes, Bob."

"Should be adequate," came the reply.

Davis was not enthralled by the controller's answers. They did not answer his query about "long and wide." He could feel hope's tenuous grasp starting to slip. He took a deep breath and wrote it off to fever, infection, and fatigue. He dipped his left wing ever so slightly and began the slow course correction. It took about ten minutes to get Davis on the vector for Hondo north-south. Davis found the exercise very taxing.

"Brooks, in a couple of minutes an aircraft is going to show up off your left wing. Don't panic or anything—just keep flying straight and level. They are going to look your aircraft over for any damage or anything that might make landing a problem. Be sure to look right at them."

"Is it the guy with the Cessna?"

"No, Brooks, it's actually going to be a military aircraft."

"Not the Cessna?"

"No. The Cessna will meet up with you when you are closer to Hondo."

Davis thought about it for a moment. "I'm pretty sure that there is no damage to the plane. It's practically flying itself."

"Don't worry, Brooks. Merely a formality with this kind of emergency."

"Whatever you say, Bob."

Davis was convinced of the mere formality thing until the armed-to-the-teeth F-15 pulled up 100 yards off his port wing. Davis needed some reassurance from his new pal Thacker.

"Hey, Bob, are you there?"

"I guess you can see the military aircraft about now."

"Oh yeah. You didn't tell me that it would look so hostile."

"Oh no, Brooks, they're not hostile. Just a couple of good boys out of Del Rio. Listen, Brooks, you are going to have to apply more power to speed up. An F-15 generally doesn't like to fly as slow as a Cessna."

Brooks adjusted the throttle, and the little plane accelerated.

"That's great, Brooks. Are you looking at them?"

"They are photographing me, aren't they, Bob?"

After a slight pause, Thacker replied, "You are very astute, Brooks."

It did not take a CIA operative to realize what was happening.

"I suppose that in this increased terror threat environment you can't be too careful."

"Like I said, Brooks, you are very astute. Smile pretty."

Davis did just that. He turned to the fighter and waved and gave them a thumbs-up. In the F-15, the weapons officer in the back seat focused a high-definition digital video camera on the plane and zoomed in on Davis' face. When he got twenty seconds of clear video, he turned off the camera and returned the wave and thumbs-up. He satellite up-linked the video to the FBI Intel group in Quantico, Virginia. Their technical gurus sent the images through their facial recognition software driven by their Kray supercomputers. It took the Kray 450 milliseconds to map Davis' face and compare it to the images of the contractor's face that resided in the computer's memory banks. It then performed a long series of probability calculations and reported simultaneously to Homeland Security and the FBI San Antonio field office that there was a 62.488 percent chance that the guy flying the Cessna over South Texas was the man known as Brooks Davis. It further reported that there were no external modifications of the plane that could be identified as a threat. Interior views of the aircraft were deemed inadequate to determine the mathematical probability of a threat inside the plane other than the pilot. The probability was low because the subject in the plane unlike the database photos had a substantial growth of beard and a large scar on his forehead. That coupled with refractive errors caused by shooting the video through the ballistic Plexiglas of the F-15 and the aircraft safety glass of the Cessna made a conclusive match difficult.

Back at Homeland Security, it was Lindsay's call. The sixty-two percent probability was just too low to make him warm and fuzzy about the intentions of the man flying the Cessna. When the F-15 pulled up and away, Davis did not know whether to be relieved or to stand by for the air-to-air missile. When nothing happened immediately, he tried to be optimistic.

"Are they satisfied that I'm the real thing?"

"It will take some time for analysis," lied Thacker.

"What's the news from Hondo?"

"Our instructor pilot is fueled and taking off as we speak."

"So, I'm lined up for a straight-in landing?"

"That's the plan for now."

"What if I can't make the landing on the first try?"

"Then we will have you regain altitude and fly a sort of rectangular pattern and try again."

When Thacker said "rectangular," Davis' mind flashed back to his classroom at flight school. He remembered that after an aborted approach, you would make a new approach by conducting four ninety-degree turns to get to the starting point of a new approach.

"Oh, Bob! You are talking about all those ninety-degree turns. I don't know about those turns."

"Brooks, you worry too much. If you can steal a plane and fly it under the radar out of Mexico, you should be able to land on a nice flat runway without breaking a sweat."

Davis pondered Thacker's comments for a moment. He was about to ask another question, but the controller spoke first.

"Brooks, we've got an FBI guy on the horn. He needs to talk to you. We're patching him through now." A new voice came online.

"Mr. Davis, I'm Martin Collier, the special agent in charge of the San Antonio field office."

"Good to hear from you. What can I do for the FBI?"

"As you can imagine we are very pleased that you have resurfaced. I would like to ask you a series of questions. Some will sound odd and maybe somewhat personal. But they are questions that only Brooks Davis should be able to answer."

"I get it. Is the guy in the plane old Brooks Davis, or some terrorist in disguise?"

"Exactly. So, bear with us. What is your wife's maiden name?"

"Turner," replied Davis without hesitation.

"What is your youngest son's middle name?"

"William."

"What grade is he in and where?"

"Fourth. St. Matthew's Catholic School. His teacher is named Evans," he added for good measure.

"What color is your wife's favorite nightgown?"

Davis was startled by the question. He thought for a moment.

"White, I guess. She usually wears one of my tee shirts."

"Before Mr. Epstein, whose house did you build and where?"

"Spurs power forward Jeremiah Fellows, in the Dominion. You satisfied yet, Collier?"

"Almost. Are you armed?"

Again, Davis was caught a bit off guard.

"Well, yes, as a matter of fact, I am."

"What kind of weapon do you have?"

"Actually, I have three."

"What kind of weapons?"

"I've got an AK-47, a custom rifle in 7mm magnum, and a .40 cal pistol."

Collier made a gesture to Agent Dayton, who rushed out of the room, and then he quickly changed the subject. "I'm satisfied that you are you. But what happened to Epstein?"

"I'm pretty sure he died of a heart attack that was brought on by all the dope they shot us up with."

There was a pause. "Do you know where in Mexico they took you?"

"East of the town of Jimenez in the state of Chihuahua. I've got topo maps in my backpack. If I live through this, I'll show you the building I escaped from."

"You told the controller that you fought your way out of Mexico. Why did you have to fight? Why did you not find some authority and get help?"

Davis answered like he was lecturing a dense student.

"Because the fucking Mexican Army is in cahoots with ISIS, and they are both in cahoots with the cartels, and in my humble opinion, everybody else is on someone's payroll. If I went to anybody, they would have probably given me right back to the terrorists. And somebody needs to find a son of a bitch general named De La Garza and shoot that bastard for me."

Collier wrote a note and handed it to another agent and whispered, "Call the director and get him up to speed on this. The State Department will also want to know this ASAP.

"Brooks, we really need to concentrate on getting you down in one piece. We've got a lot to talk about."

"Collier, how is my family doing?"

"About as well as can be expected when the old man has been missing and presumed dead for six weeks."

"Six weeks! I've been gone six weeks?"

"Almost exactly."

"How time flies when you are running for your life."

"Speaking of your family, I'll call them and give them the news."

Davis thought for a moment.

"Don't call them."

Collier was surprised. "You don't want us to call them?"

"No. Not yet. I don't want to get their hopes up...prematurely. I can't stand the idea of a moment of elation taken away if I crash and burn trying to land. I would rather call them myself if I make it."

Collier understood. "That will be one memorable Easter Sunday call."

"It's Easter Sunday?"

"That's right, Brooks."

Davis was suddenly absorbed in his own personal thoughts. Tears flooded his eyes. He could not believe that he had escaped the sure clutches of death on Easter Sunday. He knew that he needed a miracle to pull this off, but to have it delivered on this day was particularly uncanny, and in no small way a little unnerving. Someone was truly watching over him very closely.

Thacker contacted the guide pilot out of Hondo to give him instructions and a radio frequency on which he could communicate with

Davis. The instructor pilot was named Mike Ruiz.

"You say this dude has never landed a plane?" asked Ruiz.

"No, never. It is going to be interesting," replied Thacker.

"Be advised that we have got strong wind gusts from the west-north-west. I can assure you that if we don't get a lucky few minutes of calm at just the right time, he is probably going to be blown all over the place."

Thacker considered the dilemma and advised Ruiz, "Try to be upbeat with him. We don't care if the Cessna is never the same again, so long as Davis comes out with a pulse."

"I'll do what I can," replied a skeptical Ruiz.

Ruiz was vectored to meet about forty miles south of Hondo. He brought his identical Cessna along Davis' starboard side. He made the introductory call.

"Hey, Brooks, how ya doing?"

"Slightly freaked but under reasonable control."

"Man, you really know how to put some excitement in an otherwise quiet Sunday morning."

"I promise I'll never do it again. What's your name?"

"Mike. Mike Ruiz."

Ruiz went over the plan as they approached Hondo. Essentially Davis was to concentrate on the runway while Ruiz issued specific instructions about flaps, throttle, and position of the control column. As they approached, Davis could see the small town in the distance. The airport was on the west side of the town and Davis was soon able to see the two north-south runways that were joined together by a single east-west strip to the north. On Ruiz's command, they throttled down and started to lose altitude.

Suddenly the little Cessna began to be tossed about in the strong, gusting winds. Davis' mind flashed back to his first flight as a student. The problem was both crosswinds and very powerful and erratic thermals that caused the plane to rapidly rise and fall.

A particularly strong gust caused Davis' plane to lurch toward

Ruiz. Ruiz realized that he had made a serious error. He should have stationed himself on the upwind or port side of Davis. He quickly corrected and regained a safe distance between him and Davis. Downrange, the planes were well off the centerline on the north-south runway. He tried to talk Davis back on course to regain the centerline, but their altitude was getting critically low. Davis was clearly panicking and becoming more erratic. As they crossed Highway 90 Ruiz could see that it was hopeless.

"Brooks, go ahead and throttle up. We are going to have to go around and try again."

Davis's heart sank. He relaxed his white-knuckled right fist from the control column and pushed the throttle toward full power, and slowly pulled back on the control column. The little Cessna obediently climbed to the north.

After they were clear of Hondo and back up to 1,000 feet, Ruiz again described the four spaced ninety-degree turns to reestablish the approach position. After he had a taste of the crosswinds and the small length and width of the Hondo runways, Brooks' confidence was approaching absolute zero.

"Mike, I don't think I can do it. That strip is narrower than the dirt strip I took off from this morning. I've got no room for error. We've got to find a bigger runway."

Ruiz thought for a moment. "What's your fuel status?"

Davis found the gauge. "A little more than three-fourths of a tank."

Ruiz thought that he had better get back with Thacker. He automatically went back to the proper communication style.

"This is Cessna George Michael one two niner niner to ATC, over."

"This is Thacker. Go ahead."

"I think that Davis is right. If we have a wide, long runway we can make an approach with lots more room for error. Fuel is no problem, over."

"The closest things that fit are Kelly and San Antonio International. SAT is out because 21 left is closed because of a ground problem and that's causing civilian traffic to stack. Kelly is very long and very wide, but Homeland Security will have to make that call."

"Why would Homeland Security care where we land?" asked Ruiz.

Davis was monitoring the frequency and replied, "They think I might be a terrorist in cowboy clothing. They don't want me close to any population centers."

"Get outta town!" replied Ruiz. "Is that right, Thacker?"

"It would just be better if we get Brooks down as quickly as possible."

"Better for whom?" asked Davis. Thacker was too slow to reply so Davis addressed Ruiz. "Mike, let's just get on with the ninety-degree turns."

Ten minutes and one ninety-degree turn later that nearly ended up with Davis inverted, the rapidly weakening contractor was at the end of his emotional rope. He thought that the terrorists and their colleagues were bad enough, but when US authorities were making life more difficult, there were few remaining options. Somewhere deep inside of Davis' psyche a switch flipped off in the part of the brain that makes one willing to cooperate with authority.

The first ninety-degree turn sent Davis on a nearly due east heading. East was toward San Antonio and his home and family. He looked down and to his right and could see the dual ribbons of US Highway 90. It suddenly struck him that the highway crossed a few hundred feet from the north end of the main runway at Kelly, USA. Kelly was formerly Kelly Air Force Base. In its military heyday, Kelly was the major service depot for the Air Force's entire inventory of heavy air lifters. Brooks remembered the hundreds of times he saw behemoths like C-5 Galaxy and C-141 Starlifters on approach to Kelly. He now realized that the flying behemoths required huge, long runways to take off and land. He quickly made up his mind.

"Hey, Bob. I've made an important decision. I'm going to fly to Kelly and land there."

Thacker replied immediately. "That's a negative, Brooks. We can't clear you for a landing at Kelly."

"Bob, you're not hearing me. I don't need any clearance. My suggestion is that you earn your pay and get everybody the hell out of my way."

"Brooks, please let us help you. Or…"

"Or what, Bob? Are you going to take away the pilot's license that I don't have and don't intend to get?"

"No, it could be much worse than that, Brooks."

That caused Brooks to think a bit.

"Well, Bob, if Homeland Security thinks that I'm such a big threat, I guess that they will have to order those good old boys from Del Rio to shoot me down. And when the FBI and NTSB comb the wreckage and find what's left of my carcass, they are going to have to deal with my wife. And I can assure you that on a bad day, she can make ISIS look like a bunch of choir boys. Ruiz, are you listening?"

"I'm reading you loud and clear, partner."

"I think we have a good plan. We just need the right runway. Will you stick with me and talk me down?"

"Oh, hell yes. We can fly very tight, then they will have to shoot both of us down. And when our newly elected, first-ever Hispanic president gets word that a bunch of gringos at Homeland ordered the shootdown of a courageous and defenseless Hispanic pilot who selflessly volunteered to help things out, well shit, there will be some serious outrage from the Latino community."

Brooks laughed. "Ruiz, I like how you think! You are a true American."

"I want to caution both of you—this is not a good plan," interjected Thacker.

"Well, Bob, we are pointing at Kelly, so are you going to help or hinder us?"

Thacker did not respond. He was getting Lindsay on the line.

"I guess that we will take that as a 'no help,'" said Davis.

"Then it's on to San Antonio. I've always wanted to land at Kelly!" replied an enthusiastic Ruiz.

When Lindsay got word of the plans of the renegade contractor and his accomplice, he put the orbiting F-15 on standby for possible shooting orders. He then called Ratzner. Within a few minutes, a five-way conference call involving Lindsay and Ratzner of Homeland Security; G. Collins Meyer, the secretary of Defense; FBI Director Clarence Scott; and Collier was underway. Meyer wanted to know who was the surest whether the man in the Cessna was friend or foe.

Lindsay and Ratzner were not happy enough with the facial analysis statistics. They were suffering from the unrelenting criticism that they had been getting since the nightmare had begun. While Davis and Epstein were missing, ISIS was successful twice more. Homeland was at a point where if anything looked out of the ordinary it was terrorism until proven otherwise. If the proof was not definitive, they felt obliged to act vigorously and protect the many even at the expense of the few.

Collier and Scott were happy enough with the sixty-two percent probability of positive identification when coupled with all the correct answers that Davis had given. FBI analysts at Quantico had already studied the tape of his question-and-answer session and confirmed that Davis' voice inflection indicated no unusual stress. They were in the process of pulling voice prints off recordings of Davis' cell phone transmissions that were made before the kidnappings for comparison, but that would take time. The FBI was in favor of letting Davis attempt landing at Kelly.

The secretary of Defense ground his molars together. He hated it when his advisors were giving advice that was 180 degrees apart. It meant that he would have to make the call. If he guessed right, whether it was to shoot down a despicable terrorist or to help a beleaguered American make his way home against all odds, he would be a hero. If he guessed wrong, he would not be able to deflect much of the blame. While Meyer paused as he tried to decide, Collier took the opportunity to put in a final plug for the contractor.

"Sir, we know that the instructor pilot is clean. He is just caught up in an unusual event. That coupled with Davis' correct answers makes it very strong in favor of the subject being legitimate. I would hate to think of the outcry if we kill him."

As an afterthought he added, "We will be accomplishing exactly what ISIS tried but failed to do."

The two Cessnas were flying in a formation as tight as that Ruiz thought to be safe. By the time that the secretary of Defense had made up his mind, the renegades could see the skyline of San Antonio in the distance. Ruiz started working Brooks into small course corrections that would allow them to be on a northwest to southeast heading in line with the huge runway at Kelly.

As they reached the far western suburbs of San Antonio, Davis called his partner.

"Hey, Mike, we are flying over well-populated areas. Do you think that means that they won't shoot us down now?"

"That would be my guess. You ought to just ask Thacker—I'm sure he's listening."

Thacker replied immediately but reassumed his professional air traffic controller persona. "You are now designated as emergency flight formation alpha one two niner niner. Please come right ten degrees and descend to 700 feet and hold."

"Roger, right ten degrees and descending to 700 feet," replied Ruiz.

Ruiz started describing his approach and landing strategy to Brooks.

"Alright, Brooks, let's try this a little different this time. I'm going to fall behind and climb above you so I can give you precise left and right rudder and control column instructions. It will be like I'm landing you by remote control."

"Remote control! God, I wish we really had remote control."

Ruiz throttled back and let Brooks pull away. When he had the separation the way he liked it, he climbed to a point about forty feet higher than Brooks and synced their airspeeds. On the ground, many people caught sight of the two Cessnas flying in such a peculiar formation, but almost no one recognized that a huge drama was about to come to a resolution.

CHAPTER TWENTY-EIGHT
Terra Firma

Davis could now see the runway at Kelly in the distance. It made the Hondo runway look like a two-lane country road. It was as wide as a multi-lane freeway and seemed to go on forever.

"Now that's a runway!" said an enthusiastic Davis.

"A blind guy with Parkinson's could land there, so don't disappoint me."

Ruiz coaxed Davis' heading onto the centerline of the runway. Thacker handed George Michael 1299 off to the air traffic controller in the tower at Kelly. An anonymous voice came online.

"This is Kelly control. Emergency flight George Michael one two niner niner, you are cleared for final approach and landing. Emergency vehicles are standing by. Formation leader, you are now in control for landing. Be advised, you have intermittent west-northwesterly winds gusting fifteen to eighteen miles per hour. Good luck one two niner niner, over."

Ruiz conducted the landing just like he did when a student was sitting next to him. He really liked the unique perspective provided by flying above and behind his student. He always tried to keep his students calm by interjecting casual bits of conversation with his landing instructions.

"Hey Brooks, did you say that you built Jeremiah Fellows' hacienda in the Dominion?"

The question startled a white-knuckled Davis for a moment.

"Ah...yeah. Neoclassic Mediterranean."

"What did it set him back?"

Davis shook his head and thought, *I'm probably going to die in a few minutes and this guy wants to know how much some jock paid for his mansion.*

"About $2.5 million."

"Shiiit! It's obscene that a dude has that kind of money to throw around. Press lightly on your right rudder pedal, Brooks." Davis obediently made the correction.

"Is your wife a home type or does she have a profession? Keep your wingtips level."

"She's an RN by training but she helps me now."

The Cessnas were on the final leg of the glide path. Davis marveled at the size of the runway as it grew in the windscreen. He could clearly see Highway 90 passing from east to west at the northwest end of the runway.

"Come off the throttle a little more and give me two clicks of flaps. We are going to maintain eighty knots until we cross over the highway. Then slowly cut the throttle and let it sink on its own. No forward push on the control column."

Davis followed his instructions in silence. He could not answer if he wanted to. He could feel his heart rate ramping up as the engine RPM was going down. As the plane settled toward the ground the crosswinds became more noticeable but did not seem as bad as Hondo. He noted that he was drifting off the centerline. Without advice from Ruiz, he applied additional pressure to the right rudder and corrected the glide path himself. Ruiz was impressed. "I think you're bullshitting me about never landing before. I think you are just padding up the story for your memoir."

"If I get to write my memoir, you will be prominently noted." As an afterthought Davis added, "And you will never have to buy a beer again the rest of your life."

They crossed Highway 90 in perfect formation. Ruiz offered final advice.

"Remember, let it sink on its own. Do not land on the nose wheel first. When I tell you, I want very gentle back pressure on the control column. You want the wing wheels on the ground first. If you bounce, do not overcorrect. Just let it settle down again on its own. When it's rolling, then slight forward pressure on the column. When the nose wheel is down, kill the throttle, shut off the engine, and let it coast. Don't worry if it coasts off the runway into the grass. Are you ready?"

At first, the somewhat transfixed Davis nodded in reply but said nothing.

"Are you ready, Brooks, or did you nod off?"

Davis finally got out a weak, "Ready."

Ruiz thought that his student needed a bit more levity before wheels-down.

"Okay, Brooks, I'm going to stay above, behind, and to your starboard when you land. That way I should be able to stay out of the fireball and debris field."

Despite the tension, Davis had to laugh.

"You're a real freaking comedian, Ruiz."

"Jimmy Failla has nothing on me. You are centered up and level. Start your throttle down."

Davis' plane slowly sank to the runway. He briefly worried about running out of runway, but Kelly was just too long. When the wheels hit the concrete, the Cessna bounced about ten feet back in the air. Ruiz's voice crackled in the headphones.

"Steady, dude! Don't overcorrect! Let it settle, let it settle!"

The Cessna's wing wheels kissed the runway and the nose wheel obediently followed. Ruiz added power to his plane. As he regained altitude, he passed over Davis and then looked back.

"Throttle off! Kill the engine!"

Davis was wild-eyed. He was on the ground and apparently not going to die. The bounce had pointed the nose of the plane to the port and the Cessna rolled into the grass and came to a stop. With difficulty, Davis released his grip on the control column. He fumbled with the door latch and stumbled out of the plane. His knees were so weak that he immediately collapsed to the ground. He could not get to his feet, so he simply crawled away from the plane on his hands and knees.

He got to a sitting position and turned to look at the little Cessna that had so flawlessly brought him home. From that day forward Cessna aircraft would be the lasting symbol of his Easter miracle.

Davis did not see the caravan of emergency vehicles with flashing lights that raced toward him until they arrived on the scene. Two black unmarked SUVs led the way. Before they came to a complete stop the doors came open and eight black-clad FBI SWAT team members disembarked and all pointed MP5 submachine guns at the wayward pilot. When the first team member saw Davis' holstered pistol he screamed, "Gun! Gun! Gun!"

Davis was startled and shouted back, "Where? Where?" A chorus of "Get on your belly!" and "Arms out!" and "Do not go for that weapon!" rang out.

Finally, Davis realized that they meant him. He joyously followed their orders and peacefully surrendered. The pistol was torn from the holster, and he felt two or three pairs of hands pat him down. They pulled the folding knife out of his pocket. When they were finished one of the FBI men reported, "No electronics!" That seemed odd to Davis, but he was suddenly too tired to ask why they were interested in electronics. They handcuffed his hands behind his back.

Two of the federal men picked Davis up by the arms and brought him to a standing position. Other agents were carefully examining the cockpit of the Cessna. They brought out the backpack and the rifles. One called out to the apparent agent in charge, "An AK and a 7mm magnum like he reported. Both loaded."

The agent in charge of the SWAT team was named Killingstadt. He had the most no-nonsense face that Davis had ever seen. Killingstadt addressed Davis.

"When we take that backpack apart are we going to find anything that would cause us trouble?"

"Like what?" asked a confused Davis.

"Like a booby trap for example."

Davis carefully cleared his throat. "The three weapons, the backpack, and the ghillie suit are my contributions to the plane. Anything else you find should be blamed on the man I stole the plane from."

"So, there is nothing that will blow up or anything like that?"

Davis laughed and shook his head weakly. "Collier certainly is a careful man. No, the plane is not hauling any threatening materials. Now that I'm not behind the wheel, everything should be safe."

Killingstadt spoke into a radio. "The subject is secure. No overt threats noted. The subject appears to need medical attention."

Davis could hear Collier's voice. "Very good. Take him to University Hospital. We will notify the ER."

At about that time, Ruiz flew low over the scene. He waggled his wings in salute to Davis. With his hands secured, Davis could only nod back at his instructor. Ruiz, changing his mind about landing at Kelly, turned west and headed back to Hondo. He figured that if they wanted to arrest him, they could come to his house.

Davis was loaded in one of the FBI vehicles. They headed for the hospital code three. No one spoke to him during the trip. When Brooks asked if the handcuffs were necessary, all he got was a sideways glance from the agent to his right. He decided that being home and in one piece on the ground was all that was important, so he kept quiet and enjoyed the scenery on the way to the hospital.

He was taken to a nondescript side entrance to the emergency room. The agents continued to flank and support him. He was taken to a treatment cubicle where a medical team and three obvious federal men were waiting. Davis picked out Collier immediately.

"Good morning, Special Agent in Charge Collier. I can't tell you how good it is to be alive to meet you."

Collier smiled and nodded. He instructed the SWAT men to remove his handcuffs.

"That was some great flying for a rank amateur," said Collier.

"I'm glad you liked it because you will never see me do it again."

"We've got a lot to talk about. But let's let the docs start working on you first."

While the doctors gave orders about bloodwork, the medical team seated Davis on the side of a gurney and began to get him out of his filthy clothes. He put up his hand and spoke up loudly. "Stop!" After he had everyone's attention, he addressed the doctor who appeared to be in charge.

"Let me tell you what we are going to do. First, I want to go somewhere where I can get out of these clothes and take a shower. A long, hot shower. I'll need anti-bacterial soap and some kind of shampoo and a toothbrush and toothpaste." He looked at the doctor's crisp surgical scrubs. "Then I want a pair of those scrubs. I would really like a nice private room somewhere. And money is no object." Davis pointed to the festering wound on his head. "Then I would like a consult with the best plastic surgeon on the staff. After that, you can do whatever tests and treatments you want. But this is the way we are going to do it." He looked at Collier for support.

Collier smiled and addressed the doctors. "Let's make it happen." Within ten minutes, Davis was in a VIP suite on the tenth floor.

When Davis was ready for his shower, he looked in the mirror. The beard, weight loss, disheveled hair, and horrible wound on his head made him nearly unrecognizable. When he stepped into the shower the warm, clean water felt almost foreign. After the cleanup, he donned the set of scrubs and sat on the side of the bed. Collier and Agent Dayton had stayed quietly in the background until they were alone with Davis. Davis looked at Collier and Dayton and slowly shook his head.

"I've got to tell you, it's sort of freaking me out. At sunup this morning I was sure I was a dead man, and now I'm home. It's all too fast. It's very, very weird."

"You ready to call your wife?" asked Collier. Davis recoiled in surprise.

"She doesn't know yet?"

"You said you wanted to tell her yourself."

Davis stared off into space for a moment. "Make the call."

The Davis family was just sitting down to a large Easter lunch. All of Davis' immediate family was there as well as some extended family and close friends. The family had been to early Mass at St. Matthew's. When Father Hoolihan saw Molly and her family arrive, he spoke to her and asked if there had been any word. When they said that there had not been, Hoolihan said that he would include a special prayer. Molly sat through Mass in a trance-like state. She did not hear much of the service until the priest asked the congregation to join him in a prayer for an Easter miracle. They prayed that wherever Brooks was he was happy and that everyone would have the strength to accept God's will. At that moment, Molly privately hated the priest. How dare he pray for a miracle. There were no miracles in this day and age, especially if ISIS had you.

Everyone was seated around the formal dining table when the phone rang. James got up to take the call. Every time the phone rang since the nightmare began, everyone in the family agonized about whether this would be the call that they found Brooks' remains. James picked up the kitchen portable out of its cradle and said hello.

Collier recognized James' voice.

"This is Special Agent Collier. Is this James?"

"Yes, sir."

"I have some very interesting news. Hang on a second—I'm going to put someone on to tell you about it."

Collier handed the phone to Brooks. He took a sip of water and cleared his throat.

"Jim."

"Yes."

"Listen very carefully. Do not react. Do you know who this is?"

James' lips began to quiver, and his eyes welled with tears. He nodded his head and managed, "Yes, yes, I do."

"Hang tough, buddy. You've got to do this for me. Take the phone to your mom. Put it on the speaker and set it in front of her and tell her this. 'Rumors of your husband's untimely demise have been greatly exaggerated.' Can you do that?"

"Yes...yes I can."

James placed the phone in front of his mother. She immediately saw the tears in his eyes and her heart sank. The call that they had dreaded for so long had come. James looked at everyone at the table and then his mother.

"Mom. Rumors of your husband's untimely demise have been greatly exaggerated."

There was a long pause of dead silence from the table. Finally, Molly managed, "What on God's green earth are you talking about?"

James pointed at the phone and said, "You are on speaker."

Molly stared at the phone and then her deranged son. She spoke up. "This is Molly Davis. Who is this?"

From the speaker, a tired but unmistakable voice addressed a very confused wife.

"Hi, babe! I made it home."

Molly gasped with recognition but was stricken temporarily speechless. Zane jumped out of his chair and declared definitively, "That's Dad! That's Dad! It really is!" A water glass was knocked off the table and shattered on the floor. Everyone talked at once. Andy leaned back in his chair and assumed a trancelike pose. Molly stood up and demanded silence. She picked up the phone and put it to her ear even though it was on the speaker.

"Brooks Cameron Davis! Please tell me that you are free and alive and that you are somewhere nearby!"

"Free, alive, and at University Hospital, my dear, dear wife!"

She was rapidly becoming overwhelmed.

"What? Where? How did you? Are you really...okay?"

"Honey, I'm getting better by the second. I'm a little hard to look at for the moment, but I'd be hard-pressed to be doing any better. Please get over here as soon as you can, but be safe. We can't lose each other now."

CHAPTER TWENTY-NINE
Reunion and Repairs

All the rules about only two visitors at a time went out the window when Davis' family and close friends showed up on the tenth floor. Davis' head wound was being examined by the plastic surgeon when they arrived. At first, Molly thought that they had escorted her to the wrong room. The thin, bearded man with the horrible wound on his head certainly was not Brooks. She apologized for bursting into the room and tried to leave.

"Where are you going, honey?" asked Davis. At the sound of his voice, she stopped and spun around. She was speechless for a moment and then blurted out, "Dear God! Is that you, Brooks?"

Davis laughed and replied, "In the flesh. What flesh there is."

The family embraced in a group hug and tears began to flow. Molly stepped back and looked at her husband.

"You are so thin. I can't believe that it's you."

Davis started the ordeal at six feet two inches and a solid 212 pounds.

"They just weighed me. I'm 151 pounds. I lost sixty-one pounds in six weeks. I don't recommend the diet plan. Very dangerous."

"What happened to your head, Dad?" asked Zane.

"Mountain lion."

"Oh, that's rad!" replied the son.

"Oh, dear God! I've got to sit down!" replied the wife.

Davis pulled a chair over for her and held her hand. "Don't worry, Honey. This is Dr. Bishop, the plastic surgeon. He's going to start working on me tonight."

Bishop comforted Molly and explained that Brooks' quick action with the mesquite thorns had kept the subcutaneous blood supply to his scalp alive. He said they would begin debridement and cleaning up the infection in preparation for definitive plastic surgery in a few days.

"He will have a sexy scar to show off to his grandchildren when he tells them the mountain lion story."

After nearly an hour of joyous reunion, a nurse came in with equipment to start an IV. She used the treatment as an excuse to get the crowd moving out of the room. Collier announced that it was important to start the debriefing immediately and emphasized that everyone had to leave the room. Brooks voiced an objection.

"I really want Molly to stay."

Collier responded, "I know that you need to be together, but we may be covering some very sensitive information."

"Martin, you must understand. Molly and I have no secrets. She will know the whole story sooner or later." As soon as he said it, Brooks' mind flashed back to a hilltop confessional. Molly gave Brooks a small, almost forlorn smile but said nothing.

Collier thought for a moment. "Mrs. Davis, can we count on your discretion? It is imperative that any information about Brooks' ordeal be carefully screened from the media. Remember, he escaped ISIS, and they won't like that. And they have infinite patience and long memories."

Molly held Brooks' hand and nodded her understanding of the dangers. A third FBI agent arrived with portable recording equipment.

"Brooks, we would like for you to start with a simple description of the events, starting at the time you and Epstein were placed in the van and taken away. We already have a detailed description of the kidnapping and killing of the roofer, Charles Garza." Davis grimaced at that bit of news.

"That was Chuck that they killed?"

"I'm afraid so."

"He was a good man. He had eight kids."

"So, let's begin there. For the first cut, I want you to try not to get bogged down in details. Cover the overview of the six weeks. We will be recording, and our analysts will pore over the information during the night and start a list of very detailed questions we will have for you tomorrow."

A nurse entered the room carrying a modest tray of food. She smiled and said, "I know that you are very hungry, and this doesn't look like much, but if you eat too much, too fast you probably won't keep anything down." The tray looked great to Brooks, but he had other more pressing things on his mind. He glanced at the agent with the recording equipment.

"Are you recording now?"

"Yes."

He looked at Collier. "Could you turn it off for a moment?"

Collier nodded at the agent, who shut down the equipment.

"What's on your mind, Brooks?"

"I need to know right now how what I say could potentially affect me legally."

"What do you mean, Brooks?"

"I went through a great deal escaping and then fighting my way out of Mexico. Some serious things happened along the way. Very serious. I need to know that everyone recognizes that I was the victim and the things I did were done strictly in self-defense." As an afterthought, he added, "If you get my drift."

It did not take Collier long to get the drift. He sent everyone out of the room except Brooks, Molly, and himself. He closed the door to the room and pulled a chair close to Davis and his wife.

"I think I understand your concerns."

"I don't mind telling you, Martin, that when I saw the recording equipment, I thought that the next thing you would do would be to Mirandize me. And if that happens, I guarantee that I will lawyer up immediately, and not say another word to you."

Molly's anxiety level was rapidly rising. She had never thought that Brooks would have to worry about anything if he was lucky enough to escape.

Collier thought for a moment. "Brooks, I think that would be a smart thing to do. That's what I would do. I'll tell you what I recommend. We will put the primary interview off tonight. I'm going to call the US Attorney's office and set up a meeting with them tomorrow. I'm also going to call Ruben Santiago. He is a partner at Morrison & Oliver. He is an international litigation expert. He knows Mexican law as well as US law. I want you to tell your story to him in private first. Then, we can start our interview. If Santiago thinks that there will be a problem, he can represent you and be present to offer guidance. How does that sound?"

Brooks looked at Molly, who nodded her agreement. "That sounds good. I don't mean to be a pain in the ass, but there is just too much at stake."

That night Davis underwent the first surgery on his mangled head. The next surgery would be a couple of days away.

At 10:00 a.m. the next morning, Collier returned with Santiago and a US attorney named Richards. After introductions, Collier excused himself and left the room. Molly was present and obviously nervous. She had spent a sleepless night worrying about hearing the story of her husband's ordeal. Her gut told her that it must have been horrific. Davis's alarming appearance was testimony to what he must have gone through.

What followed was an abbreviated version of the six weeks in Mexico. Davis emphasized that while Epstein was the target, he was the target of opportunity. With Epstein's untimely death, the terrorists were left with the country boy from Uvalde.

When Davis described the rape by al-Kahat, Molly broke into sobs. The lawyers could only shake their heads in disbelief. He told them that each time he was forced into a fight, he was certain that he was about to die. When he told them about the reward poster, Richards interrupted and asked if he had a copy. Davis said that there was one in the backpack that was in FBI possession. Richards immediately got up and left the room to find Collier. When he returned, he said, "I've instructed Collier to copy and protect the wanted poster. That is a critical piece of evidence."

Richards assured Davis that he had nothing to fear from the US side of the border.

"Brooks, there is no need to worry. You are the victim of a federal crime on US soil. Whatever you had to do in Mexico is out of our jurisdiction. We can't prosecute you for anything."

Santiago agreed but with a caveat.

"You've got no problems here at home, but the US and Mexico do have an extradition treaty. If their authorities feel that there was any criminal wrongdoing on your part in Mexico, they could ask for extradition and under the general terms of the current treaty we could possibly have to comply. At first glance, all your actions except stealing the plane were clearly self-defense actions. And since you did not wreck the airplane, you can give it back. No harm, no foul."

Davis stared at Santiago for a long moment and then replied, "Everyone needs to understand from the get-go that I'm never going to cross our southern border again. Period! End of discussion."

Molly had heard that form of punctuation from her husband before. He could be extraordinarily adamant under certain circumstances.

"Hopefully, when the information from the FBI gets to Mexico City, they will understand the unusual circumstances and recognize your actions as self-defense," said Richards.

Santiago added, "I know their system. I can assure you that they will convene their equivalent of a federal grand jury. They will want Brooks to testify, probably in Mexico City."

Davis closed his eyes and started to slowly shake his head.

"You must understand, Brooks, they will see this as a case of corruption at the highest level. My God! A general in their military on the take with ISIS and the cartels. President Acosta will have a stroke."

"Well, so long as they convene their grand jury here in San Antonio, I'll be happy to tell them what a dirtbag General De La Garza is. But like I've already said I'm never going to cross the border again. Any more discussion is a waste of time."

The lawyers could not criticize Davis for his stance, but they both had a feeling that international complications were coming down the road.

CHAPTER THIRTY

News Flash

The news of Davis's fateful return came out on the evening of Easter Sunday. When the 5:00 p.m. local news played without mentioning the event, a nurse from the University Hospital's emergency room could not believe it. She got on the phone and called her brother, a cameraman at Channel 12, and told him that Davis was alive and relatively well on the tenth floor under FBI guard.

When Mike Ruiz's wife got the story from her husband, she immediately called Channel 4 with the news, hoping to win their "news tip of the month" program. She got the word out just before the FBI showed up and told Ruiz that the events of the morning were considered a matter of national security and that he should keep any information to himself, or they would look at his wanton disregard of FAA orders with greater scrutiny.

It was after 7:00 p.m. before channels 4 and 12 had solid confirmation. Regular programming was interrupted by live reports from outside the University Hospital. Collier barely had time to notify Epstein's family in Isreal of their loss before the media circus began. The information was on the wire and had gone national by 7:15 p.m. News teams were dispatched to the Davis home and camped there for days, trying to get the next great scoop.

At 8:15 p.m. the FBI announced that there would be a news conference at 9:00 p.m. Central time. At 9:00 Collier entered the hospital auditorium for the news conference. Collier's game plan was to keep it simple and avoid questions.

"We have the initial information about the Epstein-Davis case. At this hour we can confirm that Mr. Brooks Davis is in this hospital and is currently undergoing surgery for a nonlife-threatening head wound that was sustained after his escape from captivity at the hands of ISIS. We are sad to report that Mr. Raymond Epstein died during captivity, possibly from a heart attack. That cannot be confirmed because his body has not been recovered. We all wish to offer our sincere condolences to the family and friends of Mr. Epstein.

"We can confirm that after the dual kidnapping that occurred on February 17th, the terrorist elements took both Mr. Davis and Mr. Epstein out of the country to an isolated ranch in the state of Chihuahua in northern Mexico. It was there that Mr. Epstein died.

"Mr. Davis was able to escape and evade recapture. This morning, he was able to commandeer a light aircraft and fly back across the border. He was vectored by the FAA to Kelly USA, where he landed shortly before noon today. He is currently described as in fair condition. We expect to begin the interview and debriefing process sometime tomorrow.

"Since Mr. Davis is currently in surgery and we will not be able to interview him until sometime tomorrow, we have no more information for you at this moment. Since this is an ongoing investigation, we will not be taking any questions at this time."

As Collier left the podium, an unsatisfied press shouted out questions anyway.

"Mr. Collier, is it true that Mr. Davis is not a pilot and had to teach himself how to fly?"

"It was reported that two Cessna aircraft were flying in close formation on approach to Kelly this morning. Was Mr. Davis in one of those planes?"

"What has been the response of the Mexican government to these allegations?"

Like the seasoned FBI man he was, Collier ignored the questions and promptly departed the room.

At that moment in the White House, President Martinez picked up the remote and turned off the Oval Office television. The director of the FBI, the attorney general, and the secretaries of Defense, State, and Homeland Security were with the president.

President Martinez addressed Director Scott. "Your man in San Antonio certainly knows how to maintain control of a news conference. But tell me, Clarence, what do we really know at this hour?"

"Apparently ISIS did not take Epstein's heart condition into consideration, and the stress of the kidnapping and trip to Mexico killed him before they could cut his head off. Davis is the wild card here. The terrorists broke from their normal form when they took him. We do not yet know what that is all about. In terms of his escape, either he was very lucky or he was a whole lot more than the bad guys bargained for."

"Is he ex-military?" asked Malcomb Washington, the secretary of State.

The secretary of Defense and the FBI director both shook their heads simultaneously. "No military history at all. An Eagle Scout and a former Scout Master is as close as you get," replied Scott.

"And what was the deal about the plane?" asked Martinez.

"He was still a hundred miles from the border and in bad physical shape and knew that he would never make the border. As a last resort sort of thing, he stole the plane this morning and flew home. The amazing thing was that he had only one flying lesson some twenty years ago."

"Incredible! What else has he told us?"

"Not much. Collier reports that he wants a consult with a US attorney and a private lawyer who is familiar with Mexican law before he gives any details."

The president and the secretaries looked quizzical.

"He is worried about self-incrimination. Davis was well-armed when he landed. Apparently, he had to fight his way out of Mexico. We are assuming that there were several dead folks of both Arab and Mexican descent scattered along his trail out of Mexico."

The president's brow knitted with concern. He could understand Davis killing terrorists but why Mexicans?

"Why did he have to fight to get out of Mexico? Why not go to the local authorities for help?"

"He's implicated a Mexican Army general named De La Garza as a co-conspirator along with ISIS and the cartels. It was apparently very clear to Davis that if he escaped, he could not turn himself over to Mexican authorities because of such high-level corruption. It was a case of get out on his own or die in Mexico."

Martinez did not like the sound of it but recognized the problem. He asked the secretary of State, "Should we talk to Acosta now and get ahead of the curve on this? This smells like trouble to me."

"I would recommend we wait. As far as we are concerned, our man is the victim. Let Acosta clean his own house. When he wants something from us, he will call. Privately we can give him appropriate intel and publicly we can announce that we are working closely with our good neighbors to the south on this problem."

Martinez looked at Attorney General Bryce Daniels. "You are awfully quiet, Bryce. What is your take?"

"Well, Mr. President, I was just thinking. The country is up to our collective ears with bloodthirsty terrorists. This Davis man, just a common man, comes along and shows everyone that the terrorists and their allies can be defeated the good old American way, by delivering a really good ass-kicking. I predict that when the story gets out, and mark my word it will, we will have a real-life red, white, and blue Eagle Scout hero on our hands. This is just what the American people need badly right now. But..."

"But what?" queried the president.

"What are you going to do if Mexico thinks he is a killer and demands that we honor our extradition treaty? Are we going to let the Federales cross the border and collect up our hero to face the Mexican judicial system?"

The Oval Office fell silent. Martinez started rubbing his temples. He made eye contact with each of his advisors.

"This kind of shit is supposed to happen only during the last six months of a president's second term. You tell everyone that until further notice, I do not want to hear the word *extradition* uttered out loud by anyone."

CHAPTER THIRTY-ONE

Home at Last

Brooks spent a total of seven days in the hospital. The FBI and State Department interviewed him daily between various surgeries and treatments. His family spent as much time with him as the Feds and doctors would allow.

The afternoon he was discharged from the hospital was the beginning of a long party. Food and drink were in abundance, and every friend and family member brought more. James even invited a certain green-eyed blonde from UTSA. To Molly's approval and Andy's chagrin, she wore a bra for the occasion.

As the evening wore on, Molly noted that Brooks' usual level of animation was fading fast. Her first thought was that Brooks was more debilitated than he was letting on and that his medical problems were not limited to a near scalping and malnutrition. She thought that he had a bit of that "thousand-yard stare" that soldiers who have seen the worst of war often exhibit. More than once, she would feel his eyes across the room, and when she smiled back, or mouthed the words "I love you," he would reciprocate with a haunted little smile and then look away.

When they finally got to bed, Brooks quickly turned off the bedside light, casting the room into darkness. Just as quickly, Molly turned the lamp back on. Brooks gave her a quizzical look.

"You're not getting off that easy, cowboy."

Brooks gave her a nervous look. "What?"

"What's on your mind? Something is really troubling you. If you are too tired to talk about it, then I need a really good preview for tomorrow. So again, what's on your mind?"

Brooks inhaled deeply and absently touched his freshly repaired head wound. He remained quiet.

"So, you have some hideously bad news about your physical health that you are not sharing with me?"

Brooks recoiled and gave his nosey wife a disgruntled look. "No! Other than suddenly looking twenty years older, and skinnier than a rail, I'm just fine, thank you."

Molly didn't give him a reprieve. "Okay, so you have some hideously bad news about your mental health?"

Brooks groaned and rolled on his side facing Molly. "You have always had such a devious way of forcing me into conversations that I don't want to have, or maybe I'm not ready to have."

Molly smiled and quietly replied, "Ah, progress. Is it 'don't want to' or 'not ready for'?"

Brooks looked at her blue eyes. He was so happy to see those eyes again. He thought how intuitive she had always been and how easily she could pick him apart whenever she wanted to.

"I guess it is a combination of both. I know that there are some things that I need...*we* need to discuss, but I don't want to, so I'm not ready."

Molly gave him one of her strategic silent pauses, knowing that he would inevitably keep talking. Sure enough.

"Repeatedly facing one's imminent death, then killing people to prevent it, causes you to re-evaluate your whole life. You are forced to look at everything you have ever done...the good...the bad...but mostly the bad. It is the ultimate come-to-Jesus meeting. It is a gut-wrenching, all-humbling experience when you face a lifetime of sins and failures all at once."

Brooks went silent, but Molly wanted to hear more. "Go on," she encouraged.

"You ask God for forgiveness, but when you've done terrible things, short of God Himself coming down on a cloud and touching you and telling you, "I truly forgive you; go and sin no more," I don't really know if it's true."

After a bit, Molly tenderly touched his face. He squinted his eyes shut, thinking of all the days and nights in Mexico that he longed for that touch. But now he knew what his real problem was. He neither deserved this woman nor her forgiveness.

Without a word, Molly turned out the light. She drew herself close to Brooks and gave him her RN's diagnosis. "Physically, you're on the mend. Mentally, you are about to find out everything you never wanted to know about PTSD. But, cowboy, you are a spiritual wreck. Tomorrow I want you to make an appointment with Father Hoolihan."

Brooks nodded but remained silent. After another quiet pause, Molly asked, "Did you notice that Tina wasn't at the party?"

Brooks inhaled sharply and immediately hoped that Molly didn't notice. "With all the people coming and going, I really didn't give it much thought," Brooks lied. "I guess that is a bit odd."

"Not really. When we all thought you were dead, and I was the new CEO, I fired her. So, it wasn't odd that she wasn't there."

"You fired her?"

"Yeah, long story. I know you are exhausted—let's sleep. The kids will be at school tomorrow and we will have the house to ourselves. I'll tell you all about it then." Molly gave Brooks a gentle kiss on the lips. "I love you. I'm so glad you are back home with us."

Brooks returned her kiss and slowly caressed her back but was unable to speak. His inability to find the right words was matched by his inability to find much sleep that first night.

On the other hand, as Molly drifted off to sleep, her last thought was, *There may be some hope for THIS Brooks Davis.*

CHAPTER THIRTY-TWO
Sort of a Final Exam

Brooks didn't sleep much that first night at home. Dweezel, the family Jack Russell, kept jumping on the bed to make sure that the master of the house was really back in bed with the mistress like he was supposed to be. Brooks could tell that the little dog's stubby tail was wagging at warp speed every time he found the master's bed occupied appropriately. Molly was unaware and slept well.

At 6 a.m., Brooks gave up on sleep and got up and started the coffee. He took Zane and Andy to school and was elated that such a simple chore made him feel so alive and restored. When he got back to the house, James had already left for morning classes. It was just him and Molly, a pot of coffee, and plenty of alone time to talk.

Molly fixed her magnum-sized mug and sat down across from Brooks. She smiled but didn't start the conversation. After twenty-plus years with this woman, Brooks knew that it was up to him.

"It's wonderful to be home."

"It's a miracle and we all know it."

They both nodded and sipped coffee. Molly remained quiet. Brooks knew the drill.

"I thought I would sleep better, being in my own bed with you. That damned Dweezel kept jumping on the bed to see if it was really me."

Molly chuckled. "I don't think it was the dog."

He studied her face for a clue. "You don't?"

"No."

Brooks absorbed the quick certainty of her answer. A dull drill bit started to bore a hole in the back side of his heart, and his coffee was clawing its way back out of his stomach. "You're right as always. It's the crap with the Mexican government, or what our government might do."

"Maybe."

"Maybe? Or maybe what else?"

"I don't think it is the Mexicans or our government. Maybe something closer to home, Brooks."

"Like what?"

Molly got up to top off her coffee cup and offered the pot to Brooks. He shook his head. She sat back down and decided on a subject change.

"You know Brooks, you never asked me why I fired Tina. Considering how important her position was in the company, I thought that it would be the first thing you would want to know about."

Brooks forced himself to look into those deep blue eyes. His gut slowly tightened even more. He thought, *Oh, Honey, I know why you fired her, and you are just dragging the confession out of me.*

"Well, Molly, that is the real reason I didn't sleep much last night. My guess is that she said something to you that was just too aggressive and hurtful for you to let go. So, what was it?"

"She lied to me."

Brooks wasn't ready for that. "What did she say?"

"She said that you and she had an agreement to sell her the company, and you would bankroll the deal when you were ready to retire. That's bullshit, right? You and I never had that kind of plan, right?"

Brooks digested that for a moment. "I never said that to her, Molly. That was certainly bullshit. That was someone trying to take advantage of you during a horrible situation. What else did she say?"

"Nothing."

Brooks experienced a moment of premature hope. "What did you say to her? Did you fire her right then?"

"No. I said that I would have to think about it and then I sent her back to work."

"So, when did you fire her?"

Molly stared at her husband for a long moment with a neutral look on her face, while drumming her fingers on the tabletop. The look was just like how he saw her face in the windscreen of the Cessna just before takeoff. The look and the drumming were not lost on Brooks.

"Brooks, do you really want to know all the details? It might be better for you to accept my decisions as they are, so we can move on and let our family heal. So, what's it going to be? You want the blow-by-blow, gory details, or do you want to let it go?"

Brooks could not speak, and his face was like an illustrated book.

"Neither one of us is stupid, Brooks. If you need to know anything else, go have a discussion with Bob Goldsmith and then go play a round of golf with Dwight. They are the last people I've talked to about Tina Landry. I've made my decision to never speak of this again...ever."

Brooks' mind went to Dwight and the Chicago trip. There was only one reason why Molly would ever discuss Tina with Dwight. Brooks hung his head. None of the guilt and pain he felt in Mexico even remotely matched what he felt now. He finally found his voice. "There is no reason to forgive me, but I am so very, very sorry."

Molly gave it some thought and took a swig of coffee. Molly and Brooks made eye contact for a long moment while they each reviewed the last twenty years of their lives together. Brooks was in a state of paralysis. He could not move and could barely breathe. She finally placed her hand on the back of his hand and softly stroked it. Brooks looked at her hand in no small amount of disbelief. His eyes slowly returned to Molly's face. He thought, *Are there humans who are capable of God-like levels of forgiveness?*

"I had decided to privately and quietly hate your memory forever. But Bob Goldsmith offered me some advice about how hating you might affect our sons in the long run. He said that there may be some value in having a hero figure for a dead father. I was really torn. But then, you weren't dead, and I heard the stories of how you went to war against great odds to get back to your family, and I had second thoughts. So, I decided to give you a test, a big test, a sort of final exam."

"A test?"

"Yes. If you came home and immediately asked about Tina, then you would have failed the test. And our boys would not have their superhero father."

CHAPTER THIRTY-THREE
The Problem of a Free Press

At FBI San Antonio, the counterterrorism task force met for an update on the Epstein-Davis case. Collier let Agent Dayton run the meeting since it was his first major case since arriving from the academy.

"As expected, ninety percent of the communication traffic from known and suspected terrorist groups and individuals that we are monitoring at this time concerns Davis. Typically, they are expressing their displeasure that Mr. Davis is alive, and their colleagues are not. At this point, there has been no overt threat against Davis or his family. Our ISIS experts say that if they stay true to form, they will put Davis on the back burner for twelve to eighteen months. Then when everyone is lulled into a false security they may or may not resurface and exact retribution."

An agent's hand went up. "What determines the 'may' or 'may not' part?"

"If they have an immediate need to flex their muscles and they have the necessary assets in place, they could make a move against him. But realize that they must have both the need and the assets available for Davis to be at significant risk.

"There may be one possible caveat brewing worth noting. NSA, CIA, and our own digital intel systems are picking up bits and pieces of new information about Davis and his family that could be broadly interrupted as continued or increasing risk. So, for now, we are not going to step back from an overt presence in this case."

Another agent asked, "What about Epstein's body? What's the latest there?"

"That's currently being handled by the State Department. They are trying to get permission for a cadaver team to have access to the area around the ranch house to look for Epstein and possibly any other victims. When Davis was playing dumb about not understanding Spanish, he reports that discussions between General De La Garza and the terrorist leader made it sound like the other victims may have all been transported to the ranch and killed there. Permission has not yet been granted for our access so that avenue is presently closed."

"Why are the Mexicans refusing our help?"

"Probably a couple of reasons. First, they have egg on their face that this happened on their turf. They want to demonstrate that they can clean up their own mess. Second, they have a bunch of killings to sort out. Think about it. Would we want a bunch of foreigners mucking about one of our ongoing investigations?"

Another agent inquired, "What's this thing going around about the Davis case and the DEA?"

Collier did not wait for Dayton to answer. "When you enter General De La Garza into the Homeland Security Database it reports that the general, through the Mexican Narco police, made a request for search assistance to help track down a notorious contract killer utilizing the DEA's high-altitude drones. It appears that the whizzos at DEA spotted Davis out in the bush somewhere and promptly gave his position to the general. Were it not for the fact that Davis was better than the guy they sent to kill him, our DEA would have been at least partly responsible.

"The DEA very nearly helped the Mexicans accomplish what they could not do for themselves. It goes without saying that we do not want that information out. If it leaks, I promise that the full assets of the FBI, DEA, and Homeland Security will be put into play to hunt you down. Is there any part of that that anyone does not understand?"

Everyone understood, but the same agent asked, "Does Davis know about that?"

Collier leaned toward the agent. "Have you seen a mushroom

cloud forming over Leon Springs, Texas? Well, you will if Davis ever finds out."

Dayton continued. "For now, the San Antonio field office will continue to provide surveillance and security for the Davis family. For a man who is obviously handy with weapons and field tactics, we were surprised to find that Davis does not have a concealed carry permit. We have frankly advised him to get one. He and his wife are currently undergoing a fast-track program to obtain their permits.

"On the home front, our problems are growing with the media. Everyone already knows that Davis is the only kidnap victim to survive, and they all want to interview him and hear the whole story. How did he escape? Why didn't he go to the Mexican authorities? Those sorts of things. Some air traffic controller has already leaked the story of his flight out of Mexico. The media's collective mouths are watering to get the rest of the story. They smell a Ramboesque adventure and want to be the first to get it. Our informants are reporting that at least two of the major networks are offering six figures to the reporter who breaks the story. That is a powerful incentive, so they are not about to let it go.

"We are going to be able to run with our current no-comment position because it is an ongoing investigation only so long. They want Davis in front of a camera. SAIC Collier will continue to be the only person in this field office who is approved to make statements to the media."

An agent asked, "Is Davis itching to tell or sell his story?"

"We don't think we are in any trouble there. We have strongly advised against any interviews. His most recent comment to us on the subject was, and I quote, 'Fuck the media.' His wife and kids are following the old man's lead. We've also recommended that he not name General De La Garza publicly under any circumstance."

"We can't realistically expect that to go on for much longer," replied the same agent.

Collier again spoke up. "Chelsy Sullenberger, the airline pilot who was forced to ditch in the Hudson River, was able to refuse to be interviewed for the better part of a year while he collected on the book deal."

"How about Davis? Are the book deals rolling in?"

"Five so far," said Dayton.

"If the book is as interesting as our interviews, they will sell millions. If you throw in a movie deal, Davis stands to come out smelling like a room full of hundred-dollar bills," replied Collier.

Ciudad Camargo, Chihuahua, Mexico

De La Garza's phone rang. His trusted captain's voice had an air of urgency.

"Trevino in Mexico City is on the secure line. He reports that there may be some significant problems brewing."

Trevino was one of several people in the federal government who was on De La Garza's payroll.

"What is on your mind, Raul?"

"The American State Department has been in contact with Acosta. Your name is being connected with our friends in Juarez and the debacle with the American."

The general thought for a moment before responding. "We have managed our security on this end very well for a long time. We are insulated. We can dismiss the American's story as the mindless ravings of a lunatic murderer. There is no physical proof left in place."

"Acosta's people are starting to take the intelligence from the Americans seriously. I wanted you to know immediately so you can stay ahead of, how shall we say, any difficulties."

"You are an effective associate, Raul. Keep me informed."

De La Garza hung up the secure phone. He turned in his great leather chair and stared out of his office window. He thought that this whole affair should have never gone beyond the Arabs. He still could not believe that some unknown Texan had killed El Serpiente. He thought about what the Federals might want to do. Any investigation in Mexico would require that the American testify in Mexico City.

He smiled grimly. It would be very simple to kill the man if they brought him to Mexico. All that would be required would be money, and he had more than he could ever spend in a lifetime. However, if the man was killed here, it would make the American's story seem even more plausible. No, it would not be a good idea if the man testified in Mexico City. It would be better if he were shut up permanently while he was still in Texas.

The evil smile returned. Maybe they could even make it look like ISIS finishing up the work that they started.

The FBI director and the special agent in charge of the Bureau's counterterrorism department had named the national task force investigating the ISIS kidnappings and murders soon after the president of FOX was killed. The ISIS Action Task Force, or IATF as it was more commonly referred to, was assigned nearly twenty percent of the Bureau's total manpower assets. Because of the horrific and ongoing nature of the threat and the huge amount of continuous media coverage, the president had no choice but to dedicate a good deal of his time to staying on top of the situation. He met every other afternoon with the FBI director, the secretaries of State and Homeland Security and Defense, and his press secretary, Alicia Tovar. Since the Mexican president had not yet made an official request for the extradition of Davis, the attorney general was not yet included in the briefings.

Martinez addressed the FBI director.

"Clarence, what is the latest from the IATF?"

"Not much change for now, Mr. President. Davis has been out of the hospital for a while. Other than the media trying to get to him, things are quiet in San Antonio. It has been three weeks since the last kidnapping and killing. If ISIS stays with their playbook, another kidnapping could occur at any time. If the Davis situation has made them think twice, they may cease activities for a while. Our Mideast terrorist analysts as well as our colleagues at Central Intelligence are predicting that they go silent for a while and study how the US-Mexico response plays out. We are in contact with our opposite numbers with the Mexican Federal Police but are getting the runaround. They do not want our help investigating the crime scene. We are not sure, but there may be some kind of turf war going on between the Federal Police, the Army, and the government in Mexico City."

Ratzner agreed. "Something is stewing down south. It may be the confusion that resulted from the early reporting of events in the Mexican media."

"How so?" asked the president.

"The downing of the helicopter by Davis was initially reported as an aircraft malfunction or pilot error sort of thing. Then after the Special Forces platoon was taken out, the media was told that it was an organized cartel attack. Some elements of the Mexican media questioned if the helicopter crash was linked to the ambush of the platoon. The Army apparently told the reporters to back off or risk permanent health problems. Then the two dead peasant women were reported as victims of some sort of cartel assassin. Then there was the matter of the stolen aircraft. When the story was leaked that it was an American, the chap in Mexico picked up on the story while watching Nuevo Laredo television. He is now making an official demand for the return of the plane because the pipeline company he works for wants to take the value of the plane out of his pay."

The secretary of State agreed. "Over at State, we think that the peculiar quiet out of Mexico City is due primarily because they are trying to separate the truth from the lies before Acosta comes to you. I am sure that he does not want to jeopardize your friendship by going off halfcocked."

The press secretary spoke up. She always spoke directly to the president. Her critics said that she had a way of pretending that she was always alone with the president.

"Mr. President, you should not wait. You must get ahead of this thing while you still can. Davis is very big news. Other than the sound bite of your call to him while he was still in the hospital, you have been essentially silent on the subject. Agreed, you have publicly demanded that ISIS end the violence, but everybody is on that page. John Q. Public is already aligning themselves with what Davis did. There is great political capital to be gained by publicly acknowledging Davis and his accomplishment. One of the ways the voters are going to look at you in the next election is whether you are for or against Davis. If I were eventually going to be up for re-election, I think that being clearly for Davis would get you a fair number of those right-wing gun owners who did not vote for you in the last election. The least you can do is to have Davis and his wife to the White House for lunch in the Rose Garden."

Ratzner could not let Tovar have the last word on the subject. "And I would strongly caution you, Mr. President, until Acosta sends a clear signal that they recognize Davis as the victim of both international terrorism and the unfortunate corruption that lurks in his country because of the drug cartels, you should keep Davis at a cordial arm's length." Then he looked directly at Tovar. "Because if things go bad, all of the people who did not vote for you in the last election still won't, and a potentially large number of people who did won't do it again."

Martinez looked soberly at Ratzner and Tovar. "I understand where you are both coming from. I will decide on that subject soon."

The briefing ended and the president was left alone in the Oval Office. He had his own ideas of how to get the Davis issue to a point. He pressed the button that summoned his scheduling secretary. She promptly appeared in the Oval Office.

"How can I help you, Mr. President?"

"I want to meet with the senior senator from California, here after dinner."

The senior senator from California was Miranda Acosta. She was a second-generation American who was born in San Diego to legal immigrants from San Luis Potosi. She was educated at San

Diego State with an undergraduate degree in political science and then law school at Stanford. She never practiced law, preferring to go into politics immediately after graduation. She appealed to the predominantly Hispanic population of Southern California and was elected to the US Senate after a meteoric rise through lesser state political offices. She was twice divorced and had no children. She never gave up her maiden name in either of her marriages. She also had two secret ambitions. She hoped to develop a section of the American Southwest where Hispanic culture and the Spanish language were the norm, not unlike the French-Canadian areas of eastern Canada, and she wanted to be the first female president of the United States. Senator Acosta was also the Mexican president's first cousin.

"Good evening, Mr. President. To what do I owe the honor of this after-hours visit to the Oval Office?"

The president received her offered handshake and turned the handshake into a kiss on the back of the hand. He had done the same thing on election night, acknowledging her tireless work getting him elected. He showed her to a sofa.

"Miranda, I have an important job that only you can help me with."

"I am at your service as always."

"I need you to visit with President Acosta. And it must be done quickly and quietly."

"What should my cousin and I talk about?"

"This Davis affair."

"You know, Mr. President, with all these vague snippets of information being given to the media, I had a feeling that there was substantially more to the story. So, what is the story, Mr. President?"

Martinez got up to pour himself a scotch. He offered one to the senator, but she declined. He took his time with the drink, trying to decide how much of the story he needed to reveal.

"Davis has named a very senior Mexican Army general as being an accomplice to ISIS and is on the payroll of the Juarez cartel."

"I presume that President Acosta has already been given this information?"

"Yes, we shared intel early on."

"I don't know how I can help."

"We need to know for sure, like cousin to cousin sure, that President Acosta is not going to press for the extradition of Davis."

"Over a stolen airplane?"

"No. Not because of an airplane." Martinez paused, wondering if the FBI director and Ratzner would approve of his including the senator in the circle of privileged information.

"No. Not because of some dinky Cessna. What I am about to tell you is considered national security level information and not for further dissemination."

Acosta unconsciously leaned closer. "I understand, Mr. President."

"Davis had to fight his way out of Mexico and left a substantial trail of bodies in his wake."

Acosta recoiled slightly. "Terrorist bodies?"

"A few terrorists, but mostly Mexicans."

The senator's eyes narrowed at the revelation. Before she could speak, the president added, "When Davis recognized that an army general was in league with ISIS and the cartels, he assumed that if he escaped, he could not trust any authority to go to for help. And honestly, when you give it any amount of thought, he was probably right. His story is that everyone he killed was armed and actively after him. He claims that he acted purely in self-defense."

"How many people are we talking about?" asked Acosta.

"Total? Terrorists and Mexicans?"

"Mexicans. I don't care about terrorists."

"About twenty."

Acosta recoiled further. She thought for a moment and wished that she had not turned that drink down.

"That seems like an awful lot of so-called self-defense."

The president shrugged. "The circumstances were certainly

extraordinary. Extraordinary circumstances beget extraordinary actions."

The senator suppressed her obvious disgust and got back to business.

"So, what do you want me to do?"

"Clear your schedule for tomorrow and the next day. Be ready to fly out on our unmarked Citation first thing in the morning. We will notify President Acosta that you are coming for a special diplomatic discussion and ask that your visit be kept quiet. When you meet with him, try to get a feel for how they are viewing Davis' actions. Do they perceive his actions regarding Mexican law as self-defense with extenuating circumstances, or as in any way criminal? In essence, are they going to charge him in absentia for anything, and publicly demand extradition?"

The senator leaned back onto the plush sofa and slowly nodded her head.

"So, what we need to know is whether we can put our home-grown hero on parade, or are we in for serious diplomatic complications with our neighbor to the south and very uncomfortable political complications here at home?"

The president took a long pull at his single malt.

"That pretty much sums it up."

He stood, indicating that the meeting was essentially over. He ushered Acosta to the door of the Oval Office. Before he could open the door, she spoke up, this time in Spanish.

"Mr. President, I must know something. How do you feel about this Davis fellow personally?"

The president switched to Spanish without blinking.

"He is just a guy caught up in events that are much bigger than he is."

The president studied Acosta's face for clues of what was going on in the back of her mind. He picked up her hands in his.

"All life lost to violence is a tragedy, but I'm sworn to protect and defend the people of this country, not Mexicans."

As Senator Acosta left the Oval Office, her first thought was, "Wrong answer."

Senator Acosta was shown into President Juan Acosta's palatial office through a quiet hallway without fanfare. At the same time, a serving cart with a Sterling tea service was rolled into the room. While President Acosta's staff was in the equivalent of the Oval Office, Senator Acosta greeted the president with all the pomp that his staff would expect.

"Mr. President, it is so kind of you to adjust your schedule to meet with me on such short notice. I bring the best regards of President Martinez to his old and trusted friend."

"Madame Senator, I shall always make time for the emissary of President Martinez. May I offer you tea or coffee?"

The senator asked for tea while the president took coffee. After the cups were presented, the president looked to his chief of staff and said, "You may leave us now."

The chief of staff gathered everyone and ushered them out of the office and closed the door.

When the president was sure that the door was closed, he and the senator stood and embraced each other affectionately.

"Mirandasita, my sweet, sweet cousin. I have not seen you since before your president's election. You look wonderful."

"Have they decided to make you king yet?"

"No, but I am working on it! I just have to have a few more enemies killed, and then I can be fitted for the crown."

The cousins laughed and retook their seats. The president took a sip of his coffee and said, "Let me guess. Martinez sent you here to find out how we feel about your Señor Davis of San Antonio."

The senator smiled and nodded. "Juan, there is no doubt why you were elected in a landslide. You have always had an uncanny way of cutting to the chase. Yes, he wants to know if he will be charged with anything."

The president laughed out loud. "Is he serious? This man Davis killed more than twenty Mexican citizens including two peasant women. What are we to do? Ignore the carnage?"

"Davis was a victim of ISIS and apparently the Arabs were aided by some very high-level Mexicans."

The president reluctantly nodded. "Yes, yes. I know that someone had to have colluded with the Arabs. That is under scrutiny. But the fact remains that your man Davis took it upon himself to fight his way out of our country rather than finding reliable help from the proper authorities. The American press has always preferred to report on the very small percentage of corrupt Mexican officials while ignoring the thousands who are not."

"I don't disagree about that," replied the senator.

"Miranda, I have a fast-growing problem on my hands. The northern papers are reporting that an American assassin was sent to Chihuahua to kill some people in revenge for a drug deal gone bad. And then two dozen dead citizens later he sneaks back across the border. The families of all those dead people are demanding something be done. They are petitioning the governors of Chihuahua and Coahuila for now, but their demands will soon be made in Mexico City."

"But, Juan, you don't actually believe what the papers are saying?"

"Of course not. The editors of the papers are all probably owned by one cartel or the other. They are being told what to publish. But our Constitution, like yours, prevents us from doing anything about it. The problem is that what the common people read is essentially what they believe."

"Are you aware that a general officer in your army may be owned like the newspaper editors?

"As I said, our federal police are working on that as we speak."

"So, Juan, when I go home to my president, what do I tell him?"

"Tell him the truth."

"Which is?"

"That he was elected not because of his swarthy good looks, but because of the efforts of *my* country with *his* problems with illegal immigration from the south and the flow of illegal drugs through this country to *his* drug-hungry citizens. We are doing everything to which we agreed on this side of the border. Our efforts have been making the statistics improve dramatically. And great statistics will make his re-election much easier. What phrase do you like so much? Tell Martinez that he owes me."

"So, Davis is going to be charged with crimes on Mexican soil?"

The president leaned forward for emphasis. "Not yet decided. Tell your president that the thing he can count on is me not sacrificing my political career for his. Tell him that your Davis is only five bodies short of the record of this country's most notorious serial killer. Tell him this. He may have to decide whether he should sacrifice one man for the greater good of both of our nations."

The president smiled broadly, leaned back in the sofa, and sipped his coffee.

To signal that he had said his piece on the Davis subject, he said, "Enough business talk. Tell me, how are my Aunt Sophia and Uncle Hector, the proud parents of the senior senator from the great state of California, formerly a northern territory of Mexico, doing these days?"

On the flight back to Washington, Senator Acosta spoke with the president on a secure communication line. Martinez wanted the bottom line.

"Are they going to seek extradition?"

"Not yet decided, but political pressures on President Acosta are building rapidly. People want someone to pay for all the loss of life. The political cartoons in northern Mexico are showing caricatures of you with President Acosta on a leash sitting obediently at your heel. Many Mexicans believe that they gave away too much to the US during the last elections. Nothing has changed for the common people south of the border. They see you as picking up most of the political capital."

Martinez responded, "A close look at the ledger shows that the American gains have been more rhetorical than substantive. It seems to me that the common people of both countries are more alike than we would like to think. Everyone wants everything fixed yesterday."

"Mr. President, I feel obliged to let you know that in the Southwest the sentiment of the Hispanic voters is turning against Davis. His apparent heroism is now being revealed to be more akin to mass murder than the noble American defeating the terrorists. President Acosta's parting advice to you was that it may be better in the long run for you to appear strong and demonstrate that hero or not, Davis must explain his actions within the context of Mexican law and Mexican public opinion. If you want your legacy to be the development of a real and lasting co-prosperity sphere between the US and Central America, this may be the litmus test. Protect Davis and it will be business as usual. Make Davis proceed through the Mexican judicial process and your standing in the international community will grow."

Martinez thought for a long moment. "That all sounds good, but the Electoral College won't be counting many votes from the international community in two years."

CHAPTER THIRTY-FOUR

Red Herring

De La Garza's operation in Texas was going to be complex because it called for simultaneous operations to be accomplished on the same night in two different cities. The first operation started in Austin with the kidnapping of a University of Texas professor of Middle Eastern Studies named Azizi. He was a thirty-two-year-old bachelor who was born in Pakistan. He happened to be on an FBI watch list only because he attended the same mosque and was acquainted with three men who were relatives of legitimate ISIS members in Iraq and Jordan.

De La Garza knew of the man because he was the next-door neighbor of one of the Juarez Cartel's distribution specialists. The distribution man worked with the Mexican Mafia smugglers who brought product across the border and into the cities.

At De La Garza's request, the cartel's enforcement people contacted the Austin distributor and ordered him to enlist the services of Mafia hit men in Laredo. Their task was to kidnap the professor and force him to load and fire a silenced Heckler and Koch P2000 automatic to ensure that the weapon was covered with the professor's prints and his hands were covered in gunshot residue. He would then be handcuffed, gagged, and placed in the black Chevy Suburban for the trip to Leon Springs, where he would meet his fate.

Leon Springs, Texas, 3:15 a.m.

The driver of the Suburban dropped off the four-man team and the professor a half mile from the Davis home. They were all dressed in black and followed a track that was preset in a handheld GPS unit. The only trouble that they encountered was a barking dog of one of Davis' neighbors. A well-placed, silenced 9mm round fixed the problem. When the Mafia team was 200 yards from the Davis house, they used a Russian-made infrared scanner to locate the first of two FBI agents assigned to night security around the Davis home.

One of the hit men quietly stalked the first agent. When he was forty yards away, he fired the silenced Heckler and Koch, aiming just above the top of the agent's bulletproof vest. The round entered the agent's neck, exploding his larynx and right common carotid artery. The shock of the round knocked him to the ground, and he bled out before he could trigger the alarm to his partner. The hit man relieved the dead agent of his .40 caliber Glock 22 sidearm and his field radio.

The remaining Mafia men and the professor gathered around the dead agent. They pulled a black ski mask over the head of the doomed Pakistani. They walked the professor twenty feet away from the dead agent. The killer of the FBI man placed the muzzle of the agent's Glock in one end of a small plastic box stuffed with cotton and then shot the professor in the forehead. Another man peeled the piece of duct tape off his mouth and then carefully replaced the ski mask. They replaced the Heckler and Koch in the professor's right hand. The Mafia man then returned to the agent and placed the Glock back in his hand and fired a second round into the silencer box to ensure that there was gunshot residue on the agent's gun hand. To any crime scene investigator, the evidence would be clear. A deeply planted Muslim extremist bent on retaliation was killed by the heroic but dying FBI agent.

The killers only needed to find and eliminate the other agent and Davis and his family, and their mission, would be complete. They would each be $1 million richer and would be in the very good graces of their cartel brothers and one very happy Mexican Army general.

The Davis House, 3:40 a.m.

Dweezel Davis, the family's Jack Russell terrier, was always the first to recognize a threat, and he was rarely wrong. He was in his bed in the kitchen. When he first heard the scratching noise his first thought was raccoon. Dweezel hated those filthy bandits. He ran to the entry hall and the front door of the house. He pressed his nose forcefully into the door seal and inhaled deeply. His encyclopedic nose immediately recognized human scent, not the scent of those damned raccoons. He had memorized the scents of all the new humans that were now hanging around since the main human had disappeared and then returned. These were new humans, and they stank of nervous sweat. Something was not right. The main human needed to be informed.

Brooks had just gasped awake from the recurring dream about the two women with machetes. Once again, he could not clear the pistol from his holster before the first blade split his skull. He rolled to his right to see if he awoke Molly. Her deep rhythmic breathing told him that she was not disturbed.

He had dismissed the doctor's advice that after surviving such a grim ordeal he should begin seeing a good psychiatrist to help him through the post-traumatic problems that were sure to come. Molly had agreed with his doctor, but Brooks was not about to waste money on a shrink. But now that the knife-wielding women were a routine fixture in his REM sleep, he thought that he might have to reconsider.

He closed his eyes and once again asked God's forgiveness as well as the forgiveness of all the loved ones of the people he killed. He was halfway through his nightly Act of Contrition when Dweezel jumped on the bed and growled.

In the moonlit bedroom, Brooks could see the dog staring in the direction of the bedroom door. Another low growl was issued from the dog. Brooks rose up on one elbow and whispered to the dog.

"What's happening, Dweez?"

Davis realized that the dog's hackles were standing on end. The sight made the hair on the back of Davis' neck go equally erect. He slipped out of bed and went to the master bedroom closet. The FBI had installed a bank of monitors that were displaying the images produced by ten strategically placed day/night cameras. The night images were shown on high-definition gray-scale monitors. The images were remarkably clear.

His eyes went to the image of four men gathered at the front entry of the house. He knew that the security detail consisted of only two agents. He stared at the monitor and was able to see that the men were armed with compact weapons with long, curved magazines. They wore some sort of elongated goggles on their heads. Davis immediately thought of night-vision devices. On another monitor, he could see the motionless body of someone sprawled on the ground. Davis burst out of the closet and shook his wife awake.

"Molly! Get up! No questions! We've got trouble." He pulled open the drawer of the night table and handed her the Ruger P-89 with which she had been training.

"Get upstairs to the boys. Get them up. Get James armed—have him cover the back stairs. Tell them to do just like the FBI showed them. Tell them this is not a drill." As an afterthought, he added, "No matter what you hear, do not come downstairs unless you hear me yell Shelby Mustang." It was a reference to Brooks' favorite car. "If you don't hear that, kill anyone that comes upstairs!" A shaky Molly accepted the weapon and went to protect her sons.

Brooks retrieved the Benelli 12-gauge police autoloader that was permanently stationed in the corner of the bedroom. Dweezel was now panting with excitement. Brooks pointed in the direction that Molly had gone.

"Dweez! Go to Molly, now!" The feisty little dog ran after Molly.

Brooks pulled on jeans and headed to the great room of the house. As he moved across the great room toward the entrance foyer, he could hear someone trying to pick the front door lock. He flicked off the shotgun's safety and positioned himself behind the leather sofa.

The lock clicked loudly, and the door slowly opened. The first man entered the foyer with his weapon at the ready. Brooks could see the outlines of his colleagues following behind. He wondered how many shots he could get off before they would be able to return fire. His mind briefly wondered how wide the spread of the buckshot would be at this distance. Could he get two of them with his first round? He wondered if they could see him in the darkness with their night-vision devices. An idea materialized in his mind.

Brooks rested the shotgun on the back of the sofa and lined up on the face of the first man. As he squeezed off the first round he flipped on the table lamp.

The shotgun blast inside the room was deafening. It was followed immediately by another blast from behind Brooks. He immediately thought that he had been flanked by other terrorists. When the 100-watt bulb of the lamp went on, the light was instantly intensified a hundred-fold by the night-vision devices blinding the three Mafia men still standing. They all returned fire but were shooting blindly without effect. Davis rapidly sighted in on the head of the second man and sent him the way of the first. Another blast came from behind Brooks and the third man went down before Brooks could shoot. The fourth man threw off the night-vision device. With a moment to recover, he tried to train his weapon on Brooks, but Brooks was an instant quicker. He fired the shotgun blast at the man's knees and sent him to the floor screaming.

Brooks spun to find the source of the fire from his rear. The front bead of the Benelli came to rest on James. Brooks gasped and lowered the shotgun. James held the second tactical shotgun and was pointing the weapon at the bodies of the intruders. He had a look of grim satisfaction on his face.

"Jesus, James! Get the fuck upstairs and protect your mom and brothers!"

James looked at his father and then in the direction of the screaming terrorist. "You might want to finish that bastard off before he picks up his gun again." He turned and casually walked up the stairs. Over his shoulder, he quipped, "You're welcome, Dad."

Davis approached the fourth terrorist with the shotgun now pointing at the man's face. The man made a feeble attempt to go for his weapon. Davis adjusted his aim and shot the man's right hand off.

The crippled man started screaming, *"No mas! No mas!"*

Davis was suddenly struck by the fact that the man he was sure was an Arab terrorist was speaking Spanish, not Arabic. Davis kicked the weapon away from the man and checked the other three. Two were already dead and the third was gasping his last breaths. He stepped to the bottom of the staircase to the second floor and yelled, "Shelby Mustang." A moment later Molly appeared at the top of the stairs.

"I'm alright. Everything is under control. Have you called the police yet?"

"No. I had just gotten the boys together and then James disappeared. Then the shooting started. Where did James go?"

"He's covering the back stairs. Go back to the boys and close the door. Do not call the police. I will take care of it. Do you understand me?"

"No, but I won't call. What are you going to do?"

"Practice my interrogation techniques."

Davis returned to the wounded man. He was writhing in pain and bleeding profusely on the parquet floor of the foyer. He wore black combat utility clothing and a web harness. A combat knife was in a sheath attached to the harness. Davis removed the knife from the sheath. He placed the point of the blade under the man's nose.

"We are going to have a discussion. I'm going to ask you questions and you are going to tell me the truth. Do you understand?"

The man shook his head slowly back and forth. *"No habla inglés."*

Davis contemplated switching to Spanish but remembered that being secretly bilingual had proven to be quite valuable once before.

"Pal, you had better dust off your middle school English right quick."

Davis pressed the point of the knife into the man's groin.

"If you don't answer my next question, I'm going to remove your right testicle. Then I'm going to ask you again. If you still don't answer me, well you know what's going to happen to old lefty."

The man's face registered pain and resignation.

"Who sent you to get me?"

After a pause, the man swallowed with difficulty and replied, "A man named Ortiz from Juarez."

Davis chuckled. "Well, well. I guess that we have a bona fide, speaking-in-tongues sort of miracle going on here. I expect Ortiz is a cartel man?"

"He is from Juarez" was the man's only reply.

"Does he take orders from General De La Garza?"

"That is something that someone at my level would not know."

"Are the FBI men dead?"

The man looked away and would not answer.

"I'll take that as a yes."

Davis got up and called to Molly.

"Molly, I don't want you or the boys to come down here."

She reappeared and nodded but did not reply.

The man looked at Davis and asked, "Why didn't you kill me?"

After a pause, Davis replied, "Why should I do a piece of shit like you any favors?"

Brooks went to the staircase where James had stood and fired the other tactical shotgun at the cartel hit men. He found the first and then the second spent 12-gauge buckshot cartridge. He returned to the position where he had engaged the hit men and threw James' empty shells on the floor with his own. When the FBI crime scene investigators evaluated the site of the bloody shootout, it would appear that only Brooks did the killing. Brooks just had to make sure that James got the story straight.

CHAPTER THIRTY-FIVE
Alarm and Response

The Davis house was connected directly to the communication center of the San Antonio field office by a special line. When Davis pressed 777 on any phone in his house, an alarm sounded in the communication center. Several large displays in the com center immediately showed that the source of the emergency was the Davis house. The night watch communication specialist picked up within five seconds of the alarm.

"FBI San Antonio. What is the nature of your emergency?"

"This is Davis. There was an attack. Both agents are down. Three out of four attackers are dead. The fourth is wounded. My family and I are all okay."

The com specialist triggered a general alarm that was reserved for a special crisis when agents were down. A mobile alarm started sounding the homes of Collier and all the members assigned to the Epstein-Davis task force. At Collier's home, the alarm had been heard in the past. It made a sickening feeling form immediately in the chests of Collier and his wife. When that alarm went off, it was always very bad.

The specialist asked, "Where are you right now?"

"I'm in the foyer guarding the wounded terrorist. My family is upstairs."

"Have you disarmed the wounded suspect?"

Davis looked at the man's bloody stump where his hand used to be and his ruined knees.

"That's affirmative. He's not going anywhere."

"Go to your emergency kit and get a pair of handcuffs. Cuff one wrist to the opposite ankle. Then retreat to your assigned defensive position. Do not leave your defensive position. Do not go outside. There will be others outside and they will probably be regrouping for a second attack. I repeat, do not go outside."

"Don't worry about that for a second. How long before your people arrive?"

"The night watch people here in the office are seven miles from your house. They will be arriving in eight to ten minutes. Others will be arriving shortly thereafter. They will announce their arrival by saying FBI and the code phrase. Do you remember the code phrase?"

"Shelby Mustang," replied Davis.

"That's correct. Now secure the wounded suspect and retreat to your defensive position."

As Davis hung up, he mumbled, "Oh, he's going to love that."

Within the hour, most of the San Antonio field office personnel were on the scene. Patrols had fanned out looking for the getaway vehicle, but it was long gone. When the driver heard the shotgun, he realized that what was supposed to be a silent operation had been compromised. He waited five minutes and then drove by the front of the Davis home. When there was no one to pick up, he left and was on his way back to Laredo, lamenting the lost million dollars.

Molly and the boys were gathered around the kitchen island, looking somber and making attempts at mugs of hot chocolate.

The wounded terrorist was taken to the hospital under heavy guard. He was a seasoned enough criminal to know better than to speak to the colleagues of the two federal men he had just killed. He was caught, crippled, and totally out of luck. He just wished that Davis would have finished him off.

The bodies of the two agents and the professor had been located outside. Collier, Dayton, and Davis stood near the body of the Pakistani. The men tried to make sense of the gruesome scene. The black ski mask of the suspected terrorist had been removed by the crime scene technicians and his face photographed. The investigator called to Collier, "This guy does not look Hispanic like the others."

Collier, Dayton, and Davis approached for a better look.

"He looks Middle Eastern to me," said Dayton. The others agreed, but Collier shook his head.

"This is odd. Something is not right." He turned to Davis. "Are you sure you did not hear a shot before they entered the house?"

"I was asleep before the dog let me know that something wasn't right."

Collier went into the mentor mode and addressed his young agent.

"So Special Agent Dayton, on first look, how do you see this thing going down?"

Dayton paused for a moment, feeling like he was back at Quantico and was just about to take an important exam.

"I can see two scenarios. The first has this Arab-looking man being ISIS and recruiting some local talent, maybe Mexican Mafia types, to pull a retaliatory raid trying to finish what they started with Brooks. They successfully kill Agent Markosky over by his vehicle. They attack Agent Taylor here, who gets off a lucky shot and drills the Arab in the forehead before he dies. The Hispanic men then try to complete the raid to collect whatever paycheck they were offered. The second scenario is more vague. Maybe this is an all-Mexican-inspired deal as retribution for Brooks' actions down in Mexico. But I just can't fit the Middle Eastern-looking man into that picture."

Davis mumbled, "Red herring."

Collier turned to Davis. "Funny, that's exactly what I was thinking. Are you sure that you weren't Bureau in a previous life?"

Dayton's wheels finally caught up. "You think that this guy was along only to make it look like ISIS?"

Collier replied, "I can't wait to get this guy's prints and picture into the system. The results may be very telling."

Davis had his own ideas and did not need fingerprint confirmation.

"It's that fucking De La Garza. This just reeks of that sorry bastard!"

An agent approached Collier with a report from the roadblock that had been established as soon as the search for the getaway vehicle began.

"Sir, the news trucks have arrived and are asking for access."

The SAIC shook his head and hissed, "Shit! They can smell blood better than a pack of sharks. Tell them no! I'll announce a news conference later this morning."

Collier turned to Davis. "Brooks, we need to think about getting you and your family to a more secure location."

Davis shook his head. "I'm not giving up my home to anybody."

"Not a good idea, Brooks. Look what happened last night."

"Well then, double the guard. Let's just announce that you've moved us to a secure location out of state."

"I don't know, Brooks."

"We're not going. End of discussion. We can defend ourselves here better than someplace we are not familiar with." As an afterthought, he laughed and added, "And besides, we've always got Dweezel on alert, twenty-four-seven."

"You need to rethink that, Brooks. You and one dog might not be enough to protect your whole family."

Brooks shrugged in reply. He was thinking about a certain backup shotgun-wielding son the FBI didn't know about. The same son he was ever more worried about.

By 9:00 a.m., the forensic pictures of the professor and his fingerprints were matched up by the great computers at Quantico. Collier and the Davis case team were meeting back at the San Antonio field office.

"This must be a Mexican-inspired attack designed to lay the smoking gun at the feet of ISIS. If our agents and Davis and his whole family had been eliminated and all we had was a dead Pakistani, we would have certainly thought with a high degree of certainty that it was the work of deep-cover ISIS."

"So, who in Mexico set it in motion and why?" asked an agent.

"Davis thinks it's General De La Garza. I think he's right. Remember the DEA was helping De La Garza try to fix the position of a so-called notorious cartel assassin. Based on Davis' story and by backtracking his route out of Mexico, Davis was the guy on De La Garza's shit list. Once Davis made it home alive, the general knew that Davis would be spilling his guts to us. He is smart enough to know that his cover is self-destructing, and his plush little racket is about to come to a screeching halt."

Another agent asked, "So if De La Garza is dirty, isn't it a little late for him to be worrying about what Davis says?"

"Not if the general is trying to kill off the Federales' only credible witness before he is asked to testify in Mexico City."

The agents looked around at each other. Dayton summed up their thoughts.

"They wouldn't make him go back to Mexico, would they?"

Collier shrugged. "Now we are entering the territory of the State Department, Justice Department, and the attorney general. Definitely above our pay grades."

"What were you thinking?" Brooks had invited James outside that evening for a little father-and-son talk. James was nursing a can of Coke and did not respond immediately. "Those were professional killers. You could be so easily dead right now. I repeat, what were you thinking?"

James drank down the Coke and then crushed the empty can. "Yeah, they were professionals, and you were outnumbered four to one. I thought you could use a little help. It turned out alright."

Brooks exploded, "You are a cocky bastard. You have made your mother sick during all of this. And it's going to stop right now."

The young man replied with a disinterested shrug.

"James, you have no idea what you have done to yourself. You've killed someone. Your soul will probably never be the same again."

James quietly replied, "Like father, like son."

CHAPTER THIRTY-SIX
The News Conference

Collier's noon news conference was held in the conference center of the San Antonio field office. It was significant enough news to preempt regular programming. All the local affiliates of the major networks were present as well as KNIC, the major Spanish station in San Antonio. Representatives of the major print media and news radio stations were also represented. Dayton's attention was drawn to the news truck of XHLAR, the major television station of Nuevo Laredo, Tamaulipas, Mexico. He wondered how they were able to get the news and make the nearly four-hour trip from the border to San Antonio. He alerted Collier to the presence. Collier called Agent Dominguez over for instructions.

"Stick near the Nuevo Laredo people and get a feel for what they are reporting. Then make small talk with them before they pack up. Try to find out how they were so Johnny-on-the-spot."

Collier talked to the director while prepping for the news conference. They agreed to simply give the facts as they appeared at the present hour and not speculate or give any intel away. In general, the goal was to feed the media enough to keep them happy and appropriately confused.

Collier stepped to the podium and went right to work.

"I'm Special Agent in Charge Martin Collier. This is what we can confirm at this time. Between 3:00 and 3:30 a.m. this morning at least five men conducted a raid on the home of Brooks Davis. Utilizing infrared and night-vision devices and silenced weapons, they were able to surprise and kill two FBI agents assigned to night area security at the Davis home. Their names will be available only after notification of all next of kin is completed."

"Mr. Davis was awakened by the sounds of someone trying to gain entry into the house. Since this was not in accordance with the security protocol, Mr. Davis assumed correctly that he and his family were under attack and in serious jeopardy. He armed himself and was able to engage four armed intruders, killing three and wounding the fourth. He then notified FBI headquarters in San Antonio of the attack. First responders were on the scene within six minutes of the call.

"The names of all the attackers have not yet been verified. We expect more on those identities later today. The wounded attacker was taken immediately on arrival of EMS personnel to an area hospital where he is undergoing surgery at this hour. For now, he will remain at the hospital in isolation and under heavy guard. He will be interviewed in the presence of legal counsel as soon as he is declared medically able. We have no estimate as to when that will occur."

"Because of the ongoing nature of the threats against Mr. Davis and his family, they have been moved to a secure location for the immediate future. Because of this, Mr. Davis will not be available for interviews with the media until further notice."

That note was greeted with a chorus of groans and protest from the assembled media. The protests were greeted with a hostile glare from the special agent in charge.

"I will briefly answer questions at this time."

Hands shot up all over the room. Collier pointed to Tom Hannah, a reporter from the local ABC affiliate.

"It has been nearly two weeks since Mr. Davis' escape from Mexico and the FBI appears to be keeping a very tight lid on this case. Now there has been a major security failure at the Davis home."

Collier interrupted, "Mr. Hannah, is there a question coming?"

"Yes. Why is the FBI preventing media access to Mr. Davis? His story is important to the nation?"

Without a moment of hesitation, Collier replied to the question he already knew he would be asked. "Because, Mr. Hannah, there is a continuing Red Level threat in this country and Mr. Davis occupies a unique position at the center of an ongoing national threat investigation. The country cannot afford to lose the valuable intelligence that Mr. Davis can offer."

Before the man could ask a second question, Collier pointed to another reporter.

"If the media can't interview Mr. Davis directly, when can we expect a detailed account of his six weeks in Mexico?"

Again, Collier had a prepared reply. "The Epstein-Davis case is an ongoing, multilayered international case that requires very thorough and detailed investigation. At the conclusion of the investigation, a public report will be forthcoming."

"And how long will that take?" fired back the reporter.

"As long as it takes," replied Collier calmly. He pointed to another reporter.

The man stood and identified himself and his affiliation with XHLAR in Nuevo Laredo. Collier's eyes narrowed slightly as he took the question.

"Señor Collier, is the FBI and the US State Department aware that Mexican Police and military authorities are attributing the deaths of twenty-six people including two peasant women in Mexico to Señor Davis, and is the State Department prepared to cooperate with the Mexican government if extradition is requested?"

The conference room fell dead silent. Collier's eyes locked on the Mexican reporter.

"As I've already said, the Epstein-Davis case is ongoing. We are investigating a number of leads and allegations, and we are not prepared currently to present them publicly."

Every hand in the room was raised with urgency. Collier knew that everyone would abandon their prepared question and zero in on the damaging new revelation, so he addressed the assembled news people in general.

"Ladies and gentlemen of the media. You all must understand that early speculation in any case is rarely helpful in discovering the precise truth and can therefore be more damaging than useful. When the FBI is certain beyond reasonable doubt about the facts in this case, you will be the first to know."

With that dismissal, he ended the news conference. As he left the podium, his eyes sought out Agent Dominguez. When their eyes met, his telepathic orders were clear: Get on the XHLAR reporter and find out as much as you can.

Brooks and Molly were watching the television when the news conference came on. When the Mexican reporter mentioned the body count, Molly's breath left her. Brooks did not move until the reporter mentioned extradition. With the word, Brooks recoiled, and his eyes narrowed, causing a deep furrow to form on his forehead. Molly's hand sought out her husband's and held it tightly as if she could physically prevent anyone from taking her husband a second time. She looked at his face. She had seen that look before when Brooks was pondering a difficult construction problem. She knew not to interrupt his train of thought. After a few minutes, he got up and retreated to the kitchen. He poured himself a glass of iced tea and sat down at the island. Molly followed him. When he refocused on his wife, he held up his glass and asked, "Tea?"

Molly shook her head. A wave of nausea was building in her belly. She sat down next to him and again grasped his hand. Davis looked at the hand and then her face. He studied her face for a long moment. She was a strikingly beautiful woman when they met, and she aged so well that Davis could see little difference now. He suddenly remembered the time that someone mistook Molly for his daughter. She never let him forget by frequently calling him Daddy. Molly could not stand his silence any longer.

"Brooks, what are you going to do?"

"Truthfully?"

"Yes."

"I have no idea of what I'm going to do. But on the other hand, I know for sure what I'm not going to do."

She studied him briefly. "You are never going to cross the border."

Brooks smiled and winked. "Great minds always think alike."

Molly moved behind him and put her arms around him from behind. She embraced him and tenderly kissed the unmangled side of his head.

"Honey, you will be going up against powerful people and organizations."

"No choice."

"There has to be some way to get help."

"Molly, you do realize that I don't stand a snowball's chance in hell if I cross the border, don't you?"

Molly reluctantly nodded the affirmative.

"I'm a dead man down there. Of that, I have no doubt. So…"

"So?" followed Molly.

"So, I'm going to stay here in the US or I'm willing to die trying."

Molly grimaced. "Please don't talk about dying."

Brooks put his arm around her waist. "If it is my time to die then so be it. But if I must die, where would you rather see me die? Here in the country I love, or face down in some filthy Mexican jail?"

The wave of nausea crested in her stomach, and she could not respond.

Brooks kissed her tenderly on the lips and whispered, "See, we are always on the same page."

He picked up his glass of tea and moved toward his study.

"Where are you going?"

"I've got some thinking to do."

"Brooks."

He stopped and turned around. "What?"

"Whatever you decide, I'll support you."

"I never doubted it."

CHAPTER THIRTY-SEVEN

Hidden Agendas

Senator Acosta placed a call to her friend Sylvia Brinkman, who hosted CNN's *Focus on Washington*. Brinkman's program was a staple in the news diet of most citizens with liberal agendas. Paradoxically, it was watched by many conservatives. Conservatives tuned in because Brinkman was perceived as the enemy, and it was best to know your enemy well. Liberals watched the show because Brinkman's rhetoric was just what they wanted to hear. They also loved to watch her because she was fearlessly argumentative, and she routinely challenged conservatives to go a round or two with her in front of the cameras. She usually won such contests. She was accused by the right of having the personality of a pit bull bitch, but mostly just a bitch.

Acosta knew that the Davis case was just the sort of fodder that could create a feeding frenzy of liberal versus conservative rhetoric and the perfect person to keep things stirred up at a national level was Brinkman.

They agreed to meet at the home of one of the senator's friends in rural Virginia. After cordial small talk about pet projects, Acosta got to the point of the visit.

"Sylvia, are you aware of the facts behind the Davis case?"

"I heard the allegations by the Nuevo Laredo reporter that Davis supposedly killed a bunch of people down in Mexico."

"I thought that you should know that the allegations are indeed fact."

Brinkman absorbed that for a moment. "Who all was killed?"

"A few ISIS types, but mostly Mexicans."

"How many?"

"According to my source, Davis was only five bodies short of the Mexican record for killings by a single serial killer."

"How reliable is your source?"

"The highest reliability you can get in Mexico" was Acosta's less than cryptic reply. Brinkman was aware of the senator's relationship to the Mexican president.

"Senator, forgive me but it seems odd that you would share these things with me. Don't get me wrong, I'm thrilled that you are, but I'd love to know why."

"Primarily because we are always on the same page. My approach to my political enemies is virtually identical to your approach to dealing with anybody from the other side of the aisle. Our personalities and styles are very similar."

"Okay, so I'm the media equivalent of the senior senator from California. But that does not explain the gift of preferential information. So, what's the deal?"

"Sometimes a politician must show public support of the administration even if they see an issue from different perspectives. The Davis case is guaranteed to be the hot-button issue to come out of this round of terrorist activity. Oh, by the way, great job putting ISIS' current program at the feet of the last administration. Essentially Sylvia, I think you and I are seeing this problem in the same way, and we can help each other ensure that the resolution comes out right."

"If I can continue to get preferential information that results in the greatest media share and make my producers ecstatic and make the other side continue to cringe at the sound of my name, I'm on board!"

President Martinez took President Acosta's call in the Oval Office. The conversation was conducted in Spanish. His chief of staff and press secretary were in attendance. Since they were bilingual Martinez put the call on the speaker and Rodriguez and Tovar sat quietly and made notes. After cordial greetings, Acosta got to the point.

"Guillermo, you know why I'm calling."

Since it was a statement and not a question, Martinez responded positively.

"Of course, the Davis affair."

"Are your Mexico watchers keeping you informed of the political fallout that is building both in the northern states and here in Mexico City?"

"We are watching and listening. What we are debating is who is driving the calls for action. Is it a small group of common citizens who lost loved ones or is it manipulation by the cartels or questionable elements in your military?"

"You know how things are down here. It is a combination of factors and factions. However, the inescapable fact is that there will soon be a call to action that I will not be able to ignore or risk grave political damage."

"So, you are going to ask for extradition?"

"If Mr. Davis would voluntarily come to Mexico City and testify before our grand jury, he could present his case and formal extradition would not be necessary."

The chief of staff looked at the president and slowly shook his head. He knew that Davis was not likely to volunteer for anything.

"Juan, your northern press is calling Davis a mass murderer and worse. Is there any possibility that your grand jury would do anything other than indict? Our man was placed in an irreconcilable position. He did what he had to do to survive."

Acosta became more formal. "Mr. President, Davis killed many people here in Mexico. Some were certainly bad, but many were not. Two peasant women out collecting firewood were killed. Davis must be required to present a rational explanation for that."

"It is my understanding that the women were trying to collect more than firewood."

"Our grand jury should decide that. The greater issue is one of perception."

"What do you mean, my friend?"

"How will we be perceived by our countries and the rest of the world? Do we want our constituents to perceive that we are willing to play loosely with the rules and be accused by our adversaries of favoritism? Mr. President, this is not a case of giving a brother-in-law a job with a title. This is a case where a growing number of people are thinking that a mass murderer is getting a free ride. That should not happen on either side of the border."

"I will have to take this under advisement with the attorney general and the State and Justice Departments."

"Very well, Mr. President. I will also discuss this case with my advisors, and I will have my decision soon. I hope that one man is not responsible for undoing all the important progress that our countries have made since we took office. Keep in mind that we have lost nearly two dozen of our citizens. That will not go easily under the rug. Sometimes a chief executive must make painful individual sacrifices for the good of the majority."

"Juan, I must ask a serious question, and as friends, I need an honest answer. If Davis were to go to Mexico City to testify, can you guarantee his safety?"

There was a long pause from Acosta.

"Of course. He will be afforded the best protection."

As Martinez pressed the button to end the call, his only thought was that Acosta had paused too long.

CHAPTER THIRTY-EIGHT
Plans Set in Motion

James was in his bedroom, sitting at his desk doing his calculus homework, when Brooks entered the room and shut the door. James gave his father a quizzical look and thought that he was about to be the recipient of another fatherly diatribe about being a miscreant killer.

"What?"

"I need to talk to you."

"You've already read me the riot act, Dad. I don't need anymore."

"Oh, shut up, wiseass. I need your help. Hear me out." As an afterthought, he added a "Please."

James was taken aback. He put his pencil down and turned to face his father.

"Look, I've made a decision that I need to put some distance between me and the family again."

""What?! Does Mom know this?"

"Not yet. You're the first to know. I've got to find a way to communicate with her without anyone knowing about it. That's where you come in. Since you have a death wish and desire to be involved in my business, here is your chance to participate with my blessing."

"But why do you need to go? Is it the extradition thing?"

"Yes."

"But what if somebody else attacks the house? I don't think I can protect the family...not without you."

Brooks finally realized that his son's manhood had fully arrived while he was absent. It was time to fully acknowledge it.

"Son, I didn't recognize exactly how capable you are. And for that, I am truly sorry. You have equal parts of bravery and selflessness. Now, if you can be a thinker before you act, you will be a force to be reckoned with. As far as protecting the family, I think that between you and the tactical shotgun and Dweezel, inside the house, and the FBI outside the house, everything is going to be pretty well covered. But me getting hauled off to Mexico, that's a whole different thing."

James was quiet while he scanned his father's face. His eyes traced the healing scar on Brooks' head and thought, "My old man is truly a badass. But a good kind of badass."

"Okay, so how can I help you with this?"

Brooks dug into his pocket and removed a wad of cash. He peeled off $300.

"Go buy two pre-paid, untraceable cell phones. One for each of us. When I need to communicate, I call you, then you talk only face-to-face with your mom. No traceable or recordable communications."

James' mind went to his "desperate agreement" that he was forced into with Agent Dayton. He worried about all the surveillance assets that the FBI had, and that were probably already trained on him. He quickly dismissed the idea that he should tell his dad about the interaction with Dayton. He smiled and thought, "Now I've got one on Dayton!"

"When do you need the phones?" asked James.

"How long will it take you to get them?"

Davis sequestered himself in his study with the door closed. He dialed a number on the disposable phone. His banker, Les Prewitt, answered the call.

"Les, Brooks Davis. How the hell are you?"

"Brooks, you son of a bitch! I should be asking you the same thing."

"Well, as my dad used to say, I'm in pretty good shape for the shape I'm in."

"I would have called you sooner, but I figured that you probably just wanted to be left alone."

"You're right there, Les. Listen, I won't keep you, but I need a very serious favor, and I need it fast."

"For you my friend, anything."

"I need you to get about $50,000 in cash ready ASAP."

There was a pause from the banker.

"Brooks, is everything okay? Nobody is forcing you to do this, are they?"

"No, nothing like that. I just need some cash and right quick. It is a long, complicated story. I'll tell you the sordid details later."

"How do you want the money?"

"Fifties and hundreds, non-consecutive, and in your old beat-up briefcase. Then I need it delivered to me at the Longhorn Café in Leon Springs. How long will it take you?"

"Jesus, Brooks, this is making me very nervous. You realize that a large cash withdrawal will trigger a flag at the federal banking authority?"

"Yes, I figured it would. I'm sure the Feds will be in your office in nothing flat."

"What am I supposed to tell them?"

"Nothing but the truth, so help you God. Tell them I called, asked for a cash withdrawal and a delivery of said cash to the Longhorn Café, which is where you can tell them you last saw me."

"And you are sure that everything is alright?"

"About as right as you can be in a Red Level threat environment. How long will it take you to make it happen?"

"I can be there in an hour."

Davis hung up the phone and called a second number. A man answered.

"Fritz. This is Brooks Davis."

"Brooks! Man, I don't mind telling you, I thought you were shit outta luck."

"You should know that I'm a resilient sort of guy."

"You better be. According to the news, the boogie men are after your ass."

"Unfortunately, I've got all kinds of people that are set on having not only my ass but the rest of my anatomy as well."

"How can I help you, Brooks?"

"Do you remember when we were hunting in the Kaibab above Flagstaff?"

"I'll never forget. I broke my leg above the tree line when it was five degrees and snowing. You carried my carcass back to camp and saved my wretched life. I told you that I owed you big-time. I'm thinking that you are calling to collect."

"This is the time, my friend."

"Just tell me what I can do for you."

"I need to get lost for a while and I think your peculiar talents may be of great assistance."

Fritz chuckled. "This sounds like it could be fun."

"Can you pick me up behind the Starbucks in Leon Springs in an hour?"

"Did you say behind the Starbucks?"

"Yes."

"Why behind?"

"We've got to avoid surveillance cameras."

"Oh, this is just getting better and better."

Brooks asked Molly to join him in their bedroom. When he closed the door, her first thought was that he was suddenly in the mood for a romantic afternoon interlude. But when she looked into his eyes, she knew immediately that romance was not on the agenda.

"Honey, what is it?"

"I've got to take off for a while."

Her forehead wrinkled in confusion. "What are you talking about?"

"You know how you have always accused me of having better intuition than a whole pack of women? Well, my intuition is telling me to make myself scarce."

"Is it the extradition thing?"

"Yes. We heard it first from Santiago. Then the newsman from Nuevo Laredo. We've heard it twice. I feel sure that the third time will be the charm. The next time I hear it I will probably be in handcuffs. I've been in handcuffs, and I didn't like it. It's not going to happen again if I can help it."

"So, what are you going to do?"

"I can't tell you."

Molly did not like that. "What do you mean? Why not?"

"If I tell you, they can force you to talk, or you will be threatened with obstruction of justice. Our boys don't need you in jail."

Molly reluctantly understood the logic.

"So, if I take off and you know nothing about it, they can't threaten you. That will help me a great deal."

"But I will be sick with worry."

Brooks embraced and kissed her.

"You should have learned by now that I'm a survivor type. I assure you that if my plan works out, I will probably be safer than you." Brooks paused to caress Molly's face. "There are a couple of other important things I need to tell you. First, protect the boys. When I take off, the Feds will be questioning everyone, repeatedly, about what they know. Be wary of everyone, even people we would normally trust. Andy and Zane should be blissfully ignorant, so they should leave them alone. You and James...different story. I've already talked with James, and we have made some plans. If you need to communicate with me, you only do it through James. He is going to know how, but he is not going to tell you how. Only talk face-to-face with James...no phones."

Molly looked sick. All of this intrigue and the thought that her husband would be gone once again made her heart ache.

"I will need your help getting out of here, so you will be sort of an accomplice. But don't worry, it will be hard to prove."

"An accomplice? What do you want me to do?"

"What you do best. Just be a perfect hostess."

"When is this going to happen?"

"It's almost lunchtime, so right about now."

Molly went out to the front drive, where an FBI vehicle was stationed. During daylight hours the security detail consisted of six agents. The night detail was now ten considering FBI losses and ongoing threats. She cordially invited the agents to come into the house for soup and sandwiches.

The agent in charge of the detail thought about logistics for a moment, then called in half of the agents to take advantage of Mrs. Davis' kind offer. He would keep the other half of his men on the perimeter.

Brooks was upstairs and watched as the security men came to the house for lunch. It would be close, but he plotted his exit strategy.

Davis came downstairs and joined the agents while they enjoyed their lunch. He made small talk for a while and then excused himself. He went to the hall closet and picked up a navy blue windbreaker that closely approximated the standard FBI jacket. He also picked up the navy-blue ball cap with the letters FBI embroidered above the bill in gold thread. The cap had been given to Zane by Dayton when it looked like his father might not return.

Brooks walked out of the front door and headed east to the spot where the perimeter was left unguarded by the lunching agent. He had about seventy-five yards of open ground to cross before the safety of the tree line. Just before he reached the trees he looked to the north and saw the next perimeter guard. Brooks turned his head in the man's direction in hopes that the agent would focus on the ball cap and not his civilian jacket. He casually waved at the man, who nonchalantly waved back. When Brooks was well inside the tree line he stopped to see if an alarm had been sounded. When all appeared quiet, Davis broke into a run in the direction of I-10. As he ran, he checked his watch. He had twenty minutes to meet his banker and twenty-five to meet his getaway man.

At 5:00 p.m. Molly went outside and addressed the first FBI man she saw.

"Have you seen Brooks?"

The agent looked at her slightly askew. "No. I haven't seen him since lunch. When did you see him last?"

Molly paused for effect. "I guess right after lunch I saw him in his study. He was working on bids. He has been so anxious about how all the mess is affecting our livelihood. He just wants to go back to work."

"How about the boys? Have they seen him?"

"I picked up Andy and Zane at school at 4:00. James has been in and out today. I already asked them...nothing. We checked the house. I thought he was outside talking to you guys."

The agent retrieved his radio.

"Team leader, this is Draper. We've got a problem."

Within ten minutes the Davis compound was searched. When Davis did not turn up, the team leader called the alert directly to Collier. Collier issued a quick set of orders. The agent on site found a worried-looking Molly in the kitchen.

"All of your vehicles are accounted for, so he is either on foot or has been picked up. And you are sure that he didn't say anything about leaving?"

Molly forced herself to maintain eye contact with the agent. "He was in the study and seemed preoccupied. He did not say anything to me."

The agent studied her eyes for evidence of anything other than legitimate concern. "This is very important, Mrs. Davis, so I need a truthful answer. If Brooks left of his own volition, is there a possibility that he is armed?"

The question startled Molly because she was not expecting it. She rushed her answer. "He is not armed! Do you understand me, Brooks is not armed! You tell everyone that he is not armed!"

The agent's eyes narrowed. His training told him that her answer was too stressed. If she did not know where he was, how did she know that he was unarmed? She knew more than she was letting on. "Very well, Mrs. Davis. We will find him soon, I'm sure." He left her in the kitchen and stepped outside. He dialed Collier's direct number.

"Sir, I think something serious is up, and I'm pretty sure Mrs. Davis knows all about it."

The White House

President Martinez's intercom buzzed in the Oval Office.

"Yes."

"Mr. President, Secretary Washington is calling from the State Department."

Martinez picked up the phone and pressed the blinking line.

"What's up, Malcolm?"

"Mr. President, I've just received the official request for extradition."

Martinez recoiled a bit. "Acosta sure didn't take much time on this. What was their procedure?"

"It probably means that the criminal action started in Chihuahua. Davis was indicted and charged locally with twenty counts of homicide. The indictment states that Davis is charged with both federal and state crimes."

"Twenty counts! Federal and state! What is that all about?" asked the president.

"The charges cover the deaths of the eighteen men in the Army platoon and the two civilian women. The killing of active-duty military is a federal crime, while the deaths of the women are state crimes. It appears that the governor of Chihuahua made a public production of the indictment and made sure that the media knew that it was forwarded to Acosta so that he couldn't dodge or delay action on the case without taking a political beating."

"Why twenty counts? I thought twenty-six people died?"

"They are apparently sticking to their previous story that the men that died in the helicopter crash were unrelated losses, and nobody would want to acknowledge the loss of the hired assassin."

Martinez thought about it for a moment. "I'm sure that it will be all over the Mexican media and our media will be right behind."

"I think that we can expect the story will lead the six o'clock news, Mr. President."

"So how should we respond?"

"I think we can buy some time with the standard rhetoric that the State Department is in the process of actively investigating the allegations and developing a response according to the requirements of the current treaty with Mexico. When they start asking you specific questions, tell them that the case has moved to a priority spot on the secretary of State's plate. I can then do whatever foot-dragging that is needed."

"How fast do things have to happen?"

"In most cases, these things move relatively slowly. There is a fair amount of paper exchange between the two countries. However, our case is different."

"Why is that?"

"Mexico is already invoking Article 11 of the treaty that requests for immediate provisional arrest of the subject if there are exigent circumstances."

Martinez closed his eyes and massaged his temples.

"Exigent, like our man might be a mass murderer as far as Mexico is concerned."

"Yes, sir, exactly."

"How long can we delay arrest?"

"The treaty is vague there, Mr. President. There is not a set time frame. But again, we should expect the Mexican media to report that Article 11 is invoked and that our media will pick that up and start asking the administrations very pointed questions."

"Oh, crap! Let's get Attorney General Daniels, Ratzner, Clarence Scott, and my staff together ASAP to try to get ahead of this thing. We must have a party line before the six o'clock news."

"I'll make it happen, sir. One other thing. I'm emailing your secretary a copy of the text of Article 9 of the treaty. It could possibly help us out of this. You can take a look before the meeting."

"If it can help, why don't we just invoke it?"

"There may be a high political cost."

"How high?"

Without hesitation, Secretary Washington replied, "Like a one-term presidency, sir."

Martinez's shoulders sagged. "Oh hell!"

CHAPTER THIRTY-NINE
On the Road Again

At 5:00 p.m. Brooks was already thirty-five miles away in the hills north of Spring Branch, Texas at the home of his longtime friend and soon-to-be accomplice, Fritz Koehler. Davis could count on Fritz as an ally. Fritz did not think much of the government. His deceased wife had been attending a business meeting on September 11 in Tower Two of the World Trade Center when the terrorists struck. His daughter and only child, who was a graduate of West Point, was killed by an IED during Operation Iraqi Freedom. Fritz had always said that the only "shock and awe" he ever felt was the incredible emptiness that was the net result of failed government policies.

Fritz himself was a retired contractor of sorts. Instead of building homes, he built electronic gadgets. Before retirement, he worked for a branch of the National Security Agency making all sorts of electronic listening devices. If someone was saying something that they were trying to keep secret, and you wanted to hear it, Fritz could build the device to make it happen. He could also make it hard for people to eavesdrop on your conversation.

During the trip to his house, Davis told Fritz the highlights and lowlights of his ordeal. He also confided in his friend that extradition was a possibility. He did not have to explain to Fritz that Mexico was an all-lose proposition. When they arrived at the Koehler residence Fritz asked Davis about the contents of his briefcase. Brooks showed him the money. Fritz whistled softly.

"What's all that for?"

"Traveling money."

"Where are you going?"

"I don't know yet, but I thought you could help me with that."

"Do I look like a travel agent?"

"No, but if a man wanted to move around in this day and age of surveillance cameras without being seen, I figured that you were the man to see."

Fritz stroked his chin and stared out the window at the hill country view. He finally turned to his friend.

"Can't be done."

"Oh, man! Don't tell me that." Now it was Davis' turn to stare out the window.

"You know, Brooks, it's easier to make everyone think that you are somewhere when you really aren't."

"That sounds like a promising alternative."

"It is sort of like when you beat feet this afternoon. For at least a while the Feds thought you were at home when you were not. Now you are in Spring Branch, and do they or the bad guys know that? You were smart enough to make it nearly impossible to trace you to me. By the way, how many calls did you make with that pre-paid phone?"

"Two. My banker and you."

Fritz appeared preoccupied. He asked Brooks for the phone.

Davis produced the phone and gave it to Fritz. He quickly dismantled it and studied the internal components. "Is the phone that your son has the exact same model?"

"Yes, same phone, different number."

"The first time you use the phone to call him, try to establish a time when you can reliably call him when the phone is in motion, like when he is in the car. That will add another layer of complexity to any attempted tracking."

"I thought it was untraceable?"

"Nothing is truly untraceable, only hard to trace. And you should only call him and not vice versa. And no more than thirty-second calls. And he knows only face-to-face with his mom, right?"

"Right."

Later, while they ate supper Fritz quizzed Davis about his goal.

"So let me get this straight. You are fearful that your south-of-the-border sins are going to lead to extradition. By sneaking off, they cannot physically cuff you and ship you off, but at the same time the Feds are obliged to protect your family because you are a protected federal witness who was the subject of a coordinated attack on your home."

"Right. With me gone I don't think that the threat against the family is all that high. De La Garza wants me dead so I can't testify. ISIS wants me dead because I represent a failure in their otherwise perfect record. The wild card here is our own government. What will Martinez do if his pal Acosta calls and says it is politically imperative for me to go to Mexico?"

Fritz replied, "I would expect that Martinez would feel untold heat if he gave you up to the Mexicans and anything bad happens to you. It seems like just too great a political risk for him. He is a first-term president. He must walk a very careful line, or he won't stand a chance for re-election."

"You want to talk risk? If this does not go well, he is not likely to be re-elected, but I'm likely to be dead. His risk pales in comparison to mine. I've decided that I'm not going to get my head chopped off for any president, past, present, or future."

After supper, the two men retired to the patio and drank Jack Daniel's and smoked cigars. Each man was trying to formulate a plan.

"You know, Brooks, you can hide out here forever as far as I'm concerned but is that really practical?"

"No, not really. If the Mexicans want to try me for murder or manslaughter, they have no statute of limitations, just like here in the US. If I come out of hiding, they can just make a new demand for extradition. I got online and read the text of the current Extradition

Treaty with Mexico. There are twenty-six articles in the treaty. Article 9 is the interesting one. It says that no executive can be forced to extradite a national. That is what I need to see happen. I need Martinez to get up in front of God and everyone and publicly invoke Article 9 and refuse extradition. That should keep me on the north side of the border while he is president. Hell, if he refuses extradition, I will even vote for him next time. I'll even make you vote for him. If enough years intervene, I will probably fall off the radar and be relatively safe."

Fritz leaned back into his patio recliner and blew a smoke ring in the cool night air. The beginning of a plan was starting to take shape.

"So, Brooks, what you need to do is be physically invisible, but start influencing public opinion so Martinez has to choose in your favor."

Brooks nodded but had a melancholy look that indicated that his chances of influencing the president were slim to none. Fritz slapped Davis on the knee.

"Don't look so glum, old friend. Fritz has a plan that may not only work but be a bit of fun as well."

"Fun? What do you mean, fun?"

"Haven't you always wanted to screw around with the government?"

"I'm an American, right?"

"Well, there you go! We are the perfect partners."

Davis and Koehler adjourned to Fritz's home office and booted up his computer. Davis noted that his friend's computer did not look anything like the average home PC. Three large linked central processor units stood against the wall. On the wall in front of Koehler's desk were four twenty-eight-inch monitors. Davis studied the equipment for a moment before he realized that there were no brand logos on anything.

Fritz moved in and out of various sites apparently in search of something specific. Davis could not just sit and watch.

"What are you looking for?"

"I'm going to pull up a site that will give the coverage areas of every brand of disposable cell phone on the US market. I'm moving to that site in such a way that it will be nearly impossible to trace back to me. My IP address is sacrosanct. I don't like anybody knowing where I surf."

Davis liked the sound of that, so he watched and remained quiet. After a few minutes, a map of the contiguous forty-eight states appeared. Superimposed over the map was a complex series of irregular lines, each in a different color. On an adjacent monitor, Davis saw a key appear that matched each colored line with the cell phone company's name. Davis recognized most of the names from television commercials.

Fritz then started a subroutine, and the Texas portion of the national map appeared on the third monitor. Hundreds of colored dots began appearing all over the Texas map.

Fritz chuckled. "I'll bet you had no idea how many cell phone towers there are in Texas." Brooks just shook his head.

I'm going to tell the computer to do an overlap routine, and we should be able to see where in Texas you should be able to get reception from the greatest number of cell phone networks."

When the computer finished, a major office-size laser printer began to spit out pages of data. Fritz gathered the pages and said, "Now we need coffee."

While they sat at the kitchen table nursing mugs of coffee, they began to reduce data.

After ten minutes Fritz commented, "As you might expect, you can get virtually every brand of phone to work in the major cities. The question is, do you want to try to hide in a major city, or do you want to get lost in a small town or in a remote, unpopulated area?"

Davis thought for a moment. "On one hand, in a major metropolitan area, you can probably hide in plain sight. But on the other hand, there could be millions of eyes on you." Fritz nodded his agreement.

"In a small town, there are fewer eyes, but everybody knows everybody. Strangers stand out. And if they start putting your mug on television or wanted posters in the post office your chances of discovery rise dramatically."

Davis rendered his first wish. "If I had my choice, I'd like to kick back in the middle of some big old Texas ranch out in the boonies and just not be seen by anybody."

"Good thought. Do you know some wealthy rancher that likes you but not the administration?"

After a moment of thought a name exploded in Davis' mind. He shuffled through the papers showing the overlapping coverage areas.

"How many networks do we need for your plan to work?"

"About six or seven."

Davis consulted a specific printout. "How about eight?"

"Eight would be good! Very good! What have you got?"

Davis spun the map of central Texas toward Fritz and tapped a finger on a cluster of cell towers south of the town of San Saba.

"Interesting. Do you know someone in San Saba?"

"No, but I know the guy who owns the ranch where all of these cell towers are located."

"No shit! Do you think that he will let you hang out for a while?"

"I have no doubt. He is the only guy I know that despises the government more than you."

"Ah, a kindred spirit. We must meet. How do you know him?"

"I built his ranch house."

"Damn, Brooks! You are certainly a man in demand."

"So, what do we do?"

"Tomorrow, you give me a chunk of that cash and I go shopping for non-traceable, disposable cell phones. It will take a few days to get enough together."

"Why is that?"

"Because if I buy a bunch of phones in the same place the great computers in the sky will tag the transaction and they will start asking businesses for their security tapes. So, we must be careful. And of course, it is the cash that really makes things workable."

Brooks nodded his understanding. "I get it."

"Yes. One phone here, one phone there. A little cash here, a little cash there, and nobody knows shit. Then we get in touch with your rich pal and see how he feels about putting you up for a while and becoming an accessory after the fact."

The Davis House

That first night that Brooks took off was very subdued around the dinner table. Zane was on the verge of tears, even though Molly and James assured him that his dad was not back in Mexico and would be home soon. Andy was no help because he just sat there looking one grade better than catatonic. Molly kept giving her eldest son wide-eyed looks, and he returned with smug looks of "I know more than you know, Mom!"

After dinner, Molly put the younger brothers to work on dishes and gave James an evil command. "Upstairs!"

She slammed the bedroom door closed and demanded, "I want to know number one, how, and number two, when, you are going to communicate with your father!"

"Ain't gonna tell ya, and ain't gonna tell ya."

"And why not?"

James addressed his mother like he was talking to a slow child. "Because he said that if I spilled the beans, he would kill me."

Molly closed her eyes and slowly shook her head. She was about to berate her worthless son, but he beat her to her comment.

"And Mom, don't forget, Dad *is* a killer. So, I'm not going to take any chances."

After a long pause, she replied, "You just love this all-new father-son mutual admiration bullshit, don't you?"

James smiled and gave her a small shrug. Molly responded, "Well, I want you to communicate with your father and tell him that I may have told the FBI guy a small lie today, that may be a small felony, and that we should communicate about *that*!"

"Can't do it."

Molly recoiled. "And why the hell not? I thought you were the big-time communicator."

"Dad said no outgoing communications until he lets me know that the coast is clear."

CHAPTER FORTY

It's Not What You Know

John Long described himself as "Texas New Money." He was a University of Texas Law School graduate and was a vicious litigator in any court in the land. His claim to fame was hitting a home run in a $4.8 billion anti-trust action when he was thirty-one years old. Any sensible lawyer would have taken the immense wealth netted from that case and retired, but not Long. His success put him in a different class of litigators. He was now only presented with the most complex cases and therefore the highest potential for more home runs. He had a secret ambition. Before he died, he wanted to own more land in Texas than the fabled Captain Richard King of King Ranch fame, who had amassed 1.2 million acres. At fifty-two, he was more than three-quarters of the way there.

The phone number of Long's private secretary was one of the numbers that Brooks had committed to memory. It was easy to remember. It was the Dallas area code followed by seven zeros. Local legend had it that Long had bought the number to commemorate his net worth at age fifty.

Brooks used the first of his disposable phones to place the call. It was answered on the second ring by Long's secretary.

"The Law Offices of John Long. This is Susan Proctor."

Brooks did not want to identify himself so he resorted to a small lie.

"Susan, could you please tell Mr. Long that there is a major problem at his San Saba property."

"Who is calling, please, and what is the nature of the problem?"

"I'm one of his neighbors. Tell him that a section of his high fence has been cut and all his high-dollar whitetail breeding bucks are escaping onto my place and I'm about to call finders keepers on him."

"One moment, please."

Davis knew that the one sure way to get Long on the phone was if anything bad was happening to his prize-winning whitetail breeding stock. Fifteen seconds later Long came on the line.

"Who in the hell is this and who cut my fence?"

"John, calm down. It's Brooks Davis and there is nothing wrong with your game fence or your deer."

"That's not funny, Brooks! I nearly had a coronary! If you weren't a celebrity, I would shoot you myself!"

"I'm sorry, John, but I'm in a bit of a jam and I could use your help. I did not want your secretary to know who you were talking to."

"I thought that the FBI had you covered like a blanket?"

"Well, I took off, so they are covering my family but not me."

"What's the deal?"

"There is an indication that the Mexicans may try to extradite me back to Mexico."

"What the hell did you do down there?"

"Long, ugly story."

"Well, don't worry, Brooks—we aren't letting anyone send you anywhere. You realize that we don't do criminal stuff, but I know all the best people."

"I might need to take you up on the referral, but right now I just need a really quiet place to hide out while I get my public relations campaign up and running."

"Public relations campaign? This is starting to sound like our fearless leaders in Washington are mucking about where they shouldn't."

"That's a good way to put it."

"So how can I help? What kind of hideout do you need?"

"How about the San Saba place?"

"It doesn't get any quieter than that. When do you need it?"

"ASAP."

Long pressed the intercom button on his desk. His secretary answered promptly.

"Susan, please reschedule the rest of my afternoon. Tell them I have a family problem."

Late that afternoon, Brooks and Fritz met Long at the main gate of the ranch. Over dinner that night they filled Long in on the basic plan. He was enthralled by the idea. As a lawyer, he always appreciated a good fight between the small guy and the huge multinational conglomerate who always thought that might made it right.

The next morning Long returned to Dallas and Fritz went into San Saba to stock up on groceries for Brooks. Later that day Fritz took a large portion of Davis' cash and left the ranch heading west. That night he would be at the first stopping point and ready to test both his equipment and the initial effects of the Davis public relations campaign.

Gloria Lipton was an associate producer of Fox News Network's conservative news and commentary show *Ron Dixon's America Responds*. Since the live broadcast was aired five nights a week, she was a very busy woman. Lipton's personal cell phone rang. The caller ID reported that information about the caller was unavailable. That was a bit strange, but she answered anyway.

"Gloria Lipton."

"Good morning, Ms. Lipton. I have reliable information that Brooks Davis will be watching tonight's broadcast, and if he is invited, he will most certainly call in."

Lipton recoiled a bit and asked, "Who is this, and more importantly, how did you get this number?"

"The *who* is unimportant and I'm not going to tell you the *how*. What I will tell you is that if Dixon and Davis have a nice discussion it will be far more informative than what the FBI is feeding the media. I personally assure you that your ratings and market share will grow substantially because of the said discussion. Have a pleasant day,

Ms. Lipton." With that tantalizing bit of bait, Davis ended the call.

Lipton thought for a moment and then picked up her office phone and dialed the Fox News research department.

"This is Lipton. I have an urgent need for you to queue up the soundbite of the president's call to Brooks Davis while he was in the hospital. I will be there in five minutes."

She made it to the research department in four minutes. The sound tech was just pulling up the clip.

"I want to hear the sound of Davis' voice."

The tech obediently fast-forwarded to the appropriate spot. Lipton listened intently to Davis' voice.

"Play it again."

This time she listened with her eyes closed. When she was certain, her eyes popped open, and she rushed out to find her boss and Ron Dixon.

Van Horn, Texas

In a small West Texas town like Van Horn, it was easy to find pay phones that were not covered by surveillance cameras. For a while, Fritz thought that there were no surveillance cameras anywhere in the town. He used his first untraceable cell phone to call Davis on one of his cell phones and gave him the phone number of a secluded pay phone located on the outside wall of a nondescript plumbing store. They briefly discussed strategy.

"Tell me again how this is going to work?" inquired Davis.

"I've already attached the voice modulation unit to the wiring of the pay phone's voice mic and ear speaker. I will be ready when the show comes on. When you are ready, call the pay phone. A ready light will tell me that the VMU has captured the call. I'll then dial the 1-800 number of the show. When they answer you will be able to speak to them directly."

"And you are sure that they won't be able to tell that I'm talking through an intermediary phone?"

"How dare you doubt my science!" challenged Fritz.

"Sorry, Einstein. What about feeding the pay phone? Do you have enough coin?"

Fritz laughed out loud. "We don't need money! I have electronic coins." Fritz pressed some buttons on the side of the VMU and Brooks could hear quarters, nickels, and dimes being fed into the phone.

"Fritz, you are an evil genius."

"I work at it."

"What about a trace? How long can I talk before they can trace the call?"

"I don't think it will be a problem with this first call unless your producer lady has already tipped off the FBI. I'm sure that they are going to keep this close to the vest until they know for sure it is really you. I think we can expect the Feds to be working on calls after this first one. They will be able to backtrace this call to Van Horn and think that you are somewhere in the vicinity. They will rush investigators and techs to the pay phone but will be puzzled by why they will not be able to find your fingerprints anywhere. Anyway, by that time I will be long gone, heading for the second location."

Fritz laughed. "The weak link in this chain is how good an actor you are."

That night's broadcast of *America Responds* was the perfect setup for Davis's first call-in. Dixon's guest was Maryanna Esquivel, the lead counsel for the League of United Latin American Communities. The discussion focused on the sudden appearance of rallies and marches throughout the Southwest where the placards and participants called for Davis's extradition to Mexico. Dixon, ever the conservative, planned to take Davis' side in the discussion while Esquivel would by nature and political leaning take the pro-extradition side. Davis planned to wait for the last minutes of the broadcast before he called in. He wanted the show's end to force the early completion of his call.

After forty-five minutes, the broadcast was fielding a relatively equal number of pro and con calls. Dixon was beginning the wrap-up with Esquivel.

"So, Maryanna, to recap, if I'm hearing you and the pro-extradition groups correctly, you think that Davis should turn himself in and face the Mexican judicial process."

"That's right, Ron. If Mr. Davis's self-defense claims are true, then he should not be fearful of explaining his actions in a Mexican court. His sneaking off from protective custody is only hurting his case."

Dixon was cued that there was a commercial break coming in fifteen seconds.

"It would certainly be interesting to hear Davis' opinion on all of this. If you are out there watching, Mr. Davis, I invite you to call in and respond. We will go to a commercial and leave the 1-800 number on the screen."

While Mike Lindell, the "My Pillow Guy," extolled the amazing virtues of all of his bedroom products, Davis made the call. The connection through Van Horn went perfectly.

"Welcome back. During the commercial break, I have been told that Brooks Davis has indeed called in. Mr. Davis, you are on *America Responds*. Thanks for calling in."

"You are quite welcome, Ron. Nice to talk to you."

"There is so much to talk about. First, how are you and where are you?"

"I'm fine. Miss my family. As to the where, I will let the FBI figure that out. It really should not be that hard for them. I'm sure they can trace the call and at least know where I've been."

"Why did you leave protective custody?"

"Too many people throwing the word *extradition* around. I cannot sit around waiting for the president to make up his mind."

"What do you believe the president has to decide upon?"

"Whether or not to invoke Article 9 of the Extradition Treaty with Mexico."

It was the first time that Dixon heard anything about the specifics of the treaty.

"What is Article 9?"

"It states that no executive can be forced to extradite one of their citizens. In this case, it seems like a no-brainer for President Martinez. He should have already told President Acosta in politically correct language that the disposition of Brooks Davis is not on the table. End of discussion."

"But Brooks, how do you respond to all the discussion about all the loss of life south of the border? Are you responsible for any of them?"

"Yes. People lost their lives at my hands. I have never denied it. But every person who died was armed and intent upon seeing me either dead or given back to ISIS. We do not have to discuss what ISIS' current campaign would have meant to my neck. It was no different in Mexico than what just transpired in my home a few days ago. I defended myself and my family against armed killers. If our local and federal authorities determined that to be justifiable in the name of self-defense, then somebody needs to step up and say so in clear, unequivocal terms."

Esquivel could not remain quiet and interrupted.

"What about the two peasant women you killed? Are you saying that they were armed and represented some kind of legitimate threat?"

"Ah yes, the much-discussed peasant women. They were both armed with machetes and were motivated by a one-million-peso reward on my head."

Dixon shot back, "There was an official reward for you?"

"Yes indeed. I had a physical copy of the wanted poster and turned it over to Martin Collier, the special agent in charge of the San Antonio field office. Call him up; he may give you a copy."

"Mr. Davis, our time is up. Will you stay on the line if I can get Fox News to continue our broadcast?"

"Sorry, Ron, no can do. My ride is about to leave so I have got to go for now. Listen, if I can get to a pay phone during your broadcast,

I will try to give you a call in the next day or two. I will tell you all about getting kidnapped and terrorized by ISIS and their Mexican colleagues."

"ISIS has Mexican colleagues?"

"They certainly do. You don't think I ended up in Mexico because they took a wrong turn somewhere. The next time we talk, Ron, remind me to tell you all about General De La Garza. See you later."

Collier was called by the FBI communications center within one minute of the beginning of Davis' call to *America Responds*. By the time he had his television turned on and found Fox News, Davis was responding to Esquivel's query about the peasant women. When he heard his own name attached to the wanted poster, he could only groan and grind his teeth. With a great deal of certainty, he knew that the proverbial feces had just hit the fan. By the time he was back at his office, the communication specialist had already pinpointed the pay phone in Van Horn. The Davis case team was quickly assembled for immediate actions and strategies.

"Has Communications verified the voice print?" asked Collier.

"Voiceprint is verified," replied Dayton. In hopes of making points with the boss, he added, "I've given the El Paso field office the heads-up and they are sending technicians to evaluate for latent prints. I talked with Van Horn Police and they are sealing off the area until the El Paso team gets there."

"Did you ask the police about surveillance cameras?"

"Yes."

After a pause, Collier asked, "Well?"

"Well, the Van Horn dispatcher sort of laughed and said that the nearest camera is at the bank five blocks away."

"Great! So, we have no idea who his 'ride' is or what direction he is heading."

Dayton theorized, "Van Horn sits right on I-10. We can assume that he is not heading east back to San Antonio or south to Mexico. So, his only choices are west to El Paso on I-10 or possibly north on small state roads Texas 54 or 1111. Those are literally the only roads of any size out of town."

"Without a vehicle description, we are blind. We will have to wait for his next move," replied a disgusted Collier. "Did anyone call Mrs. Davis?"

Dayton nodded. "I asked her if Van Horn had any meaning. She said that he used to hunt out there, but the lease was well south of Van Horn. She added that there were no friends or relatives anywhere in West Texas. Davis said that he was going to continue his discussion with Dixon on the air. Can we get authorization to set up a high-speed trace on the incoming lines of Dixon's show? If we can fix his position real-time, we could call local authorities to dispatch to the location and pick him up."

Collier thought for a moment. "That might work. We won't have any problem getting a federal judge to order the tap. The White House will want Davis off the air. He has a lot to say that they would prefer not to hear on prime-time television. We have got to work fast. Davis' next opportunity to tell all occurs in less than twenty-four hours."

As the case team meeting broke up, Dayton stayed behind to consult with Collier.

"How do you feel about having to go after Davis?"

Collier eyed his young agent. "What is more important is: How do you feel about it? Are you going to have a problem pursuing him?"

"No, I won't have a problem. I am prepared to do what I'm told to do. But I must admit it seems somehow very unfair because it is so clearly a self-defense issue."

"You do not define what is and what isn't self-defense. Way above your pay grade and experience level, sonny. If the powers that be put Davis on the Ten Most Wanted List for spitting on the sidewalk, you better just cuff him and drag him in and keep your mouth shut." As an afterthought, Collier added, "Besides, I'm pissed at that cowboy. Slipping away from us made us look like a bunch of amateurs. And the director holds me responsible for all my amateurs. Makes me look like an idiot, and I don't like that."

By the next morning, the Davis flight was front-page news and the lead story on all the electronic media. Fritz was well into New Mexico when he called Brooks.

"It looks like you got everyone's attention. What do you think will happen next?"

"I think that the pro-extradition types will increase activities. I am sure that the FBI will be ready to trace the next call as soon as I identify myself. How long do you think it will take them to locate the pay phone?"

"Three to five minutes. Probably more like three. The real question is not how fast they can trace; it is how fast they can dispatch law enforcement to the scene. I've got to be able to disconnect my equipment and get down the road. We have got to make our next calls well off the interstate. I'll find small towns without police departments."

Davis was still worried. "What about state troopers or county sheriff's department types? They could be patrolling in the right place at the right time."

"I'm not too worried about it. They usually have few patrols active after sundown, especially on weeknights. And besides, I have my laptop and the Hughes Net."

"What do you mean?"

I can access the Internet with Hughes Net satellites, and then I can hack into any local police dispatcher. With a little work, I can get the GPS location of any patrols in the area."

"I thought that kind of stuff was encrypted."

"For common people, encryption is a problem."

"Well, Fritz, you certainly are not a commoner."

"It's good that you recognize that. Today is Thursday. I think that we should skip a call for tonight. Keep them guessing. We will call in Friday night and let them stew on it over the weekend. That will give me plenty of time to get down the road to the next location."

Just as Davis predicted, the pro-extradition forces expanded their rallies and marches. The first incident of violence occurred at a march in Tucson, Arizona. A small group of anti-extradition people clashed with marchers. A fight broke out and one of the anti-extradition people was severely beaten and left with both arms broken. Friends of the injured man armed themselves and returned to the demonstration. They fired into the pro-extradition marchers, killing one and wounding five. The Tucson police chief, who was an Anglo, then revoked all the permits for any additional marches or rallies for all groups either for or against extradition. Pro-extradition forces were outraged and accused the chief of ethnic bias. They ignored the ban and marched on city hall.

Trying to avoid escalation, but also trying to remain prepared for the worst-case scenario, the chief ordered his riot police to prepare but to stand off two blocks away from city hall. During a fiery speech that happened to be written by Senator Acosta's chief speech writer, a brick was thrown through a window of city hall. Within moments a car was overturned and set on fire. The police chief had no choice but to let the riot police loose on the crowd. The whole affair was thoroughly covered by not less than five television news crews. The net result was forty-four arrests, eighteen protesters, and five police treated at area hospitals.

The event went national by the six o'clock news. The police chief was fired on the spot by the Hispanic mayor of Tucson. No one ever realized that the first brick that was thrown was launched by an anti-extradition zealot who was aiming at the speech maker, not the city hall window.

What became known as the "Tucson Event" was the spark that set off national debate rumblings not unlike the earliest days of the Vietnam War. The media did their best to split the coverage of the debate equally, but some networks seemed to spend a great deal of time researching and reporting from south of the border.

CHAPTER FORTY-ONE

You Cannot Disappear in America

Livermore, Colorado, near the Wyoming state line

Fritz found a pay phone in the tiny village of Livermore, Colorado at a gas station that closed at 5:00 p.m. Livermore was one of those rural towns that rolled up the sidewalks at sundown. The nearest town of any size was Fort Collins, which sat astride I-25, thirty-two miles away. Livermore had no police, and the Larimer County Sheriff's Department had no routine patrols north of a line from Fort Collins, Estes Park, and Steamboat Springs. Livermore was on Highway 287 but was so close to the Wyoming line that the Colorado State Troopers rarely patrolled that far north, thinking that speeders could just as soon be Wyoming's problem.

At the beginning of the *America Responds* broadcast, Fritz was able to hack into the Colorado State Trooper GPS locator system. The closest trooper to Livermore was forty miles away.

When Davis called in, Dixon was hosting House Minority Calvin Whitney from Mississippi. In the first fifteen minutes of the show, the host and guest did a workmanlike job of berating the administration for their lack of response to the extradition request.

"Congressman Whitney, why do you think that the president has not gone on the record about his stance on the Davis extradition? The press secretary can use the 'president has the problem under advisement' excuse only so long."

"Well, Ron, it is really very simple. The administration is trying to get a feel for his support base both in Congress as well as the public in general. If a majority in Congress is going to line up behind the president and do whatever it takes to preserve the initiatives that he has gained with Mexico, then the president will likely go on the record and allow extradition. However, the president also must be sensitive to public opinion. Conservatives from coast to coast are already pillorying the president. But we lost the last election. I am sure that the president's people are keeping very close watch on the opinions of liberal Democrats everywhere. If they start putting themselves in Davis' shoes and a large enough number of them start thinking that extradition is not a fair response, then the president will have to think hard about the impact on not only his re-election but the midterm elections as well."

Dixon was given a cue that Davis was on the line.

"I've just been told that Brooks Davis is on the line. Let's open that line. Brooks, are you there?"

"Yes, Ron, how are you?"

"Very well, thank you. We were really hoping you would call in last night."

"I couldn't get to a phone. I was riding with a long-haul trucker on a tight schedule, and we couldn't stop when the show was on. I missed the show completely. How did it go?"

"About equal for and against your extradition."

"Too bad that the pro-extradition folks can't all experience being kidnapped, drugged, raped, and scheduled for beheading."

There was a pause during which Dixon and Representative Whitney stared at each other.

"Brooks, did you say raped?"

"Yes, I did Ron. People need to know what kind of people we are dealing with."

"Who raped you?"

"One of the ISIS types. He said it was payback for the rape of his sister in Iraq by US military forces."

"Brooks, I have to stop right here and acknowledge how difficult it must be for you to relate that kind of information publicly."

"Well, Ron, I probably would not talk about it if the guy that did it didn't find out firsthand, and in the worst way, what payback is all about."

Dixon and his huge audience absorbed that for a moment.

"The last time we talked, you said that ISIS and Mexico were in league with each other and that a certain General De La Garza was deeply involved. Can you fill us in now?"

"To be correct, ISIS and certain elements in Mexico are indeed in league with each other, but not the Mexican federal government. President Acosta is probably fighting a very difficult battle in his country against the cartels and widespread corruption. However, what I can say as an eyewitness is that at the very least, the Juarez cartel has a Mexican Army general named De La Garza in their pocket and that ISIS has been taking kidnapped Americans to an isolated ranch in the state of Chihuahua to be killed. ISIS is paying De La Garza a fee in American currency for each person killed on his turf."

Whitney interrupted. "So, you are saying that the reason that none of the bodies has turned up is because they are still in Mexico somewhere?"

"That is exactly what happened to Epstein and me. We were repeatedly drugged and sealed in some kind of container in a truck. When we finally woke up, we were in a ranch house somewhere in Chihuahua. Epstein had a bad heart condition. The rigors of repeated drugging and being off his medications killed him before they could cut off his head. I was scheduled as his replacement."

Dixon wanted to close the circle of the terrorist connections.

"So, the connection between the cartels and ISIS is indirect through De La Garza?"

"I doubt it. It is common knowledge that the opium producers in the Middle East provide product for the cartels to produce heroin for consumption in the US. The opium producers also provide financial support to many terrorist organizations. So, I think that they are all on the same page and directly related."

"The FBI has explained that you escaped your captors, made your way across Mexico, and procured a light plane and flew back to Texas. Is that essentially correct?"

"Yes, but a much-abbreviated version. I escaped the ranch house after personally taking care of the rapist. I was able to arm myself and headed north. General De La Garza used elements of the Mexican Army under his command to try to recover me to give me back to the terrorists. In my first interaction with his military, the remaining terrorists were killed. De La Garza's motivation became more personal. He now needed me dead to sever his connection with ISIS and the cartels. He sent units of the Army and then a professional assassin after me. I evaded when I could, and when I couldn't, I fought them. After six weeks, I was still a long way from the border and in very bad physical condition. When I had the opportunity to steal the plane, I took it as a last resort and flew it home."

Dixon could only shake his head. "It seems clear to me that you are the victim of international crimes, and you did what anybody would do in self-defense."

Whitney added, "It is unconscionable that any government would demand extradition for actions that were so clearly self-defense."

"You are a US representative. Do me a favor. Tell that to the presidents of the United States and Mexico. I do not pretend to know a thing about Mexican law, but they must have a strange definition of self-defense. Ron, did the FBI pony up the copy of the reward poster?"

"No. We are getting the standard line about not revealing physical evidence in an ongoing case."

"Well, keep at it, Ron. I hope your ratings are on the rise. My ride is waving at me, so I've got to go. All this hitchhiking has confirmed one thing to me."

"What's that, Brooks?"

"The people that I've caught a ride with are all one hundred percent on my side in this deal. Hell, I was even invited to a birthday barbeque yesterday. A lot of people are getting more than a little miffed at our president. His performance in this affair is going to come up in the next election. I can guarantee that. Anyway, I will talk to you next Monday if I can."

San Antonio FBI Field Office

"Where in the hell is Livermore, Colorado? Somebody get a Colorado map up on the big monitor!" said Collier when the trace results came in. He stepped up to the big screen when the images of northern Colorado appeared.

"Why is he in some backwater town that far off the interstate?" When no one answered his rhetoric question immediately, he snapped, "Opinions, people!"

"Livermore is a nothing town, but it is on US Highway 287. You could make an argument for catching a ride on a highway of that size. I'm sure that truckers heading to Laramie out of any of the major northeastern Colorado cities would take 287," replied an agent.

"Our last contact was West Texas and now he is about to cross into Wyoming. He is obviously heading north. Do we think he is heading to Canada?" asked Dayton.

Collier shook his head. "Why? Our current extradition treaty with Canada is solid. If the US declares him a fugitive, the Canadians will just give him back if they catch him. It's not like it's the '70s and Davis is dodging the draft."

"What if he is trying to get to someone out west who will help him?" asked Dayton.

"I suppose that is possible. Go see Mrs. Davis and see if she can shed any light on that. Gently remind her that if she is intentionally withholding any information, she could get herself into trouble." After a moment of thought, he began issuing orders.

"Get me in touch with our people in the region. Have them start coordinating with the Wyoming State Patrol. Have them be on the lookout for any vehicles with Texas plates. If there are two men in the vehicle, have them stopped for routine license checks."

"Why vehicles with two men?" asked an agent.

"Davis is a smart guy but I'm sure he is getting help from someone. Think about it. The calls to *America Responds* are just too well thought out. He calls at the end of the show. Never more than four or five minutes before he begs off because his so-called ride is leaving. He knows that every time he opens his mouth on a live show, we can pinpoint his position in a heartbeat, but he is always long gone when the authorities arrive. He left home on foot. He has got help, I'm sure of it."

At that moment an agent arrived with a report from the El Paso field office and handed it to Collier. He read it quickly and snapped it against his hand.

"The El Paso latent prints people report numerous identifiable prints off the Van Horn pay phone, but not one even matches a partial of Davis. They also report finding talc consistent with disposable exam gloves. Smart, very smart! I am telling you he has got help. Davis and some buddy are cruising around on a road trip spending the fifty grand he pulled out of the bank. Yes indeed, he has got help!"

Following Davis' public revelation about the relationship between ISIS, the cartels, and the renegade General De La Garza, Senator Acosta decided to ratchet up the response to direct public opinion in a direction more favorable to her personal agenda. Word went out for more marches and demonstrations. Within twenty-four hours, demonstrations occurred in eight more states demanding that Martinez and the State Department cooperate with Mexico. A call from the senator to Sylvia Brinkman got Congressman Daniel Espinosa, the chairman of the Hispanic caucus, a spot on *America Responds*. Senator Acosta wanted an immediate televised rebuttal for Congressman Whitney's appearance the night before.

Agent Dayton sat down with Molly at the breakfast table over coffee.

"So, you can't think of anyone Brooks would turn to for safe harbor?"

"Brooks is a very well-liked man. He has spent his life going the extra mile for many, many people. If you want a list of people who would help him under these circumstances, you would be best prepared for a very long list. And after his public disclosure of the rape, I can assure you that every man that knows Brooks will now lie through their teeth for him. They will be happy to send the FBI on untold wild goose chases and accept the risk. If you want a list of people who would help Brooks, I will need paper, pencil, and plenty of time."

Dayton looked into her eyes and realized that a list would be an exercise in futility. Even if the FBI used all its vast resources to find and interview all the names on the list, they would all protect Davis. He also had a strong feeling that Molly would make a great list that would include everyone except the one person who was aiding her husband. He thought of one final question that only Davis' wife could answer accurately.

"Molly, what do you think Brooks is trying to accomplish with all of this?"

Molly chuckled and shook her head.

"Brooks wants to be tried in the court of public opinion."

Dayton's brow wrinkled involuntarily.

"That can be dangerous. Is he sure that is the way to go?"

"He is sure that he stands a better chance with his fellow citizens than the whims of politicians and special interest groups."

Dayton lowered his voice.

"Molly, I hope you know that all of the agents that have been involved with this case secretly hope that it all turns out well for Brooks."

Molly placed her hand on top of Dayton's.

"And I want you to know how much we appreciate the care and understanding that the Bureau has afforded my family during this crisis. I really like you, Timothy, so I'm going to give you a heads-up.

If things go against Brooks, he has said that he prefers dying on American soil than going to Mexico. Tell your colleagues that and remind them that even though it was a surprise to me, Brooks can apparently be a very ornery and dangerous man if he thinks that he has been left with no options."

CHAPTER FORTY-TWO
Outrageous Times Call for Outrageous Plans

Davis flipped off the television after the close of *America Responds*. He poured himself a fresh cup of coffee and rehashed the thoughts of his political adversaries and the prevailing direction the political winds seemed to be blowing. He picked up a cell phone and called John Long. Attorney Long had not watched the show, but from Davis' description his professional advice was to respond in a big way.

They plotted strategy for a long time before Long came up with a plan. At first glance, Davis thought it was an outrageous plan, but these were outrageous times. He was skeptical but Long was optimistic. He was so optimistic that Davis thought he sounded like a young man planning a complex fraternity prank. However, the longer they planned, the more Davis warmed up to the idea.

"Okay, John, let's do it. I don't mind telling you it feels like I'm going to Vegas and betting the family fortune on one hand of poker."

"But Brooks, you are a hell of a poker player. What's to worry?"

With that, a gleeful Long signed off and set about putting his part of the plan in motion.

Davis called Fritz and described the plan. He was more skeptical than Davis and said so.

"Sounds like a perfect way to get caught if you ask me."

"I can't hide out forever and you can't stay on the road forever. I guess this is as good a way to make a last stand as any. So, you can be in the right place at the right time?"

"Yeah, sure. You know, sometimes it is just this kind of crazy crap that actually works. Especially if you have a billionaire at your disposal."

Following his discussion with Davis, Fritz changed his direction of travel from north to east. He made his way out of Colorado going east on I-76. Most law enforcement assets were looking for cars with Texas plates in Wyoming. When Fritz got on I-80 East just over the Nebraska line he attracted no interest. As per plan, he stopped in Cozad, Nebraska, found a pay phone, and prepared for the evening call-in.

In San Saba, Davis tuned into Fox News in preparation for that evening's public relations session. He was surprised to hear that fresh from his appearance the night before on CNN, Congressman Espinosa, leader of the Hispanic caucus, was Ron Dixon's guest that night. Davis had a lot to say to the congressman, but he knew that it was imperative to stay on plan for Fritz's sake. If he spent too much time debating the international fundamentals of self-defense with Espinosa, a rapidly dispatched highway patrolman might get lucky. With twelve minutes left in the program, Davis made the call.

"Let's take another caller. This is *America Responds*."

"Hello, Ron, Brooks Davis here."

"I'm glad that you could be with us. Have you had the opportunity to follow tonight's program?"

"Yes, it's been interesting. I haven't kept count, but it seems that most callers think that Mexico should worry more about cartels and corruption than me."

Espinosa waded into the discussion just like Dixon's producers had hoped.

"Mr. Davis, you continue to try to divert attention from the fact that many people in Mexico lost their lives at your hands. You have publicly admitted it. And for that, common justice demands that you explain your actions in a court of law, a Mexican court of law."

"Well, Congressman, as I see it the ball is in the court of President Acosta at one end asking for extradition and President Martinez at the other trying to decide what is the right way to respond. He has Article 9 of the treaty to use at his discretion. You tell us, Congressman, why do you think the president hasn't already invoked it? He has had several days to think about it and plenty of expert advice from the secretary of State, the attorney general, and who knows who else. Why do you think he hasn't used Article 9?"

Espinosa cleared his throat uncomfortably. His pause allowed Dixon to jump into the fray.

"Could it be, Congressman, that the president as a first-term president is fearful of the political fallout if he grants extradition?"

Espinosa's eyes narrowed angrily.

"It is not for me to speculate what the president's motives are."

Davis laughed out loud.

"This is not a laughing matter, Mr. Davis," snapped Espinosa.

"Well, since it is my ass on the line here, I don't mind speculating about what the president's motives are. I think that Ron is right on the money. I would bet the bankroll that the president's handlers are currently running amuck trying to get a feel for percentage points for and against my extradition. I think that the president is an intelligent man caught up in a difficult dilemma. He is fighting a new and far more difficult phase of the war on terrorism. I'm sure that he would rather be focusing on the conduct of that war and not on how to handle the so-called Davis affair."

Espinosa interrupted, "So why don't you cooperate with Mexico like an innocent man would and free up the president to conduct the war?"

The poorly veiled comment that Espinosa considered Davis anything but an innocent man made Brooks pause and take a deep breath. He looked at his watch and considered how much time he had left to keep Fritz safe. Dixon was seasoned enough to stay silent because he wanted Davis to let Espinosa have it.

"Congressman Espinosa, I'll make two final comments. And I'll thank you to not interrupt. First, I hope that I'm not the only person to notice the coincidence that ISIS has launched a major terror threat against America at the beginning of a new president's first term. Their goal in the September 11 attack was to occupy the attention of President Bush and therefore their ability to dictate the direction of his presidency. They are doing it again with President Martinez. Secondly, with respect to my situation, I think that since there are an increasing number of demonstrations occurring, maybe we should organize a nationwide demonstration that will send a clear message to the White House as to what the president should do."

Espinosa looked perplexed but Dixon loved the idea of anything that would get nationwide participation originating from his show. His producers and directors were screaming into his earpiece to not let Davis leave without setting up a demonstration.

"That is fascinating, Mr. Davis. Are you suggesting that it is time for the silent majority to finally speak loudly and in one voice?"

"Precisely, Ron."

Espinosa tried to interject in hopes of changing the direction of the conversation, but Dixon and his invisible directors would have none of it. He held up his hand, stopping the congressman.

"Wait, Congressman! Let's hear his idea! What exactly do you propose, Mr. Davis?"

"I propose that at twelve noon, the day after tomorrow, everyone that is driving any type of vehicle that is in favor of the president invoking Article 9 of the Extradition Treaty with Mexico should carefully come to a stop and honk their horn for ten minutes without interruption. Since the White House is conveniently in the Eastern time zone, I propose that President Martinez should step outside and listen before he makes up his mind. If the people of this country do not care about my predicament, it will be clear. You know what they say about silence being golden."

It was outrageous but Dixon could hear the producers and directors in the control room cheering. Thinking quickly, Dixon asked,

"Mr. Davis, if the people demonstrate in favor of extradition will you turn yourself in?"

"My ride is leaving, Ron. I have got to go. I'm counting on you to get the word out about my demonstration. Remember, precisely noon, the day after tomorrow."

Davis did not have to count on Ron. The "Davis Demonstration" was the lead story on every network and local news broadcast and page one news the next morning in newspapers across the nation.

In the Oval Office, Martinez turned off the television and then slammed the remote onto the coffee table. The secretary of State, his chief of staff, and his press secretary all recoiled in unison.

"That grandiose son of a bitch! How dare he think he can sway the decisions of the president of the United States! If Friday is a flop for that cowboy, I will sign the extradition papers in the Rose Garden at 12:11 p.m. Eastern time.

CHAPTER FORTY-THREE
Verdict by a Jury of Peers

After the latest episode of *America Responds*, the FBI director was called by the president and told to catch Davis now. The director poured every available asset into the region and began the most intense hunt for an unofficial fugitive, not officially on the Ten Most Wanted List, in the history of the Bureau.

Roadblocks were placed at ten-mile intervals both east and west of Cozad, Nebraska on I-80. State police assets both on the ground and in the air followed the small state roads north and south of Cozad looking for Texas license plates or anything that did not look quite right.

Fritz was quick enough leaving Cozad that he was not observed on State Highway 21 heading north to the vicinity of Broken Bow and the ranch of one of John Long's wealthy rancher friends. With his car safely locked in the barn, Fritz enjoyed the rancher's hospitality while they waited for Davis and Long to arrive in Long's Gulfstream executive jet.

In San Antonio, Collier was able to stay in the FBI loop but could not offer any meaningful assistance to the efforts in Nebraska.

In Washington, Senator Acosta put out the word to protest organizers to redouble their efforts. She asked her friend Brinkman to see to it that anti-Davis protests got intense media coverage in hopes of countering anything that the "Davis Demonstration" might garner.

In the early morning hours of the day of the demonstration, Long's Gulfstream landed at Frederick Municipal Airport in Frederick,

Maryland. Long's pilot rented a nondescript van in his name for Brooks and his accomplices. While Long's pilot and co-pilot remained in Frederick to fuel and prep the jet, the threesome headed south on I-270 to Washington, DC.

At 11:15 a.m., Fritz dropped Davis and Long off at the corner of 18th and L Streets. Fritz had hacked into the Metropolitan DC Traffic and Security Camera Grid and had determined that the corner was one of many blind spots. Davis immediately called for a cab. They were picked up at 11:35 a.m. Davis told the cabbie that they wanted to circle the Ellipse until noon. The cabbie glanced in his rearview mirror and offered his opinion.

"You guys want to be in front of the White House when everything comes to a stop for that Davis guy."

Davis and Long exchanged glances.

Long asked, "You think that traffic will actually come to a stop for that dude?"

"Oh sure! I think it is going to be something. Dispatch told the whole shift to make sure we keep the meters running while we are stopped."

Long offered a final inducement. "If you can position us as close to the Zero Milestone across from the White House right before noon, there will be an extra hundred in it for you."

The cabbie noticed the video camera that Long carried.

"You guys must be reporters or something."

"Photographers for CNN," lied Long.

As the cabbie pulled onto E Street, he chuckled. "This is gonna be some good shit, you watch!"

At 11:55 a.m. traffic started to slow to a stop. The cab bearing Davis and Long was about 100 yards from the Zero Milestone when the traffic came to a complete stop. Long paid the cabbie and gave him the $100 tip. Davis left the cab first and made his way through a growing throng of pedestrians. Long remained in the cab to establish a degree of separation from Davis. He wore a hooded sweatshirt and sunglasses in hopes of not being identifiable by surveillance cameras in the area of the White House. Davis crossed the street and stood near the fence with his back to Long. Long remained on the other side of the street and started the video camera.

At 11:59 a.m. some driver on 15th Street wanted to be the first and started honking his horn. In an instant, the cacophony began.

In Long's viewfinder, the famous view of the front of the White House across the perfectly manicured green expanse of the spring lawn was centered. In the foreground stood many tourists, some with hands over their ears. After two minutes of filming, Long tightened the view and focused on the back of a single man with the image of the White House over his shoulder. Davis slowly turned and faced Long's camera. Long zoomed in on Davis' smiling face. Even though his voice was drowned out by the din of horns, viewers would be able to clearly make out Davis' comment. "I wonder what he is thinking right about now?" Long stopped the camera after the comment.

Since the area around the White House was saturated with surveillance cameras, Davis and Long walked on opposite sides of the street. As they walked, Long pulled on a fresh pair of latex gloves and removed the data storage card from the camera. At Pennsylvania and Twelfth Street, he crossed the street and got ahead of Davis. He placed the video card on the backrest of an empty bus bench and never broke stride. Davis slowed his pace and stopped at the bench. He retrieved a tourist map from his pocket and pretended to get his bearings. As he folded the map, he stealthily retrieved the video card and moved on.

Davis could not resist the temptation and walked to the corner of Pennsylvania and Tenth Street to hail a cab. Only later would an FBI analyst pick out the image of a smiling Davis as he waited for a ride across the street from the J. Edgar Hoover Building.

Davis caught a cab and asked to be taken to the studios of WUSA, the CBS affiliate in Washington. As they traveled, he made small talk with the Jordanian cabbie who had been very verbal about his whereabouts when the demonstration started.

Davis entered the lobby of WUSA and approached the receptionist.

"Hi, I'm Brooks Davis from Texas. This video card needs to be given directly to your station's news director. If you lose it, I am positive that you will also lose your job."

As the news director, the six o'clock anchor, and several others watched the video clip, they were hard-pressed not to laugh.

"That Davis guy is one ballsy son of a bitch! He might as well have flipped off the president!"

One of the staffers asked, "Should we notify the White House and the FBI?"

"Yeah right! Right after we run this clip as the lead-off on the six o'clock news. Make ten copies and hide them all over the building."

After Davis and Long split up, they took separate cabs to different residential neighborhoods in Chevy Chase, Maryland. Fritz made the pickups and then returned to Frederick Municipal Airport. The pilot returned the van, and the party of conspirators took off with a flight plan to Dallas Love Field. Fritz's vehicle was left in the barn in Broken Bow for later retrieval. When Fritz voiced concern about not having transportation, Long waved him off and said that he would buy him a new car in Dallas.

That evening over steaks and Jack Daniel's, the co-conspirators watched the coverage of the "Davis Demonstration." Each network orchestrated a sequence of regional reports from each time zone as the honking moved from east to west. The reports were all the same; for ten minutes, the country came to a stop and expressed its verdict. It was the court of public opinion at its finest.

Only much later would the analysts realize that a good portion of the honking was not so much a show of support for Davis, but rather an expression of frustration at the horrible noise and traffic jams. It was just like Davis and Long had anticipated. By the time the pundits figured things out, it was too late to be able to differentiate exactly who was on Davis' side and who was not.

Immediately after the demonstration, the White House press

corps was clamoring for a news conference. When pressed, the press secretary would only respond that the president had indeed witnessed the demonstration but had no comment on the matter. She deflected that it was under the advisement of the secretary of State. The only thing that the press secretary was willing to discuss was the president's impending trip to China to discuss debt and trade deficits. After the press secretary's comments were aired, the minority leader was only too happy to render the general opinion from his side of the aisle. "If President Martinez doesn't get the message, he should probably fall on his sword now."

Under tremendous and growing pressure, Martinez's advisors recommended that he make a statement before his China trip. If he delayed, the public outcry following the demonstration would easily blunt the importance of the Asian diplomacy. The next day the White House announced a prime-time televised address by the president. He wisely chose an address from the Oval Office so he could control content and not have to take questions.

"My fellow Americans. I come to you tonight on the eve of a historic trip to China. This trip has been in the planning for many months and is of paramount importance to the economic future of the world's two super economies. During our seven-day visit, there will be an unprecedented exchange of information that will lead to the stabilization of global markets and economies. As I promised during my campaign, you can expect great prosperity to result from our interactions with our major economic partners. It is our hope that from this visit the framework for a new World Economic Congress will be constructed.

"Here at home, we continue to face difficult times. Unemployment, while improving, is still at what I feel is an unacceptable level. There is still much work to accomplish."

The president paused for an instant, not wanting to start the rest of his speech.

"Our nation continues to be under attack from the forces of global terrorism. Our enemies will stoop to unimaginable levels seeking destabilization of peace among nations, cultures, and religions. America has recently lost some of our finest citizens in these latest terror attacks. The horrific nature of the attacks is proof enough of the kind of war in which we are involved and the nature of our enemies. We are sworn to bring to bear all the resources and technologies available to defeat this new threat. Our enemies should make no mistake; we will crush them out of existence and rid the world of the evil that they represent.

"One of our citizens has perfectly demonstrated our nation's resolve in this war on terror. Brooks Davis of Texas has single-handedly taken on the terrorists and has defeated them against great odds. Some of the details of his ordeal have been reported while others have not due to the intensity of ongoing national and international investigations. During his ordeal, Davis was forced to defend himself with deadly force. Use of that force resulted in the request by our good friends and neighbors in Mexico that Davis be extradited to stand trial.

"The investigations of the Davis kidnapping and the events that transpired by the FBI, CIA, and other police agencies were completed this morning and reported to me. I am pleased to report that I am satisfied that Mr. Davis' actions were all determined to be acts of self-defense under exceptional circumstances. I have spoken to President Acosta and have invoked Article 9 of the US-Mexican Extradition Treaty, which grants the executive of the requested nation the right to refuse the extradition of one of its nationals. I am therefore pleased to report that it is the determination of this office that the Davis affair is officially closed."

Leon Springs, Texas, Sunday morning

There had been no word from Davis for five days following the presidential pardon. The San Antonio field office was still providing area security at the Davis compound. Special Agent Dayton was personally very happy about the action that the president had taken.

Collier, however, had warned the Counterterrorism team that there were too many loose ends in the Davis-Epstein case to make him even remotely happy. And if the boss wasn't happy, no one should be happy.

Dayton noted that Molly and her sons were immediately very elated at the news of the pardon but had been unusually quiet the last couple of days. The only exception was the evening before when James brought a striking young blonde lady home, apparently for dinner with his mother and brothers.

It was now 8:30 a.m. on Sunday. Dayton was completing a patrol around the Davis home. As he rounded the corner to the backyard, he could see that a poolside family breakfast was in progress. Molly was on the far side of the patio table and was flanked by Andy and Zane, who was proudly wearing his FBI cap. Across the table with their backs to Dayton were two men. Molly made eye contact with the FBI man and smiled. She held up a coffee cup and pointed to an empty seat, inviting Dayton to join the family.

Dayton was halfway to the table before all the synapses closed on the question of who *exactly* was seated at the table. He paused in midstride at the same moment that Brooks and James turned simultaneously and offered Dayton a coffee cup toast.

"Your face is priceless, Timbo!" chuckled Brooks.

"What's the report from the perimeter? Any boogiemen lurking out there?" added James.

"Be nice, you two!" said Molly as she filled the cup for Dayton. "I'm sure we need to have a little talk—right, Timothy?"

Dayton took a deep breath and slowly shook his head. "Oh, you have no idea." He scanned the table and stopped at Brooks.

"You are good, Davis, damn good. You may be off the hook with the president, but I assure you that Collier will not let you go until you tell him how you did it, and how you got back to the house through all the security."

Brooks leaned toward Molly and asked, "I guess we shouldn't tell him that I've been home for more than twenty-four hours."

Dayton recoiled and grimaced. He looked at Molly for confirmation. She smiled prettily and slowly nodded while sipping her coffee.

James added, "Dad wanted to learn a little more about my new girlfriend, so we had her over for dinner."

Brooks addressed Dayton. "Have you seen his girlfriend? This boy has great taste in women." James nodded vigorously.

"Hey, I can't help it. It's a genetic thing. Just look at Mom."

His comment precipitated a high-five from his father.

Dayton grimaced. "Yeah, don't tell Collier any of that. He is going to have our asses as it is. He will send all of us back to Quantico if he knows that you have been here for more than twenty-four hours...and...and...having parties.

Dayton scanned the people around the table once again. "You are all good. Does anyone want to tell me anything now, when it will count the most? Might keep you out of some trouble." He looked at each of the people around the table. Dayton got a mix of shrugs and headshakes. After a quiet pause, Zane slowly raised his hand, seeking to be acknowledged. Everyone turned to the nine-year-old. Ever the interrogator, Dayton asked, "And what do you want to tell us, Zane?"

"Well...ah...you know James' new girlfriend? Now I know how to tell if a girl doesn't have a bra."

At the moment of that revelation, Andy was into a sip of milk that was now coming out of his nose. James and Zane were exchanging a fist-bump. Molly had her head in her hand and was mumbling about living with animals. Brooks was smiling with fatherly pride. He looked at Dayton and said, "Aren't they the greatest?"

Dayton looked ill. "Look, Brooks, I really have to notify Collier. If he finds out you've penetrated our security perimeter and you have been here for more than a day, he will ship us back to Quantico and then who knows where."

Brooks waved him off. "Dayton, you worry too much. You took good care of my family—I owe you. Call your boss. We will work it all out."

Dayton called Collier and let his boss know of Davis's return.

"Well, sir, he just walked right up, sort of like he left.... Yes, sir, I'll tell him."

Dayton powered down his cell phone. "He's going to want the names of the people who helped you."

Davis sipped his coffee for a long moment.

"Okay, you've got me. I was helped by a couple of good-ol'-boy pals of mine." Dayton opened his notebook and prepared to make notes.

"Their names?"

"Cy Vance and J. E. Carter."

"Is Cy short for Cyrus?"

"I don't know. His friends all call him Cy."

"What about Carter? What do his initials stand for?"

"I don't know. He must be a junior. We all call him 'Junior.'"

"How do you know them?"

"We go way back. I'd have to think about where I first ran into those guys."

"Are they from Texas?"

Molly stifled a chuckle into her cup of coffee.

"Nope. Cy is from one of the Virginias. West Virginia, I think. Coal country."

Brooks made a show of tilting his head and scratching his chin in pseudo thought.

"Junior, I think, is from either Alabama or Georgia...I'm not sure."

Dayton snapped his notebook closed, anxious to watch his boss conduct the official grilling.

"Can I trust that you won't disappear again?"

Davis smiled and shook his head. "I'm not going anywhere."

Dayton left the patio and once again dialed Collier. He wanted to give his boss advanced information.

"I got him to spill the names of his accomplices. It was as you suspected, sir. It was a couple of old friends of his."

"I knew it!"

"Yes, sir. I thought you might want to get some background material on them before you interview Davis."

"You bet your ass I do. As a matter fact, I'll bet you a bottle of Glenlivet that they are both former Intel people. Give me the names."

"I've got one Cy Vance, probably Cyrus, from possibly West Virginia, and a J. E. Carter Jr. from either Alabama or Georgia. No towns on either guy."

There was a long pause before Collier spoke again.

"Dayton, when were you born?"

"Ah, 1995, sir."

"You know, Dayton, because you are a youngster, I'm going to let you slide this time."

Confused, Dayton asked, "I guess I don't understand. What you mean, sir?"

"Davis got you again. Former Secretary of State Cyrus Vance has been dead since 2002. Former President Jimmy Carter and Brooks Davis are most certainly not good old buddies. Granted, Carter and Vance both signed the 1979 U.S.-Mexico Extradition Treaty that included Article 9 that got Davis' ass out of the crack. But good old buddies, I doubt. So Special Agent Dayton, I recommend that you sit back down with that crafty cowboy from Uvalde and start squeezing out the names of his real accomplices. And if you do not want a Quantico refresher, I suggest that you get the names before I get there."

Epilogue

Two years later

President Martinez's bid for re-election was an abysmal failure. He lost in a landslide. Like Jimmy Carter before him, a well-timed attack on American sovereignty and citizens and a poorly played military and diplomatic response against Middle Eastern perpetrators ended badly for a sitting president. What most Americans had forgotten in the decades since Carter was what the real goal of the terrorists was. Muscle flexing. They wanted the whole world to see that a well-played chess game would allow a small Muslim country to dictate who the loser of an American presidential election would be. Determining the loser can be as important as influencing who holds the reins of power after the votes are counted.

It did not matter that those eight years of Reagan and Gulf Wars I and II were not necessarily so great for Middle Eastern terrorist organizations, but having a hand in the outcome of a US election was a sure indicator of power on the global stage.

Birjand, Iran

Akmed al-Sirjan was joined for a celebratory luncheon by the regional leaders of ISIS. The leaders represented six different Middle Eastern countries. As they dined, they watched the American election night wrap up on satellite television. Since everyone spoke passable English, they chose to watch FOX primarily because al-Sirjan was terribly smitten with Sandra Smith.

When Martinez gave his very early concession speech, al-Sirjan and his guests all cheered. It felt good to flex dormant muscles once more.

As soon as Martinez finished and left the podium with his tearful wife and children, al-Sirjan fingered the remote and turned off the television. There were objections from his guests, but he silenced them with a raised hand. When he had their attention, he spoke.

"There is no reason to linger over this carcass. The bones are picked clean and are bleaching in the sun. We must move on to our next project. I must admit that while we were successful in seven out of eight operations, the real surprise was that the most important results were the product of our only failure. The survival of Brooks Davis was the source of much political capital for the Great Satan. It should serve to remind us that even the humblest of warriors, if he is persistent and cunning, can bring down even the most powerful. We owe Brooks Davis a large debt of gratitude. And when we kill him and his family soon, the US will once again know the power of Islam."

The condemnation of Davis brought on an enthusiastic round of "Death to America" and "Allah Akbar."

Once again Akmed al-Sirjan asked for silence with a raised hand.

"Let us now move on to greater projects. Daud, tell us how the stockpiling of fissionable material is progressing."

The End

Acknowledgments

If you are a veterinarian by profession, and a writer by avocation, what do you *really* know about writing and publishing? "Very dang little!" as the cowboys would say. This is particularly true for me since the last official English Composition and Creative Writing course I completed (with so-so results) was at Texas A&M in 1969. So, it follows that a list of acknowledgments would, by necessity, be substantial.

I will begin the list appropriately with Cathy, my life partner for more than fifty years. She is not just a wonderful wife, but also my at-the-ready subject researcher and plot and character critic. She is ever so handy to have around.

Similarly, thank you to my daughter, Dana, for your valuable input as a beta reader of the manuscript, and to my son, Adam, as my faithful IT guy. And thanks for not suggesting that your father may have gone over the hill with *Article 9*.

Special thanks to two friends and fellow authors, Julia Brewer Daily, author of *Fifth Daughter of Thorn Ranch* and *No Names to Be Given*, and Joel Maldonado, US Border Patrol, Ret., and author of *The Binding Oath*. I met both of these great people at author presentations at my local library. Julia is a podcaster (Authors Over 50), and Joel is a font of accurate information about the southern border and the politics thereof. They inspired me and pushed me down the path of writing this book.

A special tip of the hat (cowboy hat!) to a superlative group of beta readers that I have taken the liberty of naming the Literary Critics of the Grape Creek Confab. They include Randolph Stewart, DVM, PhD; Mack J. Boyd, DVM; Cotton Elliot, sheriff of King County, Texas, Ret., and Willian Robert (Billy Bob) Harlin, DVM. No finer bunch of literary critics have been spawned in the Lone Star State.

And finally, no debut novel by someone with a medical background and not an MFA degree gets to market without a huge amount of professional help. I will name them in the order I met them. They are all equally indispensable.

Sara Kocek and David Aretha of Yellow Bird Editors. It was Sara's admonition that my protagonist needed some serious flaws or I would run the risk of losing 50 percent of my readership—the female half—that got this rank amateur into some serious rewriting.

Martha Bullen of Bullen Publishing Services a) knows her stuff, b) is available to her clients even when she's on another continent, c) knows how to pull a large team together on a tight schedule, and d) doesn't hold a guy's greenhorn status against him.

Christy Day of Constellation Book Services really knows how to take an author's ideas and translate them into a spectacular book cover and interior design.

Jeremy Avenarius for wrapping it all up in a great website.

Thanks, everyone. I owe you. See you soon with my upcoming book, *Aberrant Artifacts*.

About the Author

DANIEL HOLUB has had several rewarding careers. He has worked as a medical researcher, a veterinarian, a rancher, and a novelist.

After earning a Master of Medical Science degree from Emory University and a Doctor of Veterinary Medicine degree from Texas A&M University, he became a member of the Cullen Cardiovascular Surgical Research Laboratories of the Texas Heart Institute under famed heart surgeon Denton Cooley, MD. A long and productive career in a private veterinary practice followed his years in research.

After retirement, Daniel pursued a new avocation of writing fiction. His debut thriller, *Article 9*, shows that he is as accomplished behind his laptop as he was in the exam room and the surgical operatory.

Daniel is a Vietnam era veteran and a proud Texas rancher. He lives in the Texas Hill Country with his wife, Cathy, and their two cats, Sadie Sue and Francie La Rue. To learn more or contact him, visit www.danielholub.com.